DELTA PUBLIC LIBRARY
402 MAIN STREET
DELTA, OH 43515-1304

D0422892

WES
MAC

AUG 26 2008

MASTER OF THE MESA

Hawk Nielson was fast-shooting and ruthless, the most powerful man on the range. His holdings spread over thousands of acres and his power spread from one end of the Mesa to the other. His enemies numbered all the men he had stolen from and cheated and crushed.

Vard Whitlock had more reason to hate him than most. Land and money were all Hawk cared about—until his wife bore him a son. At last he had an heir. His pride almost matched his greed. Now Vard knew how to strike back at the grasping cattle baron, he just had to wait for the right moment. When it came, he kidnapped the baby and hit the trail. Then he settled down to work out the revenge that justice demanded for Hawk Nielson. It took twenty-five years, but when it came, it caused the bitterest fight the men of the Mesa had ever seen.

MASTER OF THE MESA

William Colt MacDonald

DELTA PUBLIC LIBRARY

First published in the UK by Hodder and Stoughton

This hardback edition 2008
by BBC Audiobooks Ltd
by arrangement with
Golden West Literary Agency

Copyright © 1947 by Allan William Colt MacDonald.
Copyright © by Allan William Colt MacDonald in
the British Commonwealth.
Copyright © renewed 1974 by
Mrs. Allan William Colt MacDonald.
All rights reserved.

ISBN 978 1 405 68210 7

*The characters in this book are entirely
imaginary and have no relation to any
living person*

British Library Cataloguing in Publication Data available.

Printed and bound in Great Britain by
Antony Rowe Ltd., Chippenham, Wiltshire

CONTENTS

CONTENTS

I

CALAMITY FOR COWMEN

TWENTY-FIVE years is a long time for a man to wait for his revenge. It is doubtful if the average man would hold a grudge that long. Only one who felt himself deeply injured could nurse a grievance for a quarter of a century. Perhaps Vard Whitlock was something more, or less, than an average man. It may be that he considered himself harder hit than some of the others who had encountered a disaster equal to his own. At any rate, he waited that length of time before moving against Hawk Nielson in an effort to square the ancient account.

When the final reckoning came, there were those who maintained that Hawk Nielson had paid far more than he deserved. Whitlock, himself, was never sure, towards the last, that the whole business hadn't got out of hand. His plans had been aimed solely at the downfall of Hawk Nielson; it was only through the merest chance that others were not injured. After all, it is sometimes most difficult to determine where revenge leaves off and new injuries commence. . . .

Ordway wasn't much of a town during those days of the late eighties, though a growing cattle industry held forth promise of the larger settlement to come. But at that time it was just another of those small cow towns so typical of the South-west. Most of its life centred about the two saloons and the former Butterfield stage station, the plaster flaking from the ancient adobe walls, which was employed as a combination post office and way stop for a smaller stage line which had leased the building. For the rest, there were a few miscellaneous business buildings with false fronts and a scattering of shabby dwellings flanking the narrow, dusty road that had become known as Main Street. At that time, in fact, it was the only thoroughfare that could properly be called a street.

However, Ordway was fairly prosperous as towns go. It was the only settlement of the kind in the whole length and breadth of the Cascabel Mesa country—in reality a great plateau, rather than what is commonly known as a mesa. Consequently Ordway got all the business from the neighbouring ranches, and any place within a radius of fifty miles was considered within the town's neighbourhood.

And then, just as the various cattle-raisers had reached the point where they contemplated sitting back to take things easy, calamity struck their herds in the form of disease and drought. A stubborn epidemic of screw-worm was followed by two scorching years without rain. Cattle dropped by the thousands, their buzzard-worried carcases dotting the parched range like flies. The actual flies hovered in thick clouds above the blackened, rib-thin frames of dead and dying animals.

The only man untouched by the disaster was Hawk Nielson, the biggest cattle-owner in the Cascabel Mesa country. The Creaking River had its source on Nielson's holdings, which swept clear to the towering jagged peaks of the Medicine Bonnet Range, and even if the stream did trickle out, farther on, to a thin thread of water that soaked quickly into the arid land, Hawk Nielson had enough for the requirements of his outfit. Also Nielson had money—plenty of money—and he was gaining more each year. At the first cry of screw-worm he had rounded up his cattle and kept them apart from the animals of neighbouring ranches. Strangely enough, his method was successful, and Nielson's Forked Lightning brand thrived, while other men went under, or at best saw failure staring them in the face.

Gradually the word went out that Nielson was willing to buy land if anyone cared to sell. Several men did care to sell—nay, were eager to sell at almost any price. Nielson secured their holdings for about a tenth of their actual value. He even gained a great many cattle in this way, weak, gaunt creatures, to be sure, but on his own land the animals quickly recovered their former condition. Other men—there were eight or nine of a more optimistic breed—felt certain they could survive the disaster if only they had the requisite money to carry them through the coming fall and winter. Once more Hawk Nielson was on hand with an open money-sack. He loaned to everyone who asked—and received more than good security on their notes.

Whether Nielson's influence was due solely to hard work or to something less honourable no one seemed to know. On one point, however, all were agreed: Hawk Nielson was a hard, ruthless man, but just how hard and just how ruthless they didn't realize. Mostly, these days, he seemed to be money-crazy and to have an all-consuming obsession for power.

Contrary to the expectations of the optimistic, the following year produced nothing to improve matters; there was a repetition of the drought. It was then that folks realized just how merciless Hawk Nielson could be. When extensions of notes were asked for, Nielson only laughed and refused. By the end of July he had foreclosed on several outfits. Left now were only the Bench-W, Horseshoe-T and Bearpaw outfits, next to Nielson's Forked Lightning brand the largest ranches in the Cascabel Mesa country. Notes on these three outfits fell due the thirty-first of October.

As early as August the owners of these ranches had known it was going to be impossible to meet their obligations. They went to Nielson pleading for more time, and Nielson refused them with a curt, " Pay up or get out."

Thus the matter stood on the evening of October 30, when Steve Taylor, of the Horseshoe-T, and Tod Ranson, of the Bearpaw Ranch, stood in the bar of the Brown Jug Saloon moodily sipping glasses of lukewarm beer. Behind the bar was Herb Brown, the neat, slightly built proprietor of the Brown Jug. Herb looked thoughtful; business of late had been unusually poor. The few men in the bar-room attested that fact. And of late months the request, " Put it in the book, will you, Herb ? " had become increasingly frequent.

The swinging doors of the saloon were pushed aside and a scarecrow figure of a man in patched and faded overalls entered. He was Gabe Houston, former owner of the 13-Bar Ranch. Gabe had been the first to lose his outfit to Hawk Nielson, but folks thought little of it at the time. Houston never had been one to attend strictly to business, and the 13-Bar had been considerably run down even before Nielson took over. He was an undersized, gnarled little man with grey hair and sweeping grey moustaches. His pale blue eyes were weak, and when it came to whisky his resistance was none too strong. A few people recollected a younger, up-and-coming Houston, but that was before his wife's death had caused him to grow careless in his habits. Nowadays he was tolerated because people felt sorry for him. Shiftless, yes, but under ordinary circumstances he wouldn't have harmed anyone. Now and then he gained a few dollars here and there; he had no regular occupation since he'd lost his 13-Bar. Gradually he had become embittered.

Taylor and Ranson turned their heads when Houston entered and gave him a brief greeting. Houston replied and made his way to the bar, his loosely slung holster banging against his right leg when he walked. He asked for his usual of Herb Brown. Brown hesitated a moment: it was some months now since Gabe had paid anything on his account. Then Brown shrugged and set out a bottle and glass. Gabe poured his drink, downed it, and muttered something that sounded like, " . . . a plague of locusts eatin' up the range, that's what he is."

Steve Taylor frowned down from his six feet plus and asked, " What you mumbling about, Gabe ? "

" What's a plague of locusts doing ? " Tod Ranson said. He was a chunkily built man, nearing middle age.

Houston scowled and blinked his eyes. " Hawk Nielson," he jerked out. " Just like a plague of locusts—he keeps devourin' and devourin', like he aimed to eat up this whole blame range. Take my 13-Bar spread, f'instance: neatest little outfit in seven counties. And then the blight descended —Hawk Nielson, human blight——"

" Do you suppose he's human ? " Taylor asked moodily.

" Human octopus," Ranson grunted angrily. " Long arms —always reaching out—grabbing, grabbing, twisting the life out of the men who settled this country."

" A octypuss ! " Gabe Houston slapped his leg. " Just the name for that thievin', robbin'——" He broke off. " Well, he's done his worst to me, can't harm me no more. But I worry about you fellers. You seeing any light ahead ! "

Steve Taylor cursed and turned back to his warm beer. Gabe stole a quick look at Herb Brown, serving a pair of customers at the far end of the bar, then tilted a quick drink from the bottle Brown had been so careless as to leave untended before the little man.

" Light ahead ? " Tod Ranson said slowly. " Not very much, Gabe. Hawk Nielson's got us on the hip, and I calculate he figures to throw us hard."

Steve Taylor suppressed his wrath long enough to take part in the conversation. One hand went involuntarily to the gun at his hip. " What I'd like to do——" he commenced, and then fell silent.

Gabe Houston hadn't missed the gesture. " It's what every decent man in the country would like to do, Steve."

" No use thinking of anything rash, Steve," Ranson said quickly.

" The question is," Houston persisted, " what do you actually aim to do ? "

" I don't reckon it's up to us, Gabe," Taylor said wearily. " The question is, what will Nielson let us do ? There isn't much hope as I see it. My note falls due to-morrow. Likewise Tod's and Vard Whitlock's. You know Nielson, and you know what happens when a man can't pay up. Damn him, anyway, for a money-squeezing vulture."

Houston nodded. " Just like a plague of locusts—always devourin'."

Tod Ranson put in quietly, " Still, you can't always tell what will happen. You see, Gabe, me and Steve and Vard have scraped together all the money we could and sent it out to Nielson by Vard. Our notes all fall due at the same time, and Vard Whitlock being the best head of us three, we calculated maybe he could talk Nielson into accepting what money we could raise and extending our notes."

Gabe Houston showed more interest. " Think Hawk will do it ? " he asked. " Might I could get together a few dollars and get my 13-Bar back. If Nielson does that with you, he couldn't refuse me another chance——"

" The hell he couldn't," Taylor stated harshly. " Nielson would refuse a crust to his starving mother. Ain't that so, Tod ? "

Ranson said in tired tones, " To tell the truth, I'm not hoping for much. I'm just glad I haven't a family to face after to-morrow."

" I'm with you on that." Taylor nodded. " If I had a

wife or child, for instance, I don't know but that I might take things into my own hands and——"

"Do you think you're alone in feeling that way, Steve?" Ranson said earnestly. "But we won't get anyplace stepping beyond the law. Whether we like it or not, Nielson has acted within his legal rights——"

"Legal rights! Bah!" Taylor spat a derisive brown stream at his feet.

Herb Brown came down the bar to announce that the house was buying a drink. This time he removed the bottle when Gabe had finished pouring. The conversation turned to other matters, the men being anxious to get their minds from the trouble at hand. Abruptly the staccato pounding of hoofs along the dirt road drew their attention.

"That will be Vard, I'm hoping," Taylor commented. He and Ranson and Houston swung round to watch the entrance.

Saddle-leather creaked outside, footsteps sounded across the plank walk before the saloon. In another moment the swinging doors were pushed open and Belvard Whitlock, known as Vard, stepped inside the bar-room. "Wind coming up, going to get colder," he announced shortly to the room at large. His gaze wasn't meeting those of Ranson and Taylor.

Whitlock was a tall, rangily built individual close to thirty years of age. He had a lean, sinewy jaw and intelligent blue eyes. His hair was dark, his closely shaven lips thin and firm. He wore denim shirt and overalls, a battered Stetson, and cow-country boots. A holstered forty-five six-shooter swung at one hip. He moved a bit wearily to the bar, nodded to his friends, who were eyeing him anxiously. Herb Brown made haste to set out Whitlock's favourite bottle. Not until he had downed his drink did the others speak, then, "How'd you make out, Vard?" Ranson asked.

Whitlock shook his head and poured a second drink of

whisky. "I didn't make out," he answered slowly. "Didn't even get to see Nielson."

"Did he refuse to talk to you?" Taylor asked angrily.

"Nope—didn't even get that close to him." Whitlock hesitated a moment. "You see, Nielson is by way of becoming a parent. His wife is giving birth to a baby——"

"Gesis!" Taylor exclaimed. "Was that girl at the Forked Lightning Hawk Nielson's *wife*?"

Whitlock nodded. "Leastwise that's the way I got it from one of the Forked Lightning hands. Nielson keeps his affairs so much to himself—and his crew is just like him—that a man never knows what's going on at the Forked Lightning. It comes out that now Hawk's main idea, nowadays, is to have a son and heir. I gathered he's crazier on that idea than he is on grabbing money——"

"And was the baby a boy?" Gabe Houston asked.

"It hadn't been born when I left, so I can't say. All's I know, it had better be, or there's liable to be a dead doctor found on—— You know that drunk sawbones that's been hanging around since he was kicked off'n the stage a week back? . . . Yeah, that's the doctor Hawk has got out there——"

"Dr. Sandford Gallatin, he called himself," Ranson snorted. "Cripes! I wouldn't let that boozy son take care of a rope-burned cayuse." He swore wrathfully. "Goddammit! I always felt we should have got a regular doctor to come live in Ordway. There's some things that can't be cured with a cud of tobacco. And that"—he cursed again—"is entrusted with the birth of a child. My God! You'd have thought Nielson would have known better, brought somebody here——"

"If you," Taylor pointed out, "haven't anything more than Nielson's wife to be worried about, you're lucky. What do you care?"

" But a woman," Ranson said weakly.

" Can't tell," Whitlock put in. " This Doc Gallatin may be all right when he's sober."

" Is he sober to-night ? " Ranson asked.

" Sounded more worried than drunk to me," Whitlock replied. " Apparently he's having his troubles. I could hear Nielson's voice from within the house, bellowing at the doctor there'd be hell to pay if the baby turned out to be a girl rather than a boy. Gallatin seemed half out of his wits. I finally heard him pleading for Nielson to go away. He even promised Nielson it would be a boy. I guess he was ready to promise anything to get rid of Hawk."

" Who wouldn't be ? " Gabe Houston put in. " I'd sell my soul in hell to get that bustard off'n our range. Just like a plague of locusts, he is, always devourin'——"

Whitlock paid no attention to the older man's customary complaint as he went on, " If it's a boy, Nielson is coming to town with his crew to celebrate pronto. That being the case, I figured there was no use waiting out there to see him. Besides, if things don't pan out like he wants—if it's a girl—Hawk will be too ugly to talk to anyway. He's sure got Doc Gallatin scared witless. Hawk Nielson is on a rampage this night, and I wouldn't want to the one to cross him."

" Maybe if it's a boy," Gabe Houston put in hopefully, " Hawk will hit town feeling good. Maybe you boys can get what you want if he'll just listen to a mite of reason."

Whitlock nodded. " I had something of the sort in mind when I left."

" But good God "—Ranson shook his head worriedly—" that drunken Doc Gallatin . . . and a woman with a child. . . ." He roused himself, glared around. " Maybe Hawk Nielson does need killing."

2

HAWK NIELSON

WHITLOCK looked sharply at Ranson. " That doesn't sound like you, Tod. Generally, you're right peaceable and——"

" It makes my blood boil"—Ranson flushed—" to think of a man treating a woman—any woman—in that fashion——"

He broke off as a rattle of firearms from down the roadway interrupted the words. There came more shots and the fast drumming of horses' hoofs. Several wild cow-puncher yells punctuated the sounds. The approaching horses drew nearer, then were jerked to a halt before the Brown Jug. Hoofs stamped; men whistled and yelled. A sudden gust of wind floated a haze of dust past the swinging doors of the saloon. Heavy-booted feet clomped on the plank sidewalk.

Whitlock exclaimed, " Hawk Nielson and his crew! "

" Sounds like it must have been a boy! " Taylor jerked out, the excitement of the moment taking hold on him.

Tod Ranson voiced a brief, " Thank God. Maybe now Hawk will listen to our side. . . ." And added a moment later, " I wonder if Doc Gallatin done all right, after all? He must have been sober."

The sounds outside were continuing, and above them rose Hawk Nielson's booming voice, violating the night with joyful profanity.

Abruptly the swinging doors crashed open, and Nielson rocked in, carrying in his right hand a partly emptied bottle of whisky. He was a big man, well over six feet, with ponderous shoulders which threatened every minute to burst apart the seams of his blue woollen shirt. He was slim through the hips and moved across the floor with a light pantherish step. His Stetson was tilted back on a head of unruly blond hair, and beneath the bushy brows his eyes were grey and piercing. A hawk nose and a wide, thin-lipped mouth accented the powerful jaw. That one word sums it up—powerful. Powerful in muscular make-up, powerful in avid, brutal determination. Even now, though he was still far from thirty, there was nothing of the untried youth about him. His was a fighting life, and his face, his whole bearing, was that of a man who had lived hard, troubling himself not at all where the rights of others were concerned.

What Hawk Nielson wanted he took. Powerfully framed, vigorous, he stood inches above any other man in the Brown Jug. No one had ever downed Hawk Nielson in any sort of fight, nor had the man yet been found who could drink him under a table. He was, in very fact, the master of the Cascabel Mesa country, but a very unpopular master.

At Nielson's heels as he crashed through the entrance trailed several cow-punchers, all filling the bar-room with their drunken yells. Nearly all carried bottles. Nielson alone appeared unintoxicated. He strode towards the bar, his spurs jangling across the board floor, then suddenly paused and tossed into the air the bottle he'd been carrying. Even before the bottle had commenced to descend, Nielson's right fist reached for the six-shooter at his hip. The gun swept out, up, in one lightning-like movement. Orange fire spurted from the muzzle. Whisky and broken glass scattered in all directions, spattering the onlookers. Jarred by the concussion of the heavy weapon, one of the kerosene lamps suspended above the bar tilted abruptly to one side; smoke commenced to blacken the chimney and mingle with the powder smoke drifting overhead.

" Up to the bar, you crowd of lice-bitten, whisky-guzzling cow nurses ! " Hawk Nielson roared. " Bar-keep "—to Herb

Brown, who had been righting his oil lamp—" pull all your corks and throw 'em away. Every man in this place gets a bottle for himself, and we're drinking your place dry this night!"

He brought one hand out of his pocket, glanced at the fistful of gold coins and bills it held, then hurled it madly with one sweep of his arm in the general direction of Herb Brown, who was already setting out bottles.

"There's a fledgling hawk been hatched in the Forked Lightning nest not two hours back," Nielson thundered. "A he-whelp that snarls and kicks. His colour is red, and I'm guessing he weighs ten pounds on the hoof. A hawk with hoofs and claws. You've never seen the like. The King of the Range he'll be someday. Drink up, you flea-ridden pack of horse-forking bustards. You're drinking to Hawk Nielson's son. Let 'er go-o-o! Sluice down your gullets! It's a giant among men you're drinking to this night!"

The very ceiling vibrated with the sound of Hawk Nielson's tremendous tones. The din was deafening. Everyone talked at once; the room swam with tobacco smoke and echoed to profane words. With his sombrero pushed back on his blond head and a black cigar clenched between his strong white teeth, Nielson slouched back against the bar, only relinquishing the bottle long enough to enable him to replenish the exploded shells in his six-shooter.

Whitlock, Ranson, and Taylor had drunk the health of the Nielson son and heir with the rest of the crowd, hoping against hope that the Hawk would now be able to see their difficulties in a fresh light, and thus be persuaded to renew their notes.

Gabe Houston drew near. "Er—Hawk—what you naming the youngster?" he inquired.

"What's that?" Nielson darted a searching look at Houston. "What should he be named, but after me? . . . No, not Hawk. Pitt. Pitt's the name." He cast a quick look around the room. "I'm betting there's not a half-dozen men in this town know that's my name. But Hawk's a better moniker, truer to our nature. And still, Pitt's not a bad name. There was a great English statesman named Pitt. I could tell you a story——" He broke off suddenly and said roughly, "Forget it! I never did like the rattle of skeletons in closets. The name will be Hawk. He'll be known as the Son of the Hawk. What a pair we'll make when he gets his growth!" He whirled savagely round. "Bar-keep! Keep those bottles coming." Another shower of money went skittering along the bar.

Whitlock had been awaiting an opportunity to speak, and when it came he approached Nielson. "I hope mother and son is doing well, Hawk," he remarked genially.

Nielson gave a short laugh, and sent Whitlock a quick look from beneath his bushy brows. "The son couldn't be any healthier," he answered curtly. "The mother's done for."

Whitlock didn't comprehend at first. "You mean . . . ?"

"She's dead." Nielson said, brutally frank. "Doc Gallatin couldn't save 'em both."

Whitlock shrank back as though from a blow, still not quite understanding the man's attitude. "Cripes, Hawk," he stammered. "That's certainly hard luck."

"Is it?" Nielson's lips tightened. "I've got a couple of Mexican and Indian women out there for nurses. The boy will be all right." Abruptly he swung away from Whitlock and shouted for another bottle.

Whitlock realized right then it would do no good to ask for mercy regarding the note on his ranch. He pushed through the crowd, which was increasing all the time, and sought out Taylor and Ranson, who were talking to Gabe

Houston at the far end of the room. The three men listened while Whitlock related his conversation with Nielson. " And," he concluded, " it certainly looks as though we were up against it, fellows. Any man that hard wouldn't give us a chance for our money."

" You didn't even mention our notes, eh ? " from Steve Taylor.

" I didn't see any use," Whitlock pointed out. " If he's that unconcerned about the death of his wife, he certainly wouldn't be in the mood to listen to our plea for more time. We're just plumb finished, as I see it."

Taylor looked stubborn. " I'm not going to give up without trying, anyway," he stated, hard-voiced. " I'm going to speak to him myself. And I'm going to make him listen, too."

Tod Ranson had a look on his face that Whitlock had never seen there before. " I'm going to help you make him listen, Steve," Ranson announced. " He's had things his own way too long, and any man who'll treat women——" He swung suddenly on Whitlock. " You going to side us, Vard ? "

Whitlock shook his head. " You and Steve and I have been friends a good many years now, Tod. Ordinarily I'd back you both to the last ditch, but this time I think you're making a mistake. You'll just be beating your brains out against a stone wall—and it may lead to just about that. Take my advice and don't try it."

Steve Taylor flared suddenly, " First time I ever knew you to lack nerve, Vard," and instantly regretted the outburst. " I'm sorry, Vard, damnably sorry. I shouldn't have said that. You know I didn't mean it."

"I know you didn't mean it." Whitlock nodded, swallowing hard. " You and Tod see things one way ; I see 'em another, that's all."

" But does your way give us any chance ? " Taylor asked eagerly.

Whitlock hesitated. " Maybe we'd best take time to talk this thing over," he evaded. " Come on, the three of us will get out of here before we run into trouble——"

" Dammit ! " Taylor's temper was close to the surface. " I'm not afraid of trouble—not from any direction."

" That goes for me," Tod Ranson said promptly.

" Look here," Gabe Houston put in, " if you two boys are going to brace Hawk, I might's well give 'er a try too. If I could get my 13-Bar back and give him a note, I could——"

" You fool, Gabe ! " Whitlock swung savagely on the little man. " You keep your distance from Hawk Nielson. You can't get back your spread. If Steve and Tod want to try, that's their business. I've got a strong hunch Hawk will turn mean, and you wouldn't have any more chance than —than any prairie hen against a hawk."

" I'm hoping he does turn mean," Taylor rasped, " if he won't listen to reason. I'm up against it if I lose my outfit and so is Tod. We can't be much worse off——"

" He's a mean man with a gun," Whitlock reminded.

" Maybe I can get mean too," Taylor snapped.

Whitlock shook his head. " Not as mean as Hawk Nielson. No one's ever outshot him."

" There's always a first time," Tod Ranson put in. He was as angry as Taylor, but he hadn't so completely lost his head. " Look here, Steve," he proposed, " let's talk to Hawk and see how he feels before we start acting proddy. No use throwing away any chance we might have. After all, you and I haven't tried yet. We've left it all to Vard."

" I'm willing to try that," Taylor replied, " but if it comes to a showdown, you'll back me up, won't you ? "

" I'll back you up," Ranson answered, " providing that

showdown isn't brought about by us. I'd like to go cautious——"

"That's all I'm asking," Taylor jerked out. "Come on, let's go talk to the tight-fisted bustard."

Whitlock's gaze followed the two men as they made their way through the crowd to the spot where Hawk Nielson stood drinking.

"Congratulations on the son and heir, Hawk," Taylor commenced briskly, "and we're thanking you for the opportunity you gave us to drink his health."

Hawk smiled nastily. "I didn't ask you to drink his health, Taylor—I *told* you to—you and everybody else in here. And no man dared refuse."

Taylor flushed, but managed to hold his temper. "Put it that way if you like." He nodded. "I don't care one way or the other. And now, I'm wondering if you can spare us a few minutes to talk business?"

"Not to-night I can't," Nielson replied shortly.

Taylor's face went red. "Maybe you'll listen whether you want to or not," he flared, throwing discretion to the winds. "All Tod and I are asking is a simple yes or no to our question: are you going to give us a little more time on our notes?"

"No!" With that, Nielson turned away and reached for his bottle.

Impulsively Taylor's hand started towards his gun butt, but Ranson shook his head and caught at Taylor's arm. "It ain't much we're asking, Hawk," Ranson said quietly. "It's just that we'd like a mite more time to get on our feet and——"

Before the sentence was completed Nielson whirled to face the two men, a look of irritation in his face. "You two cow nurses will be off your feet altogether if you don't quit bothering me," he voiced contemptuously. "Can't you get it through your thick heads that I'm holding everything I can get for that boy that's just been born? Someday he's going to own this whole Cascabel Mesa country. So——"

"But, Hawk——" Taylor commenced.

Hawk Nielson went on as though he'd not heard the interruption: ". . . it all settles down to one thing—do you owe me the money or don't you?"

"Sure we do," Taylor answered. "We've never denied that."

"All right," Nielson said curtly, "that settles it. Pay up or get out."

"Maybe you'll force us out," Tod Ranson said, white-faced, "but I'm warning you, Hawk, such methods are going to make the Nielson name mighty unpopular in this country."

"So?" Nielson smiled icily. "And just exactly what do you aim to do about it?"

Before Ranson could make a reply, Taylor again broke into the conversation. "A lot of us decent men might take an idea to run you right out of this country, Nielson. Like Tod warned you, you'd best move slow before you push us too far——"

"Bah!" Nielson's loud laughter rose above the noise in the bar-room. "Do you know what happens to people who oppose Hawk Nielson, Taylor? I crush 'em—just like this—see?" His right hand darted to a glass tumbler that stood on the bar. His fingers tensed, tightened—then closed. The glass collapsed as though it had been the merest eggshell!

Slowly Nielson's fingers opened as he held forth for their inspection the broken pieces of the tumbler, one or two of which had cut into his clenched fist, causing the blood to flow from deep gashes. He laughed harshly. "Do you see? Sometimes I lose a little blood, but it never amounts to anything. Taylor, you and your side-kick had better move on. I'm sick of looking at you."

"Suppose we don't see it your way?" asked Taylor coolly. He knew now there could be no backing down. Other men had been listening in on the conversation. Both Taylor and Nielson realized that a weakening on either side would be fatal. There was no stopping the business now.

Nielson glared at the two men. "You've both been crowding trouble," he rasped. "I'm not blind. Do you think I didn't see you talking this over with Whitlock? Tried to pull him and Houston into it, too, didn't you? Figured four of you might have a chance against me. You fools! A dozen of you couldn't clip the Hawk's wings. Only brainless idiots would try. And you"—he directed his attention on Steve Taylor, mimicking Taylor's tones—"'Supposing we don't see it your way?' You're a complete unmitigated fool, Taylor, if you ask me what I'll do if I don't see things your way. I'll tell you what I'll do. . . . ."

The jagged sections of glass still held in his bleeding hand, Nielson moved out from the bar and never removing his piercing gaze from Taylor and Ranson, commenced to back away from them. Suddenly the hand holding the glass swung up. The next instant Taylor received the sharp, broken fragments full in his face, flung there with the whole force of Hawk Nielson's powerful arm. A few drops of blood from Nielson's cuts splashed across Ranson's left cheek.

"That's just one of the things I'll do," roared Nielson. "You've had your last warning to keep out of my path."

For a moment Ranson and Taylor just stood as though dazed. Blood had appeared from a cut on Taylor's forehead. His hand moved up slowly to finger the gash, as though he couldn't quite comprehend exactly what had happened. All this time Nielson was still backing away from the two. . . .

Abruptly it dawned on Taylor and Ranson that, with the

pieces of broken tumbler, Nielson had thrown them a direct challenge—both of them at once. No, now there could be no backing down. Nielson had asked for it. Nielson would get what he had asked for. If he dared both to draw on him, what happened would be on his own head.

Identical thoughts coursed the minds of both Taylor and Ranson simultaneously. As one man their hands swept down to the guns on their thighs.

Nielson waited, almost eagerly, his upper lip drawn back in a half smile, half snarl, until the hands of both opponents had closed about gun butts, before he moved with swift, deadly precision. His blue-barrelled Colt six-shooter came slashing up—twin lances of vivid flame leaped from the muzzle of the gun—the thick rafters at the ceiling shook with the detonations of two unbelievably swift explosions.

Taylor sat suddenly down on the floor, his gun only half-way out of holster. A dark stain seeped slowly into his shirt, over the heart. Ranson had taken Nielson's second bullet through the shoulder. As the impact of the slug swung him off balance, Nielson fired a third time. Ranson fell gasping across the seated stricken figure of his partner, knocking Taylor back to the floor. Neither man moved after a moment.

A tense hush settled on the bar-room. Powder smoke swirled briefly over the heads of the men before being whisked out through the entrance. Nielson was still waiting, gun in hand. " Anybody else want in on this ? " he demanded harshly, noting that Whitlock was now struggling with old Gabe Houston, trying to prevent the little man from drawing his gun.

" Gabe's not drawing, Hawk," Whitlock called anxiously. " He just got excited for a minute."

" Maybe you'd like something of this," Nielson snapped.

"Not me," Whitlock said. "We know when we're licked, Hawk."

He was still clutching Houston's right arm, but Houston, by this time, had changed his mind about getting into the fight.

"Good thing you got some sense, Whitlock," Nielson growled. "There'll be no trouble about this, either. Every man here saw Taylor and Ranson reach for their guns first. I just shot in self-defence."

A trace of scorn twitched Whitlock's lips. "It was done in self-defence," he agreed coldly. "You were within your rights, Hawk. The matter's ended."

"That's sensible." Slowly Nielson relaxed. He was reloading his gun when a slack-jawed man wearing a deputy's badge entered the Brown Jug and put forth the obvious query.

"Don't bother me with your fool questions, Parcher," Nielson said contemptuously. "Ask everybody else and they'll all tell you it was a case of self-defence. I had to kill 'em before they killed me."

The deputy didn't say anything, just nodded and stooped by the silent forms huddled on the floor. After a moment he stood up.

Nielson went on, "You do what's necessary about burying, Parcher, and send me the bill." He faced the room after a minute. "Come on, we'll all go down the street to the Red Steer Bar." And added with a trace of grisly humour, "This place is getting too noisy."

He headed for the doorway, followed by nearly everyone in the Brown Jug.

Herb Brown cleared his throat and said nervously, "If there's anything in signs, it looks as though the Son of the Hawk would get a baptism in blood."

No one replied. Whitlock took Houston's arm and led the

little man, unresisting, from the saloon. Outside, on the sidewalk, he stood gazing down the roadway, his eyes following Nielson as the Forked Lightning gang headed towards Ordway's other saloon. "Damn it to hell"—Whitlock spoke bitterly, self-accusingly—"I should have made them see there was another way. . . ."

3

WHITLOCK'S OTHER WAY

No one had ever learned where Hawk Nielson had come from when he arrived in the Cascabel Mesa country. He had appeared one day on Ordway's single street, driving before him a bunch of fifty cows, each of which bore palpable evidence of having had its original brand worked over to form a crudely designed Forked Lightning pattern. Straight along the street Nielson herded his cattle, looking neither to right nor left. Men looked suspiciously at his recent brandings and such phrases as " wet-blanket work " or " fast-runnin' iron " were heard on several lips. This was during a period when many latter-day cattle barons were founding their fortunes on cattle rustled from other men, so too much attention wasn't paid to Nielson's " wide loop " cattle.

It was the man himself that interested folks. At that time Nielson couldn't have yet reached twenty, but his eyes held hard lights generally found only in men of more mature years. The clothing that covered his huge frame was in tatters; the sole of one ancient boot flapped loosely. The parched, burned skin of his unshaven face was stretched tautly across cheekbones; there was a feverish glitter in his burning eyes. At Nielson's right hip swung a six-shooter, the walnut butt of which resembled to no small extent a miniature washboard. Whether Hawk himself had carved the notches, or whether he had taken the weapon from some famous gun-fighter, no one ever knew.

His pony was gaunt with fatigue, and both horse and cows were covered with a thick coating of alkali dust, the ribs of all animals showing plainly. Someone, remarking on the Forked Lightning brand, remembered that there was a Lazy-N outfit operated far the other side of the Estrago Desert. The comment was significant: a Lazy-N marking could very easily be changed into a Forked Lightning design. But the Lazy-N was over a hundred miles distant. If Nielson had come from that direction, it meant he had crossed the Estrago. Men shook their heads. It was difficult enough, risky, dangerous, just making a crossing like that alone astride a horse. No man could ever herd fifty cows across that glaring, desolate, waterless stretch of arid gypsum sink. And so, how Nielson had arrived in Ordway with his cows was something else that was never determined to anyone's satisfaction. The man had won through against overwhelming odds of some sort; that was the only point upon which anybody could be certain.

Nielson had stopped in Ordway to make inquiries about the Creaking River, where it headed and so on. He had next entered the general store and endeavoured to secure a sack of flour and some bacon. He had no money, but he offered in exchange one of his cows. The offer was refused. Cows were plentiful that year, and the proprietor of the general store wasn't in the proper mood for accepting one of those rib-thin, gaunt creatures out in front in exchange for his flour and bacon. It wasn't in Nielson to argue, let alone beg, so he just nodded and returned to his pony, standing, droop-headed and listless, like the cattle, in front of the general store's tie rail.

He was hauling himself back in the saddle, vowing inwardly to some day make Ordway pay for its inhospitality, when the local deputy sheriff appeared at his side and asked Nielson if he possessed any proof to show ownership of the cattle.

Nielson had hesitated. "Proof of ownership?"

"Yeah—a bill of sale."

"Oh." Nielson had smiled thinly and slapped the gun in his holster. "Yeah, I got one. It's made out in lead. Want to see it?"

The deputy had stepped back a trifle hastily and, being a man of discretion and little valour, had allowed that maybe it wasn't necessary. In fact he abruptly lost all interest in the matter after one sharp glance from Nielson's challenging eyes. He couldn't have known, of course, that Nielson was running a bluff and didn't have a single unused cartridge in his gun cylinder. Anyway, Nielson was allowed to continue on his way without further molestation, and folks never expected to see him again.

A month slipped by. How Nielson had managed to live during that time no one knew, but he not only lived but managed to take up holdings that included the head of Creaking River. Had he been able to foresee the years of drought ahead? If so, he was an unusually wise man. Nobody thought much about the matter then; in fact it was a source of secret amusement that he had settled so far away from Ordway, though no loud mention was made of the matter when he came to town.

Somehow he had managed to procure some money. The first time he came to town he bought a pair of six-shooters. Evenly matched weapons, they were. He never wore but one of them at a time, however. He went his way, minding his business and talking little to any man. The next time he appeared in town he bought a large supply of cartridges, bacon, beans, flour, and a team and buckboard. He knew he was being over-charged for these articles, but he said nothing.

After that, whenever Nielson got any money he managed to buy some land. Gradually his holdings increased. He still played a lone hand on his outfit, doing the work of three men. About this time three of the outfits in the Cascabel

Mesa country commenced to complain of rustling. The rustlers were never caught, but Nielson was suspected. It may be noted that all this time Nielson's herd was growing at an abnormal rate. Still, nothing could be proved against him. Nor even charged. Something in his hard eyes prevented most men from proceeding that far. He'd had two or three fights; they'd not amounted to much—so far as Nielson was concerned. Somebody fastened on him the name of Hawk, and it stuck. Nielson seemed to approve, and continued to follow the instincts of that predatory winged creature.

One night a stage-coach was held up in the next State, and money intended for a pay-roll, something like fifty thousand dollars, was carried off. The robbery was accomplished by one masked man, according to both stage-driver and express guard, who had both been wounded during the pitched battle that ensued. There'd been no passengers on the stage, and the bandit had got away, scot free, with the loot. This has little, perhaps, to do with the story, except as concerns Nielson's gradually growing power. It was noted after the hold-up that Nielson never lacked for money. Only a few people dared air their suspicions. The Hawk had laughed scornfully, carried everything with a high hand, met the suspicions contemptuously, or bullied his accusers into silence. And once more nothing could be proved, particularly when Nielson pointed out he had been in Ordway the afternoon of the day, or evening, the stage was held up. The chance that Nielson could leave town and reach the scene of the hold-up at the time it occurred, while barely possible, was extremely remote. Hawk Nielson was a slick worker, folks concluded, if he really had had anything to do with that pay-off robbery.

Now that there was no lack of money, Nielson went ahead and expanded wherever he could. His headquarters were moved somewhat nearer town, and he hired a crew of punchers—a hard-bitten lot they were, too, requiring the iron fist of a Hawk Nielson to hold them in check. As the months passed, Nielson became more and more powerful. Most people forgot their suspicions and commenced, reluctantly, to accept him, though their hate lessened not one iota. Mostly it was an unspoken fear of Hawk's fast-shooting gun, uncanny judgment, and all-round ability to win against odds that compelled people to cease resisting him. As for Nielson, he neither forgot nor forgave the inhospitable treatment he had received the first day he entered Ordway.

Then, with his money mania partly satisfied, Nielson turned to another idea: he wanted a son and heir to carry on the name and handle the outfit for him. All things considered, he was a lonely man in many ways. It commenced to be rumoured that he was the black sheep of a good family and a man of education. Who or what started that rumour no one seemed to know. It may have had some basis in the fact that a freighter, delivering at Ordway a packing-case consigned to Nielson, managed to drop the case when unloading, the fall breaking open the box. To everyone's surprise, the case proved to be full of books—books bearing strange names familiar to but one or two of Ordway's population. Shakespeare many people had heard of, of course, but who was Thomas Paine, François Villon, and Laurence Sterne? And a volume bearing the name Machiavelli—well, that certainly sounded like one of them Eye-talian names. There were other books, equally mysterious to the onlookers. Something about the volumes, however, augmented the awe in which Hawk Nielson was commencing to be held.

But books can't take the place of a son and heir, and by the time he'd pondered the matter for two years it had become an obsession with him. Women had played but a small part in Nielson's life, but now he commenced to seriously consider the sex and the sort of woman he needed for the mother of his son. With Hawk, it was a cold, calculating process: he might have been considering the various virtues of a brood mare. And finally he reached a decision: she must be a woman of breeding, one with generations of good blood back of her.

Whether he got what he wanted—though he generally achieved his ambitions—or where he got her, no one knew. He went away for three months, and when he returned he was accompanied by a quiet, gentle creature whom it was learned later he had married. That she lived less than a year after that marriage was something to which Nielson gave little thought. Love had had nothing to do with the proposition. Nielson's sole desire of the moment had found fulfilment in the tragic birth of his infant son.

And at the present moment he and his crew of punchers were celebrating the birth of that son, a birth in no wise marred in Hawk's mind by thought of the two men he'd killed a short time previously. But with Vard Whitlock it was a different matter: more now than ever he hated Hawk Nielson, and certain details of a plan for revenge commenced to formulate in his brain. He and Gabe Houston stood on the sidewalk before the Brown Jug Saloon, their angry glances following the retreating forms of the Forked Lightning men as they wended their drunken way down the street in the direction of the Red Steer Bar.

Gabe was first to speak. " The dirty varmint," he complained. " Killin' would have been too good for him. You shouldn't have stopped me, Vard, when I was gittin' ready to take out after Hawk, I coulda——"

" Shut up, you fool," Whitlock said harshly. " If I hadn't stopped you, you'd been lying dead on the floor with Tod and Steve by this time. Hawk would have taken you at one gulp——"

"I don't know's he would," Gabe protested. "Time was when I was a right good man with a hawg laig. And I ain't no fool, Vard."

"I know, I know," Whitlock said wearily. "I didn't mean it that way, Gabe. I'm just fagged out with thinking, that's all. I'm finding it hard to face the fact that my Bench-W is gone, or will be by to-morrow. I've worked damned hard on that place."

"Jest like I did on my 13-Bar," Houston agreed. "Say, you mentioned about there being some other way to square things with Hawk. What did you mean?"

The lines in Whitlock's embittered features deepened. He didn't answer at once. Finally he said, "Gabe, how game are you? Maybe there is a way, if I can count on you."

"You can count on me," the little man said eagerly. "You saw I was ready to draw on Hawk——"

"I don't mean that kind of nerve, Gabe. You were mad. You weren't thinking. You were just running your head against a rock wall, that way."

"I'll do anything you say," Houston promised.

The swinging doors of the Brown Jug were pushed open. The deputy sheriff and another man emerged, carrying between them the dead body of Tod Ranson.

Whitlock seized Houston's arm. "Come on, let's get out of here where we can talk."

Without waiting for a reply, he hurried Houston off down the street, until they reached a frame-and-adobe building which housed the general store. Here, on a sort of porch with a rail, were chairs where the two men could sit in the shadow of the overhanging roof and not be noticed by anyone passing by.

They smoked in silence for several moments before Vard Whitlock spoke: "Gabe, what can you think of that might hurt Hawk Nielson the most?"

Houston replied promptly, " What can I think of ? " He cursed. " It would sure make that varmint mad if I got my 13-Bar outfit out of his clutches. Just like a plague of locusts, he is, always devourin'—and to-night, killin' Tod and Steve——"

" Wait ! " Whitlock sighed deeply and tried to hold the impatience from his tones. " You want to even up things with Nielson, don't you ? "

The little man ripped out an oath. " I'd be willing to die right now, if I could take Hawk Nielson to hell with me."

" I don't mean killing Gabe," Whitlock said tensely. " I know a better way to hurt Nielson. Killing would be too easy for him. I aim to do something that will hurt him until the day of his death. Think hard. What would hurt Nielson the most ? "

" To lose his money, of course."

" Worse than that. What's he all wrapped up in at present ? "

Houston's eyes widened. " You—you don't mean this kid that's just been born ? "

" That's what I'm talking about—no, wait, don't talk like a fool. I don't want to kill the kid. But supposing that son and heir should suddenly disappear ? "

The little man's startled exclamation sounded through the gloom. " You ain't—you ain't figuring to steal the kid, are you, Vard ? "

" Hawk Nielson would pay a pretty penny to get it back, Gabe."

The little man shivered. " I'd sure hate to be the one to collect the money, Vard. Hawk would kill both of us."

Whitlock snorted. " Don't you think I could arrange matters so that Hawk couldn't harm either of us ? "

" I dunno if you could. It seems right dangerous to me. Hawk would trail us down and——"

Whitlock's contemptuous laugh cut short the words. " Where's that nerve you were showing a spell back when you wanted to shoot Nielson ? Just showing off, eh, Gabe ? And now you're quitting me cold."

" I ain't nuther." His pride stung, the little man screwed up his courage. " I'm with you, Vard. You just tell what you want done—but wait. What you going to do with the kid when we get it ? Weanin' a calf is one thing—stealin' a kid and takin' care of it is another. It might die on us."

" Leave that to me. I know a family of Mexes not too far from here. Helped 'em out of a scrape one time, and now they'll do anything for me. I just want some help from you, that's all."

" You'll get it." Houston cursed. " Damn Hawk Nielson ! Just like a plague of locusts, he is, always devourin'——"

" Hush up while I think." Whitlock rose from his chair and went to one end of the porch where moonlight shone beneath the overhanging roof. He drew from one pocket a small note-book and stub of lead pencil. Tearing a sheet of paper from the note-book, he quickly sketched a crude map. Then he rejoined Houston in the shadow and handed him the map. " Take a good look at this later, then burn it up. It shows certain points at which I want to find ponies waiting for me when I come riding. I'll have Nielson's kid with me and I'll be travelling fast. Don't fail me. With a relay of horses I can make fast time to—to where I'm taking the kid ; then I'll get back to town the same way. If anything goes wrong we'll both swear we were at my Bench-W to-night." He gave a sharp, bitter laugh. " It's still my outfit to-night, even if I do have to clear out by to-morrow——"

" You aimin' to do it to-night ? " Houston asked, aghast.

" The sooner the better. It's still fairly early. Hawk and his crew are away from the Forked Lightning. What better time? You just leave that part to me, and do your job of having those ponies waiting when I come along."

"But where'll I get the ponies?"

"Out at my place. They're still my ponies until to-morrow. By that time, if luck is with us, they'll be back in the corral—and Hawk Nielson's kid will be fifty miles from here. I'm heading for the Forked Lightning right now. You get going for my place. If we can slip out of town without any-one seeing us, so much the better. It shouldn't be hard. Practically the whole town is down at the Red Steer at present, helping Nielson gulp down liquor."

The two men talked a few minutes longer, then went to get their ponies, climbed into saddles and, unnoticed, quickly slipped out of town.

4

SHOTS IN THE NIGHT

In the large main room of the Forked Lightning ranch house Dr. Sanford Gallatin sat drinking at a bare wooden table. Beyond several shelves of books arranged along one wall, the room was furnished with only the barest necessities. Tables and chairs were huge, ponderous, like Hawk Nielson himself. There were no rugs on the floor, nor any pictures on the walls. A bedroom, in another part of the house, contained certain feminine touches; here it was that the dead body of Hawk Nielson's wife lay on a bed. In another room, in a small cradle, slept the Hawk's tiny son and heir, while near by a half-Indian, half-Mexican woman alternately dozed and then roused to make certain the infant was sleeping peacefully.

In the outer, main room an oil lamp cast its light on the drunken figure of Dr. Gallatin. He sat slumped in a straight-backed chair, drinking steadily from the bottle before him. He was a rather fleshy man, with prematurely grey hair, bloodshot eyes, and shaking hands, though even now the thought came to him, through a sort of drunken haze, that his hands were steadier than when he had . . .

A groan burst from his loose lips. " Blundered again," he mumbled self-accusingly, thinking of the dead woman stretched on the bed in the other room. " I got no business —being a doctor. Never wanted—hic!—to be a doctor. That madman—Nielson—had to have a son. So—had to give him—hic!—son. Wish he'd paid me—hic!—'fore he left—then I could—hic!—get out of here. I'll wager Nielson—hic!—would have killed me—if that baby hadn't been —hic!—a boy. But the mother——"

He shuddered, stretched out one hand, and managed to splash some liquor into a glass which he carried, shakingly, to his lips. A goodly portion of the whisky dribbled down his chin and on to his soiled white shirt. Again he slumped back in his chair. Dimly, from a distance away, came the sounds of a guitar and voices. For a moment Gallatin couldn't locate the sounds, then he realized from whence they came.

When Nielson had built this house a small settlement of Mexicans and Moqui Indians had been living on the south bank of Creaking River, a short distance from the building site. The two bloods had intermarried generations before and raised sheep and a few vegetables on which to live. The sheep Hawk Nielson had ordered from his range; the people he allowed to stay. Both men and women did odd jobs about the ranch house—jobs that regular punchers wouldn't accept or were incapable of doing. To celebrate the birth of the Nielson son and heir, the Moqui-Mexicans had butchered a steer, though the festivities were dampened somewhat by thought of the heir's dead mother. These people had liked the gentle woman whom Hawk Nielson married, though they had seen her but rarely.

How long Dr. Gallatin sat drinking at the table in the living-room he didn't know. Once he dozed. When he awakened, he saw the whisky bottle was empty. That didn't matter; there was a second bottle close at hand, and after some clumsy manœuvring Gallatin managed to draw the cork. He took a deep drink, then put his head on his arms on the table and slept.

He was awakened by women's voices in the room. The room swam as he struggled to his feet, then steadied. After a moment it came to him they'd been trying to wake him.

One of the women was the nurse who had been tending the baby. The other had come from the nearby Moqui-Mexican settlement but a moment before. Both women appeared greatly excited.

"But you must go at once, Señor Doctor," the nurse was insisting, her round, swarthy face shining in the lamplight.

"Where? Go where, dammit?" Gallatin steadied himself with one hand on the chair-back. "What in the devil are you talking about?"

Instantly both women started pouring forth a voluble mixture of Spanish, Moqui, and English. Gradually Gallatin managed to piece out the story:

A horse-drawn wagon, carrying a man and wife looking for homestead land farther west, had lost its way in the darkness while crossing the range, and had blundered over the high bluffs of Creaking River to crash to the bottom some distance below. It was here that Tony Tiguan, returning late to the Moqui-Mexican settlement, had discovered the accident, after hearing faint moans ascending from below the edge of the bluff.

Tiguan had found the wagon half in, half out of the water. Both horses were dead. Within the overturned wagon, crushed under the load of household goods and farm tools, lay the man and the woman. That the man had a crushed skull Tiguan didn't discover until he had brought the body from the wreckage. The woman, when he carried her out, was still conscious, and managed to tell Tiguan her story before fainting away. That she hadn't much longer to live Tiguan didn't realize. He made her as comfortable as possible, then mounted and hurried to the settlement for help, the settlement being only about half a mile distant.

It was his sister, Rosa Tiguan, who first thought of the doctor at Nielson's house and had hurried to fetch him. Between them Rosa and the Nielson heir's nurse got Gallatin started, much to the doctor's reluctance. He picked up his medicine-case and staggered from the house. Outside, Tony waited with two mules and the doctor's horse. By this time Tony Tiguan had secured a lantern, and he led the way while Rosa and the doctor came behind.

Gallatin muttered feeble curses all the way to the scene of the wrecked wagon, the curses increasing as the trio of riders made their way down a gully to reach the bottom of the bluffs. And then, as the light of the lantern fell upon the injured woman stretched unconscious not far from the smashed vehicle, the doctor's profanity changed abruptly to a deep groan of exasperation : " Oh, God ! Not two in the same night."

" Two ? " Rosa queried, puzzled, her dark eyes questioning. " What is theese you speak of, Señor Doctor ? "

Gallatin pointed a shaking finger at the woman as he dismounted. " Do I have to tell you ? "

Rosa emitted a gasp. " Ah ! *Pobrecica*—poor little woman. She is—how you say ?—*preñada*. It is that she——"

The doctor didn't wait to talk. Much as he hated the job, still he had taken a certain oath in medical school. He'd do his best, knowing, for the second time that night, that his best probably wouldn't be good enough. He dropped by the side of the unconscious woman and made a quick examination. Even his unskilled fingers told him there was no hope—too many broken bones, internal injuries. He resumed swearing in a monotonous undertone while he delved into his medicine-case for such aid as he could give.

Tony Tiguan stood at his shoulder. Gallatin paused once to tell him, " You'd better get anything you can out of that wagon. You said the man was dead ? You're sure ? "

" Come look at hees head," Tony replied. " Is crush like the melon—is no help for heem. Come make of the looking."

"I'll take your word for it."

Tony went off in the direction of the wagon, while Rosa stayed to give any help possible. After a time Gallatin's efforts were rewarded slightly. The woman opened her eyes, moaned, and whispered, "Save my baby."

That night Gallatin came as near being a doctor as he would ever be. Frantically he searched his memory for the things he had learned years before at medical college and put them to use. He cursed the inadequacy of his medicine-case, but did manage to a large extent to ease the woman's pain. Occasionally she spoke brief words. Gallatin learned that she and her husband were very poor, that they had no relations, that they had come West hoping to get a start in life. Once she asked for her husband, but lapsed into a momentary unconsciousness before Gallatin could frame any sort of reply.

Her baby was born a brief few minutes before she, too, died.

Tony Tiguan returned just as Gallatin was handing the crying infant to Rosa. Tony looked stolidly at it a moment, then, "Ah, it comes the fine *niña*. Is eet she will live?"

"That," Gallatin said grimly, "is up to you two. I'm through. I'm going to get out of this accursed country just as soon as Hawk Nielson pays what's owing me."

He picked up his case and started towards his horse. As he mounted he heard Rosa ordering Tony to get a blanket from the wagon in which to wrap the baby. "Anyway," Gallatin pondered as he kicked his mount in the ribs, "this time it wasn't my fault the woman died. It's a miracle I saved the child. Maybe this will cancel out that—that other. God! How I need a drink."

By this time a full moon sailed high overhead. Vard Whitlock, as he approached the Forked Lightning ranch house, cursed that moon. He had hoped for more darkness.

"Dammit!" Whitlock told himself. "I should have got out here earlier. Still, I had to wait long enough for Gabe to get those horses strung along the way for me. If that old coot fails me now . . ."

He paused, searching out the grounds about the house. There was no one to be seen in the vicinity, though some distance away he could discern the outlines of the Moqui-Mexican settlement on the near bank of Creaking River. Boldly Whitlock dismounted near the front of the house, after passing through the wide gateway in the fence that encircled the Forked Lightning buildings. A couple of lights burned in the ranch house; the bunkhouse was in total darkness, showing that the whole crew was in Ordway, helping Hawk Nielson celebrate.

"They're a pack of fools," Whitlock muttered savagely as he made his way to the open doorway beyond the gallery of the house. It was going to be easier than he had figured. Before entering, he produced a large blue bandanna, which he fastened across the lower part of his face in the form of a mask. Then he went into the house, walking easily on tiptoes.

He was playing in luck. Passing through the big, empty main room, in which a lamp still burned, he stepped silently into the adjoining chamber. Here a single oil lamp, turned low, burned on the rough board table. In the far corner sat the round-faced Moqui-Mexican nurse, Guadalopa, sound asleep in her chair, her mouth opening and closing gently as she snored.

Not far from the dozing woman was a hurriedly fashioned cradle in which lay sleeping the Son of the Hawk, only his wrinkled red face showing from the blankets in which he was bundled. Casting a quick glance at the snoring nurse, Whitlock made his way silently across the floorboards. Once a joint creaked beneath his foot and he stopped dead still, scarcely daring to breathe. The nurse slept peacefully on. In a moment Whitlock renewed his approach.

Finally he reached the cradle. Stooping over, he lifted gingerly the roll of blankets and tiny bit of humanity, straightened up with it in his arms. Abruptly his luck changed. The baby opened his eyes and a round, toothless mouth. The wail he raised was enough to disturb the dead.

The Moqui-Mexican woman straightened in her chair, stared dazedly about the room a moment, then, as her eyes cleared and focussed on Whitlock, she came awake with a jerk. Leaping from her chair, she threw her body between Whitlock and the door through which he was about to depart.

"There is no need to be disturbed, señora." Whitlock spoke easily in Spanish. "I but come to take the little one to the Señor Nielson that he may display it to the town of Ordway and show off his man-child. It is but the natural act of a proud father, eh?"

For a brief instant the woman was deceived by the words. She paused, then the sight of the bandanna mask across Whitlock's features quickly brought her to her senses.

"No, no, no, señor!" she protested rapidly. "You do much wrong to take away the little one. The Hawk would kill me were he to return and find it missing. I plead with you, señor, return the so small *niño* to his cradle and leave with much haste."

Her hands came out, endeavouring to grasp at the small bundle which by this time was howling lustily.

Whitlock pushed her roughly to one side, and the woman followed him, begging and entreating, as he passed through the doorway. Again he was forced to tear loose her hands as she persisted in clutching at his body to stop the kidnapping of the baby.

To the yelling of the infant were now added the screams of the woman. To Whitlock it seemed as though the noise would carry for miles and miles across the unbroken quiet of the range.

And, as if in answer to the nurse's cries, there came the staccato drumming of horses' hoofs along the trail that led to the Forked Lightning: Hawk Nielson, in town, had become uneasy at the thought of leaving the house unprotected, and he had sent two of his punchers home to keep watch against fire or trouble of any sort, though the thought of kidnapping had never entered his mind.

By this time a second nurse, who had been sleeping at the rear of the house, was aroused by the din of screams, wailing cries, and thundering hoofs. She came rushing to add her screeching to that of the other nurse. Both of them sprang like wildcats at Whitlock, but he managed to fight them off, carrying the squalling baby under one arm, while the other was employed to send the women, one after another, crashing back against the wall. He had no desire to strike them.

Gradually he made his way out of the house, fending off first one woman, then the other. He had just gained the side of his waiting pony when the sounds of the approaching Forked Lightning riders reached his ears. Flinging the nearest woman savagely to earth, he vaulted into the saddle, the baby carried in front of him. The next instant the horse had leaped into motion.

By this time the moon had passed under a cloud for a few moments and the ranch yard was in darkness. Whitlock tried to get to the gateway before the two approaching Forked Lightning riders, but in this he was doomed to disappointment. They reached the gateway first, thus cutting off his retreat. Behind him the two women were still screaming wildly, though the baby, momentarily, had ceased his wailing. Whitlock pulled his pony to a halt at one side, hoping the two riders would pass without question, though he knew in his heart that his luck couldn't be that good.

" Hey, what in hell is going on here ? " one of the riders demanded as he drew rein at the side of his companion in the gateway. " What's all the racket about ? " He peered through the shadows, trying without success to make out Whitlock's features.

Whitlock laughed coolly. " That's what I can't figure out," he replied, even-voiced. " I came here, looking for Hawk Nielson, and I reckon I must have woke up some kid back there. Then a couple of women started caterwaulin'. I must have scared 'em." By this time Whitlock was hoping against hope that the baby he carried would remain silent until he could make his getaway.

" Who are you, anyway ? " the other Forked Lightning hand demanded.

" I'm a friend of Hawk's from up Montana way," Whitlock replied, gathering his energies for a dash. He knew that was his only chance now. He cast a quick glance over one shoulder and through the gloom saw the two women approaching at a run, both of them still screaming. He went on, " It just occurred to me, maybe this isn't Hawk Nielson's place any more. Can you tell me where he is——"

And that was as far as he got when the moon emerged from behind a cloud to throw its silver radiance over the scene.

It required but an instant for the two Forked Lightning men to notice the bandanna mask across Whitlock's face. Now he knew he was in for it. His hand dropped to the gun at his side.

" Hell's bells ! " one of the men swore, noticing the bundle. " This hombre's got Hawk's kid ! "

At the same instant both men went for their guns. Whitlock's weapon came up streaming red lances of flame. Four explosions sounded almost simultaneously. One of the Forked Lightning men toppled from the saddle, his pony leaping nervously to one side. This partly cleared Whitlock's path. Holding the baby with one arm, while his other hand operated the six-shooter, Whitlock guided his pony with knee-pressure and jabbed home his spurs.

Red fire exploded before his eyes, the breeze from a leaden slug fanned his cheek as he drove straight at the single rider still barring his way. Again Whitlock fired, crouching low behind his pony's head as he came dashing full tilt at the man and horse blocking the roadway.

Too late the Nielson rider saw the danger. He tried to rein his mount clear, but Whitlock's horse, gathering speed with its first jump, struck the Forked Lightning animal on one shoulder. The horse staggered under the impact, lost its balance, and went down, carrying its rider to earth. As Whitlock swept past he turned in his saddle and emptied his gun at the man pinned beneath the struggling horse.

Neither of the Forked Lighting horses had been injured, and the one on the earth quickly regained its feet and started off in the direction of the corral, the other horse following it after a moment. Meanwhile both riders were sprawled motionless on the ground, the moon reflecting a glassy light from their wide-open, staring eyes.

By this time Whitlock was riding as he had never ridden before. Less than ten miles from the Nielson gateway, he turned his sweat-lathered pony in the direction of a spreading live-oak tree. There, awaiting his arrival, was a fresh pony. Whitlock voiced a triumphant exclamation. Gabe Houston was following instructions to the letter. Now there'd be fresh ponies at regular intervals along the route Whitlock had marked out. Dismounting, he placed the baby on the earth while he changed saddles. Within a minute he was again up and away, the baby, now once more asleep, carried safely in his left arm.

Through the night Whitlock made his swift ride. By the time he'd pounded one horse almost into exhaustion he'd reached the place where another tethered mount was ready for him. He made record time to his destination, and hesitated only a moment after delivering the baby to a Mexican family he knew he could trust. Without leaving his hot saddle, he called the family out of bed just when false dawn was streaking the sky, gave them a few brief facts, and said he'd return later. Then he started the dash back to his Bench-W Ranch—the ranch he was due to lose this day.

On his return trip he picked up the horses he had left along the route and drove them before him. While still fifteen miles from the Bench-W he made out the approaching figure of Gabe Houston. Neither man spoke when they drew rein together. Finally Gabe said, " Figured you might have your hands full with those horses. Thought I might help a bit."

" Glad you came out." Whitlock nodded. " You did a good job, Gabe, lining out these ponies for me. Thanks."

" No thanks necessary." Another moment's silence, then, " Did—did you do it ? "

" It's done, Gabe."

" Any trouble, Vard ? "

Whitlock's face clouded. " Some. I had to shoot a couple of Nielson's hands."

" Who were they ? "

" Sniper Kelly and Dog Tremaine."

" Them bustards ! " Houston swore. " Don't let it bother your conscience any. Them's the pair that shot that nester and his wife in the back when they wouldn't vacate their property fast enough to suit Hawk. What Dog and Sniper got they had coming. Sure you killed 'em ? "

"I wasn't aiming to leave evidence behind me," Whitlock said grimly. "Come on, let's hustle these broncs along. I'll pick up what few belongings I got at the Bench-W, then Nielson can have the place any time he wants to move in. You and me will go to Ordway and wait for the explosion when Hawk learns what's happened. Then, when he's about ready to go insane, a certain proposition will reach him——"

"We'll show Hawk Nielson." Houston grinned nastily. "We'll make him pay—him that been like a plague of locusts always devourin' up the range of honest men, always devourin' . . ."

They started the ponies toward the Bench-W Ranch, long shadows from the early morning sun travelling at their side.

5

AN UNFORESEEN COMPLICATION

AFTER ushering into the world the second baby of that night, Dr. Sanford Gallatin returned as speedily as possible to the Forked Lightning ranch house, the sole thought in his mind at the moment concentrated on the partly filled bottle of whisky he had left standing on the table in the main room of the house. Gallatin felt he needed a drink—a big drink—and needed it badly.

As he approached the house he suddenly heard a great deal of screaming and then the thundering explosions of six-shooters. For an instant he drew rein, reluctant to continue. "Now what in the devil has happened? Pshaw! It's probably just that madman, Nielson, returned here to finish his celebrating. If this isn't the goddamnedest country! The sooner I can get back to New York, the better. I'll drop medicine and take up something else. . . ."

He'd already resumed his journey towards the house. There was more screaming and more shots; then came the quick drumming of a horse's hoofs. The screaming commenced to let up a trifle, and he went on. As he neared the house, the two Mexican-Moqui women took form in the gloom. The instant they spied the doctor their screaming was resumed, and they bore down on him, both talking at once, and then screaming again.

"Dammit!" Gallatin said irritably. "Shut up! Both of you. Now what's wrong? Who was doing that shooting?"

They calmed down somewhat, but both talked at once. The hands of the two women kept pointing in the direction of the gateway that led out of the ranch yard.

Gallatin said, " Oh hell ! " and started his horse towards the gateway, the women running behind.

A minute later he spied the dead forms of Dog Tremaine and Sniper Kelly stretched on the earth. Both still held clutched in their lifeless fingers six-shooters from which bullets had been exploded.

Gallatin jumped to conclusions : " Nielson's gang even fight among themselves, eh ? "

He got down from the saddle. The two nurses fell silent while he made a swift examination of the two dead men, then straightened to his feet. " Nothing I can do for those two. They're both dead." The two women eyed him stolidly. " Dead, see ? " Gallatin insisted. He searched his memory for the few Spanish words he had. " *Muerto*—dead—finished—*terminado*—oh, hell ! Can't you understand ? I can't help them——"

A sudden wailing broke forth from the two women. Impatiently Gallatin seized Guadalopa by the shoulder and shook her with considerable vigour. " Now stop this damn foolishness, you hear ? Get back to the house and take care of Hawk Nielson's baby. There's nothing any of us can do here—— What ? What's that ? "

Through chattering teeth Guadalopa had stammered out the information that the Nielson infant was no longer within the house, that it had, in fact, been stolen away by a *bandido* with a mask across his face. And that the *bandido* had also made a shooting against the two dead men who lay near the gateway.

" My God ! " Gallatin's face went ashen. " The baby's gone ? No ! You're crazy. Nobody would steal a baby. Repeat that again. Dammit ! Don't talk so fast."

The doctor listened intently, the blood commencing to congeal in his veins. No, no, no ! It couldn't be true ! Abruptly Gallatin hurled himself on his horse and hurried to the house. Throwing himself from the saddle before the gallery, he rushed through the open doorway, through the main room, and into the chamber where he had last seen the Nielson baby sleeping peacefully.

The cradle was empty!

All life seemed to desert Gallatin's limbs. For a moment he couldn't think. Turning, he staggered back to the main room and dropped weakly into a chair at the table. The bottle of whisky caught his gaze and he swallowed greedily. Ah! That was what he had needed. He felt a trifle better, and took another swallow. The fiery liquor coursed through his veins. All right, the baby was gone, stolen by a bandit. But it wasn't Gallatin's fault; but wait!

A new thought struck Gallatin. He'd been left in charge when Hawk Nielson and the punchers departed for Ordway. Hawk might—*would*—hold Gallatin responsible for this. A great groan burst from Gallatin's loose lips. His weak chin quivered.

"Oh, my God, what a fix to be in! Nielson was a madman before. When he learns the baby is stolen he'll turn into a murdering maniac. He'll kill me—sure as hell he'll kill me!"

With an effort Gallatin staggered to his feet, seizing the whisky bottle as he came erect. "Got to get out of here," he frantically told himself. "Nielson wouldn't listen to reason. The baby gone. My fault, he'd call it. He'd put a bullet through my heart. To hell with the money he owes me. I'll take that horse outside and call my bill paid——"

Steps sounded on the gallery outside the doorway. Like some caged animal, Gallatin glanced about for other means of leaving the house. When he saw that only Guadalopa and the other nurse were entering the room, he nearly fainted with relief. He paused, took a long drink from the bottle, and rushed towards the doorway. Instantly both the Moqui women sent up a wailing.

Guadalopa clutched at Gallatin's coat sleeve. " Señor Doctor, where do you go ? "

" Damn you, let go of me," Gallatin panted. " I'm getting out of here—never mind where——"

" No, no ! " the other nurse protested. " You must not leave us to explain to the Señor Hawk. He would kill us. But you, the Señor Doctor, you can say just how this so bad thing has taken place——"

Gallatin couldn't understand the words, but he caught their import. Wrenching himself from the clutching grasps of the women, he flung himself through the doorway. " Tell Nielson I didn't have a thing to do with it," he flung over his shoulder. " I'm taking his horse for what's coming to me. I won't be back—ever ! "

He went pounding across the gallery floor, stumbled down the step at the edge, and scrambled into the saddle of the waiting horse. Then, pausing only long enough to take a deep drink from the bottle he carried, he urged the horse off into the night and was never again seen in the Cascabel Mesa country. Where he went no one ever knew.

Eventually the two nurses stopped screaming from sheer lack of breath. When quiet fell they could hear the rapidly receding hoofbeats of Gallatin's horse.

Finally Guadalopa said sorrowfully, " Josefa, the Señor Doctor is gone."

" He is gone," the other nurse agreed. " He will never return."

" For a doctor he was a very great coward," Guadalopa stated.

" Before the Señor Hawk Nielson many men are cowards. And I cannot blame such men too much," Josefa returned. She was a thin, wiry woman of thirty, and lacked the rounded spots of the more fleshy Guadalopa. Both women were of swarthy complexion with black hair and beady eyes ; both wore flowing skirts, a sort of coloured blouse, and a *rebazo*, or shawl.

By this time they could no longer hear the sounds of the retreating hoofs of the doctor's horse. Guadalopa sighed. Josefa sighed. Together they made their way heavily into the house, through the main room, and back to the room of the empty cradle, where they sat heavily down on two chairs and considered the problem.

Guadalopa spoke first. " The Hawk is a man of violent temper. When he finds the *niño* is gone, he will kill me."

" That is possible. But then, one has to die sometime," Josefa said philosophically.

Guadalopa looked pained. " He will also," she pointed out, " kill you as well, Josefa."

A startled light entered Josefa's beady eyes. " To kill me would be an injustice. I was at some distance away, dreaming of *mi madre* in heaven, when the *bandido* entered——"

" I also have a mother in heaven," Guadalopa said with some sarcasm. " Think you the Señor Hawk would pause to hear talk of angels before killing both of us ? "

" It would be the fine opportunity," Josefa said bravely, " for us to see once more our so holy mothers. Perhaps we too would become holy when the thing happened to us."

" Perhaps." Guadalopa sniffed, unconvinced. " Holiness, after all, is a matter that could be overdone when one is not prepared. I, for one, do not wish to die."

" With me it is the same thought."

Josefa sighed deeply. Guadalopa sighed deeply, her heavy bosom rising and falling. Then came a long silence.

Josefa finally spoke : " The Señor Dr. Gallatin——"

" That so cowardly one——"

"—of a certainty he will never return."

" Of what are you thinking, Josefa ? "

" We could relate it to the Señor Hawk that the Señor

Doctor departed with the *niño*. It would be but natural for the *médico* to take the child away. If he does not return with the *niño* it is no fault of ours."

"For what reason," Guadalopa demanded scornfully, "should the *médico* depart with the child? You speak of impossibilities. I, myself, heard the Señor Hawk order him to wait here for the money that was due him. That spineless one would wait as ordered——"

"Nevertheless, he has already departed as though a thousand devils were at his heels."

"Because of his fear of one devil with a gun," Guadalopa pointed out. "No, Josefa, we cannot deceive the Señor Hawk with so empty a tale. We must think of something with no flaws."

Another long silence ensued, broken only by an occasional sigh.

Eventually Guadalopa spoke. "He will kill both of us."

"He will kill both of us," Josefa agreed. She commenced silently to weep.

"He will do worse," Guadalopa continued stolidly. "He will kill all the people in our little settlement. His rage will be so great it will be a consuming fire. Much blood will flow——"

"It will be on the head of the *bandido* who stole the child," said Josefa brokenly.

"I think first of my own head," Guadalopa replied. "Weeping eyes perceive no solutions, Josefa. Your tears are wasted. We must think deeply."

For a time they both "thought deeply."

"I have reached a conclusion," Guadalopa said at last.

Hopefully Josefa raised her head. "Yes?"

"This," Guadalopa stated, "is a matter of much difficulty."

"And is that all you have decided?"

"That is all I have decided. But not yet have I stopped thinking."

"With no thinking at all," Josefa said disappointedly, "I have reached your same conclusion."

They were sitting, looking blank-eyed at each other, when Rosa Tiguan and her brother Tony entered, eager to tell the tale of the wagon that had gone over the bluffs of Creaking River and of the man who had died and of the woman who had given birth to a small girl-child an instant before she, too, died. Both talked excitedly, while Guadalopa and Josefa listened intently, both relieved momentarily to forget for a time their own troubles. Gradually a thought was forming in their minds. Here was the solution to the problem.

"And this newborn *niña*—where is it?" Guadalopa broke in.

"It sleeps at our mother's, in the settlement," Rosa replied. "A fine healthy child——"

"Guadalopa," Josefa interrupted, beady eyes shining, "this is a miracle!"

"A gift sent us by the saints," Guadalopa agreed. "Now I, for one, shall not die."

"Nor I," Josefa cried, "nor our little settlement. Our *madres* in heaven have come to our aid——"

"What is all this nonsense of dying?" Tony Tiguan demanded. He was slim and dark, with velvet blouse hanging outside his denim overalls. A battered Stetson covered his black hair, and he wore moccasins on his feet. Rosa, who looked much like her brother, was dressed as were Josefa and Guadalopa. "Dying," Tony went on, "is a matter for the Señor Doctor—— *Yai!* But where is the Señor Doctor?"

Rosa gave a short scream. "The small man-child of the Señor Hawk is not in the cradle. Josefa! Guadalopa! What has happened? You look strange!"

Between them, Josefa and Guadalopa told the story. Of the kidnapping by the *bandido*, the shooting of the Forked Lightning punchers, the flight of Dr. Gallatin. Spanish, interspersed with the softer Moqui, cracked and sputtered between the four, while the matter was discussed. Gradually the conversation died down.

Tony looked glum. "This is a very bad thing. The Señor Hawk will not only kill Josefa and Guadalopa—also he will take vengeance on all our people."

"What shall we do?" Rosa wailed.

Josefa turned sternly on the two. "*Silencio!* Have you no courage? But leave all matters to Guadalopa and me. To us goes the proud honour of saving our so lovely settlement."

"True." Guadalopa smiled confidently. "While Rosa and Tony display the minds of shallow-brained birds, Josefa and I, out of our combined knowledge, arrive instantly at a plan."

"A plan?" Rosa and Tony cried together.

Guadalopa lowered her voice. "It is this," she confided; "we shall place in the cradle of the missing *niño* the small girl-child that was born to-night to the woman of the wrecked wagon. Who is to know the difference? To a father, all newborn babes look the same."

"And it is a thing," Josefa put in, "that will keep the Señor Hawk in a condition of no anger. That is most necessary, if we wish to keep our homes—nay, our very lifeblood."

Excited talk sprang up among the four. Tony voiced certain protests: "But the child that was born of the Señor Hawk's blood is a man-child. This that you propose to put in its place is a girl."

A stunned silence fell on Josefa and Guadalopa. Such a complication had not before occurred to them. Guadalopa spoke first: "No matter. I was here when the child was born. The Señor Hawk saw it only after it had been wrapped in blankets. Only its face he saw."

"But already," Rosa pointed out, "the Señor Doctor has declared it to be a boy."

"Already," Guadalopa said scornfully, "the Señor Doctor is many miles from here. Almost of a certainty he will never return. He is known for a fool. Perhaps he made a mistake. Could I understand what words he spoke to the Señor Hawk, I who do not understand well the language they employ? No, it is settled. The Hawk is the father of a girl-child——"

"But even now he celebrates the birth of a boy," Rosa said weakly.

"Is that our responsibility?" from Josefa. "How are we to know what he celebrates? If necessary, Guadalopa will take an oath it was a woman-child the doctor handed her——"

"*I* will take an oath?" Guadalopa asked cautiously. "On what must I swear this thing?"

"On whatever is necessary to convince the Señor Hawk," Josefa replied promptly. "Do you lack of courage? Think, it is a matter of charity. You provide a home for a small orphan. The saints will bless you. All our settlement will be in your debt. There is no harm done. What is more, you will not have to die at the hands of the Señor Hawk."

"I will take the oath," Guadalopa stated firmly, and added mentally, "only if it becomes necessary."

"But the Señor Hawk when he returns——" Tony commenced.

"He has already stated he will not return until Ordway is entirely dry of liquor," Guadalopa cut in. "By that time, at the least, the sun will be high in to-morrow's sky."

"But," Tony persisted, "when he arrives he will see the two dead men you have spoken of—those near the gateway. How explain that?"

Guadalopa shrugged. " It is not my business to explain. If they arrive here, drunken and quarrelling, is it something that concerns me if they decide to kill each other ? I know nothing of such matters."

Tony nodded slowly. " But the hoofprints of the *bandido's* horse as it leaves—— "

" There are already so many prints in the dust," Josefa pointed out, " that they will not be noticed."

" What of the wagon that went over the bluffs ? " Rosa asked suddenly. " Could there be papers of a sort to tell that the dead woman was to have a child ? "

Guadalopa considered. " That," she said finally, " is a thing that is in the hands of the *Señor Dios*. But I do not think it should be left to chance. Tony, you will search well the goods of the crushed wagon and bring me all papers you find. I will take care of them."

" That is good." Josefa nodded. " And we must warn all of our people of the settlement that no word is to be said of this matter. It is something that could cause death, if one talked——"

" But the wagon," Tony asked, " and the man and woman who lie dead ? "

" Neither is that our business," Guadalopa stated, " should the Señor Hawk ask questions. True, we have heard of a wagon going over the edge. A man and a woman died in the wreck. You, Tony, and some other you will find to help you, have already buried the bodies. But bring me first any papers you find. As for the rest—the pots and pans and blankets—they must be left should the Hawk care to see for himself."

She waited for further questions, protests. There were none. Then she spoke triumphantly. " Go, Tony, attend matters at the wagon. Rosa, hurry to bring here the small girl-child. The cradle grows cold for want of a baby—a baby to be reared by the Señor Hawk."

Rosa and Tony quickly departed. Exhausted, Josefa and Guadalopa sank once more to their chairs, exhaling long sighs of relief.

" The saints should bless us for this night's arrangement," Guadalopa said after a time. " Look you, Josefa, we take a child of poverty, an orphan, and make things that it may be raised among moneybags."

" What is more," stated the more realistic Josefa, " you and I shall not so soon meet our mothers among the angels of heaven."

" That," Guadalopa said stolidly, " is a pleasure I can forego a little longer, my Josefa."

6

THE FIRST BLOW

It was past noon the following day when Hawk Nielson returned to the Forked Lightning, followed by only three of the punchers who had commenced the celebration with him, and these three could scarcely stay in saddles, so drunk were they. The remaining punchers were still sleeping off the effects of their intoxication at whatever spot they had "passed out" in Ordway. Of the four men who rode towards the gateway, only Hawk Nielson's eyes were clear and bright; he alone showed no signs of the vast amount of alcohol that had been consumed the previous night.

Flies buzzed above the carcases of Sniper Kelly and Dog Tremaine, their stiffened forms outlined clearly in the bright sunlight.

Nielson swore softly when his gaze lighted on the two dead men. "Damn them," he swore. "Looks like they continued that argument they started in town before I sent 'em home."

The punchers, sobered somewhat by this sight of their erstwhile companions, straightened a little in saddles and eyed the two dead men with bloodshot eyes. One of them spoke: "I allus felt it in my bones them two would tangle someday. Never figured they'd both go out at once, though."

"They sure must have been shakin' lead outten their bar'ls plenty fast," another rider observed. "Now Dog Tremaine——"

Nielson cut in, frowning, "I don't like this. You boys ride along down to the bunkhouse. I'll go to the house and see what's up."

He left the men and hurried to the house, dismounted, and strode inside. The main room was empty, but in the second room he entered he saw Josefa seated at the side of the sleeping child in the cradle. Guadalopa had returned to the settlement, for a time, to nurse one of her own children. As Nielson entered, Josefa got to her feet. Now came the first test. Would the Señor Nielson suspect? Inwardly the woman's heart was beating like a trip hammer; outwardly she was stolid, even sleepy-looking.

Hawk glanced quickly towards the cradle. "Is the baby all right, Josefa?"

"*Segura*—certain, Señor Nielson. For why should any-t'ing be wrong weeth the small *niña*?" She watched him closely, wondering if he'd notice she'd said "*niña*," a girl, rather than "*niño*," a boy. But the difference was too subtle for Nielson's detection. That another child had been substituted for his son was a thought that never entered his mind. To Hawk Nielson all babies looked alike.

He came closer to the cradle, stood gazing down a moment on the slumbering infant. Something like a proud smile touched his lips. He turned again to the woman, jerking one thumb over his shoulder. "Those two dead men out there—Kelly and Tremaine—what happened to them?"

"They are both dead, señor."

"Dammit"—irritably—"I know they're dead. What happened? Were they fighting?"

Josefa rolled her eyes towards heaven and called on the saints to preserve her. A voluble stream of Moqui left her lips. Nielson couldn't understand a word she was saying. Nielson seized her by the shoulder, shook her. "Damn you, woman, speak English!"

"W'at ees happen, I cannot say. Guadalopa and I—we hear them riding. We go to the door to listen. They are making the cursing one against the other. Then comes a thousand bangings. There are many groanings. Guadalopa and I—we reach them. Both men are of the dead. Had the Señor Doctor but remained it could be he——"

"By God! Where is that fool Gallatin?" Nielson had forgotten the doctor until now.

"That doctaire!" Josefa exclaimed scornfully. "As you say, he is the beeg fool. He ees also the coward. When comes the first shooting of theese Tremaine an' theese Kelly, the doctaire takes much of fright. He's leap to the horse an' ride like the madman. Where he goes, we do not know. As he ron to the door he say for us to tell you he ees take your horse in exchange for the money you owe heem. Guadalopa—ah, she is the brave one!—aids me in the attempt to stop him, but he knocks us to one side like the maniac. See, I bear marks of the battle!"

Unabashed, Josefa lifted her voluminous skirt and displayed a large purple mark on one buttock. "You see, Señor Hawk"—glancing slyly over her shoulder—"I have suffer' in the defence of your home."

"All right, all right," Hawk said impatiently. It was the sight of the bruise that convinced him Josefa was speaking truth, though that bruise, had Nielson but known it, had been inflicted when Whitlock, rushing from the house with the Nielson heir, had shoved Josefa rather violently to an abrupt sitting position.

"At least," Nielson went on, "you have taken good care of my son." He flung a gold coin in the woman's general direction. "For you and Guadalopa."

Josefa ignored the word "son" as she quickly stooped to retrieve the coin, then bent, solicitously, over the sleeping child, whose forehead was dotted with tiny beads of perspiration.

"It's damnably hot in here." Nielson frowned. "Do you have to keep him wrapped in all those blankets?"

Josefa straightened up and looked dumb. "The señor says?"

"All those blankets," Nielson growled impatiently. "They're enough to smother a child to death. Take 'em off!"

Josefa looked aghast. "W'at, no blankets! You want, Señor Hawk, for the so little one to catch of the chill? It would be of madness for heem to hav' no cover——?"

"Chill?" Nielson paused. "You mean he'd catch cold?"

"Eef no worse," Josefa replied indignantly, more sure of her ground now. "To the *niña* could come the sickness of the longs."

"Lung fever?" For the first time in his life Nielson was uncertain how to proceed. After all, the woman knew more than he regarding the care of babies. "Have it your own way," he grunted shortly. "So that fool Gallatin left, eh? Did he give you any instructions about the baby?"

Josefa looked blank. "Een-struc—w'at is theese you say? Oh, the *instrucción*! No, the doctaire he say that I, Josefa, and the so good Guadalopa, between us we know of theese thing more than heemself."

"That's not hard to believe," Nielson said shortly and left the room.

Relieved, Josefa again seated herself by the cradle.

In the main room Nielson paused. Momentarily his thoughts went to the dead mother of his child, covered with a blanket in the other bedroom. For a brief instant something of regret twinged his conscience. Perhaps he should have been more considerate. Half angrily he banished the thought, and turned back to the room where Josefa watched over the cradle. Again the woman got to her feet.

"There'll be an undertaker out from Ordway this afternoon," Nielson told Josefa. "At the same time he can pick up those two dead fools out by the gateway. If he wants me, tell him I've gone to the Bench-W to take over the place—no, never mind. I can see you don't know what I'm talking about. You Indians never understand a white man unless you want to. I'll tell the boys in the bunk-house."

Some trace of defiance entered Josefa. "May-bee some-time' the white man is hard to onderstan'," she stated simply. "For her in there"—she gestured to the room where the dead woman lay—"there should be burning the candle'. Guadalopa, when she return', ees bringing of the candle'. Is good, no?"

"Sure, sure, that's all right," Nielson said roughly.

"Also," Josefa continued, "there should be the so *grande* funeral. All of our settlement will be there. And for the child there mus' be—soon—the christen'. You have theenk of theese—no?"

"It'll be taken care of," Nielson said hastily. A christen-ing! That was something that had escaped his mind until now. Maybe this Moqui wasn't as dumb as she looked. A christening would mean a celebration in the Moqui settle-ment. Damn these Indians! always thinking of their own pleasures. Nielson's face hardened. "I'll take care of all that. You just see that the baby stays healthy."

For some reason he wanted to get out of the room. There was a mocking something in the Indian woman's eyes that he didn't like. Maybe he hadn't been a good husband. This was a hard country. If a woman couldn't stand the life, so much the worse for her. By God, though, folks would learn he could be a good father.

Nielson flung himself out of the room, quickly made his way to the bunkhouse, where he threw curses right and left in the direction of three listless cow-punchers. Then, giving a few brief instructions, he saddled a fresh horse and rode like mad in the direction of the Bench-W Ranch, arriving at that spot, deserted except for the horses in a corral, only a few short hours after Vard Whitlock and Gabe Houston had departed for Ordway.

For a week affairs ran smoothly. The Hawk's wife had been buried with some ceremony in Ordway's boothill. Nielson busied himself attending various businesses here and there. He visited Ordway and replied proudly to various questions relative to the well-being of his son. He would have liked to spend more time with the child, but always either Guadalopa or Josefa warned him off with much talk of the sicknesses that could come to an infant when not kept quiet. Occasionally he heard the child crying. Twice he had been able to see it when it was awake. It had blue eyes; this much he now knew. But so far he'd not had a good look at the infant.

It occurred to him suddenly that never yet had he held it in his arms. Even the night it had been born, Dr. Gallatin had passed it so quickly to Guadalopa, who as quickly wrapped it in a blanket, that he had scarcely any memory of it save that of a red, wrinkled face, tightly shut eyes, and a wide-open mouth from which had emerged a lusty howling. Nielson had just been entering the room at the moment, and he still remembered Gallatin's tired voice: "Well, you got your boy, Mr. Nielson—he's big—must weigh nearly ten pounds."

And then, after a long look at the blanket-swathed child, Nielson and his men had left for Ordway to celebrate.

Each time he came to look into the cradle, he pestered Josefa or Guadalopa as to when the child would walk, when it would commence to play, when talk, and at his questions he could feel rather than see a certain scorn creeping into the eyes of the Indian women. They made it clear it was best he should not come too near while it was small, and Nielson was afraid—for the first time in his life, afraid

—to do otherwise than they suggested. Their talk of fever and chills and smallpox epidemics sent shivers coursing down the spine of Hawk Nielson, who was commencing to realize that having a child is a very great responsibility for a parent.

And then one day when both Guadalopa and Josefa were away, leaving Rosa Tiguan in care of the child, Nielson returned unexpectedly. Rosa, intent at the time on bathing the child in a tin basin, didn't hear Nielson enter the house. He paused a moment in the doorway, listening to the Indian girl talking to the child in a mixture of Moqui and Spanish:

"And now, my little golden one, my small Dorado, we make clean beneath the arms. Ah, when the hair grows long, my little one, it will be like a waterfall of gold." Water sloshed in the pan. The child cried a little. "Hush, little one. Spare your tears, little *niña*. . . ." A wet rag slapped against the side of the tin basin. "Little Dorado of the so shining hair——"

"What sort of a name is that?" Hawk stepped suddenly into the room. "He'll be named Pitt when we have that christening—what in the devil is wrong with you, girl?"

Rosa had emitted a short, startled scream, then stood as though petrified. She knew she should cover the child, but she lacked strength to make a move. She just stood there, holding the child, who had commenced to cry.

"Is nozzeeng wrong, señor." Rosa spoke through chattering teeth. "Eet ees that you frighten' me—is all." She tried to gather her thoughts, distract attention from the child's body. "*Sí, sí*, Dorado, the Golden One—look to the head, señor. See, the small so golden hair already commence'."

But it was too late. Hawk scowled. "Who the devil's kid is that?" he growled. "I won't have you bringing your kids here——"

" Is your child, señor," Rosa whispered faintly.

" Nonsense," Hawk snapped. " This is a girl. My baby's a boy—my son. You fool Indians ! What's going on here ? Where's Guadalopa—Josefa ? "

" Sure, sure, is girl—is *niña*," Rosa faltered. " Ees much good to have the girl-child, señor. What ees theese talk of the boy ? "

" By God ! " Hawk thundered angrily. " Are you trying to tell me I didn't have a son ? " He advanced threateningly on the girl, then stopped and looked quickly around. The cradle was empty. " Where's my son, damn you ! "

Rosa staggered away from him, holding the crying child, and placed it in the cradle. Then she slumped to the floor in fear, her eyes tightly shut, waiting for the blow to fall. Hawk was standing over her, shouting, raging. The child's crying added to the noise.

Fortunately, at this moment Josefa and Guadalopa arrived. Both women turned white at the voice of the enraged Nielson. For a moment, they turned to flee, having realized instantly what had happened. But it would be impossible to escape the inevitable. The deception must continue. Firmly gripping each other's hands, they summoned their courage and entered the room.

" W'at is for all theese foolish yellings ? " Guadalopa demanded sternly, though inwardly she was quaking. " Is ver' bad for the child, Señor Hawk. You want to make die, perhaps ? "

Nielson turned on the two women like a raging hurricane. " It can die for all I care. It's not my son. Who brought that kid in here ? What are you tricky bustards trying to do, bring your own kids in here and let mine . . . ? "

" You have gone loco, may-bee ? " Josefa inquired. " Hav' we say it ees your son ? No, we say, always, eet is your daughter. We do not onderstan'——"

Another blast of cursing interrupted the words. The two women fell silent until Hawk had paused for sheer lack of breath. By this time Rosa had regained her feet and stood cowering at one side of the room.

" Goddammit ! " Nielson yelled. " I want my son. Where is he ? "

Guadalopa looked at Josefa. Josefa looked at Guadalopa. Both nodded understandingly. " Ees dronk, no ? " Guadalopa said.

" Ees ver' drunk," Josefa replied.

" W'at ees theese talk of the son, Josefa ? "

" There ees no son. Ah, too much of the whiskee ees ver' bad——"

" You blasted women," Hawk stormed. " I'm not drunk. I want my son, and you'd better speak fast before I put flame to all that lousy settlement of yours. Now, damn you, talk ! "

Josefa and Guadalopa fell silent until Hawk was once more out of breath, then Guadalopa brought into play all her nerve and no small amount of dignity.

" Señor Hawk," she said, " always you speak of the son. We have talk' much about theese theeng, an' we do not onderstan'. Why do you name theese girl-child a son——"

" Because I had a son," Hawk exploded.

Guadalopa shook her head. " Theese is the talk of a loco —a crazy man. Your wife she gives birth only to the girl-child."

That brought on another burst of cursing from Nielson, ending furiously with, " You've brought one of your own lice-ridden brats here to give it better care. I want——"

" You mak' talk like the fool," Guadalopa said scornfully. No—*silencio* !—let me feenish. You say that which is een the cradle ees of our people ? Look once more, señor, an' tell me if our people have the white skin, the blue eye', the golden hair. You are *demente* ! "

Despite himself, Nielson cast a look towards the cradle. No, that child there was no offspring of Indian and Mexican parents. Then, what in the hell . . . ? " Look here," he snarled. " You were here when my child was born. You heard Gallatin say, ' It's a boy.' "

Guadalopa shrugged fat shoulders. " Eef the doctaire say is a boy, then the doctaire he lie. No, I do not hear heem say theese—— "

" Dammit ! You were right in the room. You must have heard him ! "

Guadalopa nodded confidently. " *Segura*—I hear some talk, but eet ees not for me. I do not onderstan' well your language, señor. Besides, I am of the busy—making of care for the *niña*."

Perspiration dotted Nielson's red face. " By God ! I can't believe it."

" Is so," Josefa put in, quailing before the flaming look in Nielson's eyes, but nevertheless meeting bravely the hard gaze he turned on her. " The Señor Doctaire, heemself, before he make the depart, speak of the child as a girl. Like he was in theese room, even now, I can hear heem say, ' Take good care of theese leetle girl.' "

Nielson commenced to feel less certain of his ground. " Now look here," he commenced hesitatingly, " that doctor was a fool——"

" Who was it hired heem to come here ? " Guadalopa demanded, pressing her advantage. " Eef he was fool, why do you bring heem ? Yes, a beeg fool—somebody. But he knew enough to save hees life. When you say you keel heem if the baby is not the boy, w'at can you expec' he weel tell you ? You frighten' heem into telling what is not trut'—no ? "

He didn't admit it, but Nielson now remembered he had threatened Gallatin in various ways. By God! When he found Gallatin, he'd . . .

"That ees eet," Josefa put in sagely. "The doctaire lied to save hees own so miserable life."

"Somezing else," Guadalopa said reminiscently, "I am jus' remembaire—when the baby is born, the Señor Hawk request' to see her. But the doctaire say, 'No, no'—like that —'No, no'—an' geeve her to me so queeck to place in the blanket. Now you, too, remembaire, eh, Señor Hawk?"

The power of suggestion is great. Did Nielson remember the occurrence? He wasn't sure now. Then he commenced to have a vague memory of something of the sort. That goddam doctor had tricked him. His mind was in a whirl. All his plans for a son and heir came crashing down about his head to confuse, bewilder him. Abruptly he flung a single question at the women:

"You swear by all your saints that this—this girl-baby—is my child!"

Josefa and Guadalopa gulped simultaneously, then together they had the same idea: a small lie to save a small infant would be forgiven. Besides, nothing had been said about swearing by Moqui gods. It would be all right then.

"I make the swear." Guadalopa's head bobbed violently.

"I also swear," Josefa said brazenly, and added under her breath the single word "damn."

Nielson cast another look at the child in the cradle. His face darkened and he strode from the room with heavy steps. In the main room he dropped ponderously into a chair, his mind in a whirl. He had wanted a son; he had a girl. His heart sank. Though he didn't know it, Vard Whitlock had struck the first blow in his campaign for revenge.

In the room where the cradle stood, Guadalopa and Josefa were trying their best to revive a fainting Rosa. They whispered nervously and cast quick glances towards the room where Hawk Nielson sat lost in his disappointment.

"For a time," Josefa said, low-voiced, "I could hear very clearly the music of the harp of my mother in heaven."

"And mine also," Guadalopa averred. "They were making the duet—but I do not think I liked very much the sound of that music. I like better the soft chords of the guitar made in our settlement."

"*Es verdad*," Josefa agreed. Suddenly she blanched at a new thought that had reached her mind: "Comes the time perhaps when the *bandido* who stole the man-child of the Hawk may ask for a ransom. How then, my Guadalopa, to explain the thing we have done?"

All the blood drained from Guadalopa's face. Here was a complication that had never occurred to her. Her knees sagged. Then she got a firm grip on herself. "It is something that has not happened yet. Seven—eight days have gone by. Perhaps the *niño* has died for lack of the *bandido's* care. It may be no ransom will be asked. The Hawk is greatly hated. For revenge a man may have killed the child."

Josefa persisted, "But what if the Hawk does learn he is the father of a boy? What then is left us to do?"

Guadalopa shrugged. "That is a design we shall weave into the blanket when the wool arrives. For the time we have nothing to fear."

Both women heaved long sighs of relief. One more barrier had been crossed.

7

A CLASH OF WILLS

MEANWHILE Vard Whitlock and Gabe Houston, the morning after the kidnapping of Nielson's baby, had left the Bench-W and headed for Ordway, there to await the explosion that would inevitably occur when the Hawk learned of his loss. But the day passed without incident. Then Forked Lightning punchers who were still in town had climbed groggily into saddles, still unsteady from the liquor they had consumed, and departed for the Nielson ranch.

Whitlock and Houston were seated on the small porch that fronted the Brown Jug Saloon, talking in low voices.

"Maybe," Whitlock speculated, "Nielson doesn't know yet. It could be he went from Ordway straight out to the Bench-W to take possession. But wait until he gets home and learns what's happened. There'll come a blow-up that'll rock this town to its foundations, Gabe."

"I'll betcha!" The little man's eyes gleamed with expectation. "You figured out yet how we'll get the money for the return of the kid? How much you goin' to ask for?"

"I haven't got that part all worked out yet," Whitlock returned. "I'm just going to ask enough to pay us for our ranches. I wouldn't want to act like a crook. We'll let Hawk stew in his own juice for a spell. The longer he has to wait, the more ready he'll be to pay up. Let's go inside and get a drink."

"You got any money?"

"Certain. I've still got that money that me and Steve and Tod raised, hoping Hawk would take it and extend our notes. But he wouldn't. Don't worry, you and I got enough to live on until our bonanza comes."

Another day and a half passed before Nielson appeared in Ordway, and then it was solely for the purpose of attending the funeral of his wife and the two punchers who had, supposedly, killed each other during a drunken brawl. Whitlock had attended the funerals for just one purpose: to see what he could learn concerning the missing child. He found no opportunity to talk to Nielson, who quickly left town when the ceremonies were concluded, but he did manage a few words with one of the Nielson punchers in the Red Steer Bar.

"That was hard luck about Kelly and Tremaine." Whitlock put out a tentative feeler.

"Mebbe so," replied the Forked Lightning man. "I can't say it broke me up any. Those two was always wrangling, even if they were pards—kept the whole bunkhouse stirred up. I never trusted of 'em much."

"It was that way, huh?" Whitlock said carelessly and added, "How's Hawk's kid?"

The man shrugged. "'Sall right as far as I know. I never get up to the house to see it—fact is, I've never seen it. Hawk's got a coupla Injun women takin' care of it. Cripes! He's always talking about it. You'd think a kid had never been born before."

Whitlock considered. What the hell! Hawk always talking about the kid? Didn't he know yet it was missing? Maybe he'd been staying down in the bunkhouse with his men; maybe the Indian women had been afraid to tell him of the kidnapping. It could be Hawk didn't bother paying attention to kids when they were little. Still, that idea didn't seem hardly logical either. Frowning, Whitlock finished his drink and hastened out to find Gabe Houston.

"I don't like it," he told Gabe when he found the little man, sitting half asleep on the porch of the general store.

Gabe was only partially sober, having cadged enough drinks from customers of the Brown Jug to have attained " somewhat of an edge." He listened in silence, but had nothing to offer. Disgusted, Whitlock left him to resume his sleep.

The following day he encountered Nielson in town. Nielson said, " I suppose you know I took possession of your Bench-W ? "

Whitlock nodded. " I figured you had."

" Still sore about it ? " Nielson asked.

" What do you think ? " Whitlock said shortly.

" I know damn well you are." Hawk laughed. " But you'll get over it. It was a business proposition. You didn't pay up——"

" Forget it," Whitlock said coldly.

" I'll forget it quicker than you will," Nielson said arrogantly. " Look here, Whitlock, you've got more sense than most of the beef-raisers around here. I can use a foreman on the Bench-W. Want the job ? "

Whitlock eyed Hawk narrowly and shook his head. " I don't expect to be around here much longer. I'm pushing on—someplace."

" Where exactly ? " Hawk asked.

" That," Whitlock said quietly, " is none of your goddam business. If I told you, you'd come along and get me in your debt again."

A mighty laugh welled from Nielson's chest. He struck Whitlock a resounding blow on the shoulders. " Damned if you aren't a card, Whitlock. Well, no hard feelings, I hope."

" Like hell you hope. You don't care one way or the other, and you know it. Like you say, it was a business proposition. We'll forget it. How's that baby of yours ? "

" By God, there never was such a boy ! Wait until he gets his growth. He'll show this country a thing or two."

Whitlock forced an amused expression. "I suppose you're playing with him all the time."

Nielson shook his head. "Hell's bells! Those two nurses won't let me touch him for fear he'll get sick."

"You don't see him much, eh?" Whitlock waited eagerly for the reply.

"Sure, I see him every day. He sleeps most of the time."

Whitlock got away as soon as he could after that. "I don't like it, I don't like it," he told himself, his mind a whirl of vague speculations and surmises. "Hawk Nielson's up to something. He's covering up the disappearance of the kid for some reason. Why? What's he got in mind? Did he offer me the job on the Bench-W just to see if I'd stay in this country?"

The following day he again saw Nielson, this time in the Brown Jug. He asked again concerning the health of Nielson's son, and received again the assurance that the boy was getting along fine. Whitlock left the Brown Jug and sought out Gabe Houston, whom he found asleep in the haymow at the livery stable. He shook Houston into life and told him what Nielson had said.

"You think he's plannin' up some scheme?" Gabe asked fearfully.

"Yeah, I do—but I can't figure what it is. Look here, Gabe, you've never told anybody what we did, did you?"

"Cripes, no! You think I'm a fool?"

"I don't know," Whitlock said moodily. "Only a fool would get drunk every day the way you've been doing."

"Ain't costing you nothing. There's always friends to buy drinks for Gabe Houston. Now you looky here, Vard——"

"Shut up! I just thought of something. That map that I drew that night—you know, to show you where to leave the horses. Did you burn that map as I told you?"

" Course I did," the little man said, then added, " Least-wise I think I did. . . . I seem to remember. . . ."

" Goddammit, you're not sure, though," Whitlock said savagely. " You must have thrown it away——"

" I don't think so. . . ."

" But you're not sure. I ought to kill you for this, Gabe. That's what happened. Somehow Nielson has found that map. He's keeping quiet until he can learn who drew it. I wonder if there was any writing of mine on the other side of that page——"

He broke off. Houston was scrambling frantically out of the hay. " Where you going, Gabe ? "

" I'm aimin' to get outten town jest as fast as my bronc will carry me."

" Like hell you are, and leave me to face things alone, eh ? " He caught Houston by the shoulder and jerked him back. " Keep your nerve. If you suddenly run out now, Hawk's sure to suspect. We've got to stay here and bluff things out if anything is said. After all, it'll be me he'll be gunning for. Nobody knows it was you that handled those horses for me—unless you've made some drunken talk—— "

" I ain't, I swear I ain't." The little man's face was like chalk.

" All right, I'll take your word for it. But from now on until we leave town, don't you take another drink, or I'll wring your skinny neck."

" All right, Vard," Houston said meekly.

Two days later Whitlock encountered Nielson in the Brown Jug Saloon. Nielson offered to buy him a drink, which Whitlock refused, the thought having crossed Whitlock's mind that Hawk was planning to get him drunk and make him talk, in the hope of discovering something. " Thanks, no," Whitlock said. " I just dropped in for a sack of ' makin's.' "

"Changed your mind about taking a job on the Bench-W?" Hawk asked.

Whitlock said, "I'm not interested. Surprised you'd ask a second time."

Hawk laughed shortly. "There aren't too many men in this country with cow knowledge. Maybe I just wanted to make sure you wouldn't leave for a while."

Whitlock grunted something in reply and rolled a cigarette with fingers that trembled. He never knew what he said. By this time his mind was in a turmoil. Hawk suspected something, but wasn't sure. He wanted to keep Whitlock within reach, in the hope he'd make a false move. Thus ran Whitlock's thoughts. He could feel sudden perspiration running down inside his shirt. Every instinct told him to mount his horse and flee. Still he lingered, unable to resist an impulse to stay and, if possible, learn exactly what sort of trap Nielson was planning.

Herb Brown, at a request from Nielson, placed a bottle on the bar, and asked, "How's that boy of yours, Hawk?"

Nielson's eyes brightened. "By God, you never saw such a boy. I'm going to bring him to town just as soon as those Indian women say it's safe to take him out. You should see his blue eyes—wide open, clear. He'll make this country sit up and take notice in a few years, you mark my word."

"Blue eyes, eh? I heard one time that all babies have blue eyes when they're first born. Then some of 'em change later," Herb said.

"That so?" Hawk said dubiously. "In that case, maybe the boy will have eyes like mine, later."

Herb contemplated Nielson's piercing steely-grey eyes and mentally hoped the child wouldn't. One pair of eyes like that in the Cascabel Mesa country was enough. Still, Herb had to admit that Hawk had been a trifle more human since the child was born—not much, but a trifle.

By this time Whitlock had left the saloon, extremely worried. Nielson wasn't reacting to the kidnapping at all as he had expected. Still covering up the disappearance of the child, eh? Whitlock frowned. By this time his nerves weren't any too steady. He wasn't sleeping well nights, either.

"Lord," he told himself, "if I could only make out what he's planning. I'm commencing to feel like the mouse the cat had cornered. I'll say one thing for Hawk; he's a damn good bluffer. You'd never guess he'd been hit a body blow. Gesis! I don't like this business at all. Why doesn't he rage around? Why doesn't he accuse somebody, make threats? I figured by this time he'd have a posse scouring the country for the man who stole his kid. But does he suspect me, or doesn't he? I'd give ten years of my life to learn if Gabe really destroyed that map. If we had any sense, Gabe and I would mount our horses and get out—or I'd get out alone. Maybe stealing that kid wasn't such a wise idea. Hawk always was a cool, calculating bustard. Offering me a job, eh? He had something in mind, all right.

"What is it?" Whitlock continued his speculations. "Hawk has been hard hit, but he's not going to show he's been hurt. But he can't keep the kid's disappearance quiet forever. He'll crack eventually. Then he'll start offering rewards. By God! I'll get him yet. All I got to do is to keep my nerve. I'd be a fool to run out of town."

Three days more went by. Whitlock had dropped into the Brown Jug for a bottle of beer and noticed that Herb Brown and a couple of customers were somewhat excitedly engrossed in a conversation.

Herb said, "Vard, did you see Hawk Nielson?"

Whitlock shook his head. "Why?"

"The old Hawk is back," Herb explained. "You know, he's been almost human since that kid of his was born. Now he's turned ugly again. Jack there"—jerking a thumb towards one of the customers—" ask him a simple question and Hawk nearly took his head off."

Whitlock's heart leaped. The mighty Hawk had cracked at last. Now there'd be some action. Whitlock laughed shortly to conceal the exultation he felt. " I knew it was too good to last," he said. " What was the simple question Jack asked him ? "

" I only said "—Jack took up the conversation—" ' How's that boy of yours, Hawk ? ' and he turned on me with a face like a thundercloud and wanted to know what business it was of mine——"

" Furthermore," Herb interrupted bewilderedly, " Hawk states that he hasn't any son, that it's a daughter, and where in the blankety-blank did this town get an idea he had a son ? "

" Wh-a-t ! " Whitlock burst out. " What did you say ? " Herb repeated the words. Whitlock's jaw sagged. Finally he stammered, " Was Hawk drunk ? "

" You should know better than to ask," Herb replied. " Hawk never gets drunk."

" But . . . but . . . why . . . ? " Whitlock commenced.

" Don't ask me," from Herb. " We can't figure it out. Everybody in this town has heard him boast that he has a son. Suddenly he says it's a daughter. Ever hear anything like it ? "

" I—never—did," Whitlock said slowly. Once more his mind was a whirlwind of mad conjectures. Now what sort of trap was Hawk Nielson setting ?

" Cripes A'mighty ! " Herb continued. " He was in an ugly frame of mind. He swears he'll knock the block off the next nosy so-and-so that asks about his kid, and that he's tired of answering fool questions—says he'll put a slug of lead through the guts of the next bustard that asks how his boy is. And everybody's just been trying to be polite. How do you figure it out, Vard ? "

"I'm damn'd if I do." Whitlock frowned.

Ten minutes later he was on the street again. Two or three men he met stopped to talk about Hawk's abruptly changed manner and actions. All Ordway was in a state of confusion regarding the sudden transition in sex of Hawk's child.

Whitlock continued on his way, a certain exultation swelling in his breast. So, the Hawk's colossal bluff had broken down at last. Whitlock laughed triumphantly. But why Nielson should insist he had a daughter instead of a son was something Whitlock couldn't comprehend. He was just crossing Ordway's single street when he saw Nielson emerge from the general store and round the tie-rail to get his horse.

Common sense told Whitlock to keep out of Nielson's way, but some inner devil, perhaps an urge to torment his enemy a little, made Whitlock change direction and overtake Hawk just as the big man was climbing into his saddle. Hawk pretended not to see Whitlock on the sidewalk and Whitlock had to call twice to him. "H'are you, Hawk? How's that boy of yours?"

A look like a thundercloud passed over Nielson's face. Very slowly he turned and stepped to the road again. His steps were deliberate as he came around the end of the tie-rail, his arms swinging loosely at his sides. "You should know better by this time, Whitlock," Nielson said, his tone like a jagged sliver of ice. "You know I haven't a son, or you should. Everybody else in town knows I have a daughter. Better think it over, Whitlock. You've known for a long time I have a daughter, haven't you?"

Right then Whitlock should have agreed with Nielson's statement, but the temptation to needle his enemy was too great. At long last Whitlock felt he held the whip hand. Hawk might have most of the money in the Cascabel

Mesa country, but Whitlock was determined to prove to Ordway that he possessed fully as much nerve as the Hawk. That was where he made a fatal mistake.

"What kind of a bluff you trying to run on us, Hawk?" Whitlock laughed coolly. "Maybe you can fool a lot of people in Ordway, but I don't fool worth a plugged peso. I don't scare easy, either."

He stood facing the powerful Nielson, meeting eye to eye the powerful frame that towered over him, feeling, momentarily, complete master of the situation. He could read the danger in Nielson's face, but Whitlock was determined he wasn't going to be bullied as the rest of Ordway had been bullied. He laughed sarcastically. "Seems to me, Hawk, you change your mind awfully sudden. I myself heard you bragging about your son. Yes, it was a son, not a daughter."

Nielson's face flamed. "You'd better admit damn pronto that you're a liar, Whitlock."

For an instant Whitlock was tempted to reach for his six-shooter, but he quickly dropped that idea. That was exactly the thing Hawk wanted him to do. "It won't do any good to call me a liar, Hawk. You don't work me into a fight that way. Think it over, Hawk; your own mind will tell you who's the liar. And I'm still insisting you claimed to have a son——"

That was as far as Whitlock got. Nielson's gun had swept from his holster and described a short, swift arc in the air, the heavy barrel of the weapon landing suddenly against the side of Whitlock's head. The next instant Whitlock found himself sprawling on the sidewalk. A crowd gathered at a distance, but didn't dare come near.

"You're still a liar!" The words came dimly to Whitlock as he struggled to retain his consciousness. He fought his way to hands and knees and slowly came erect, gripping the tie-rail for support, swaying a little as his head gradually cleared. Nielson spoke again, harsh and challenging: "Your hawg leg's in your holster, Whitlock. Make your fight."

"I'm not—looking for—a fight," Whitlock half whispered.

"Yellow, eh?"

Whitlock didn't say anything, just swayed there, gazing into Nielson's burning eyes.

"You spineless bustard!" Abruptly Nielson flung his own gun at Whitlock's feet. "Go for your iron any time you like, Whitlock. I'm giving you your chance. Now have you got the nerve to draw?"

Here at last was Whitlock's opportunity. He knew he could draw and shoot before the big man could again reach his gun on the sidewalk at Whitlock's feet . . . but wait! There might be some trick in this: perhaps Nielson had a second gun concealed about his person. Even so, Whitlock told himself, it was worth the chance.

But Whitlock had hesitated just an instant too long. Something in the Hawk's terrible eyes made him pause. Whitlock suddenly realized he lacked the will, now, to make the necessary movement towards his gun-butt. The sheer power of the big man was dominating Whitlock's every thought. The whole street swam dizzily, and Whitlock's limbs seemed powerless to make a movement of their own volition. He moistened his dry lips and gasped again, "I'm not looking for a fight."

Nielson growled contemptuously, "There's no fight left in you. And you are a liar. You never heard me state I had a son."

"I never heard you state you had a son," Whitlock said dully.

"Keep that thought in mind," Nielson growled. "Now get out of my sight."

Whitlock turned and, reeling like a drunken man, still

groggy from the effect of the blow on the head, staggered off down the street. The crowd that had gathered parted to let him pass, scarcely noticing him go by as it stood gazing in awe at Hawk Nielson.

With no more words to any man, Hawk Nielson again mounted and rode out of Ordway. " That'll show 'em," he muttered savagely. " *I'm* the liar, all right, but no one in Ordway will have the guts to say so to my face. There'll be no laughter at Hawk Nielson's expense. Hawk Nielson is still the boss in these parts."

He threw spurs to his horse and rode furiously in the direction of the Forked Lightning.

That night Vard Whitlock and Gabe Houston took their departure from Ordway.

8

A PLAN TO WOUND

VARD WHITLOCK had been badly shaken by his encounter with Hawk Nielson. It required a month for him to get back his nerve, and in that month he did a great deal of thinking and reached certain conclusions, one being that the enmity he had formerly held for Nielson was as nothing, now, compared to the great hatred he felt for the man. Now it would take more than Hawk's money to square the account; in addition, Whitlock wanted in some way to hurt Nielson deeply, give him a wound from which the big man would never recover. Whitlock was still puzzled, however, over the Hawk's insistence that he had had a daughter born. There was something in that direction that needed a great deal of explaining, and Whitlock decided, if possible, to ferret out the answer to the problem.

With this in mind, he set out one morning from the little Mexican border town where he and Gabe Houston had been "holed up" for the past month, and paid a visit to the Mexican family with whom he had left Nielson's baby the night of the kidnapping. The family received him with welcome eyes. It was a fine, healthy child, Whitlock was assured, and doing well. The family had asked no questions concerning where or how Whitlock had picked up the baby. So deeply were they in Whitlock's debt for something he had once done for them—it was a life-and-death matter and needs no explaining here—that they were willing to do anything for their benefactor.

Whitlock asked certain questions and discovered, as he had been vaguely aware, that the Mexican man had friends and relatives in the Mexican-Moqui settlement near the Forked Lightning. He was in fact a blood relation of Tony and Rosa Tiguan. He was acquainted with the two nurses, Guadalopa and Josefa. Whitlock gave him some money and he left his home, promising to learn what he could about the Hawk's " girl "-child. At the end of a week he returned with the full story of the substitution of a girl baby for Hawk Nielson's son. The Indians had told him things they would never have mentioned to a white man.

Now Whitlock had the explanation for Nielson's actions. Things commenced to clear up, and already a certain plan was taking form in Whitlock's mind. More money exchanged hands, and the Mexican couple agreed to move to the Mexican border town where Gabe Houston awaited Whitlock's return. They started out the next morning, taking the baby with them. The woman had a child of her own, but a month older than Hawk Nielson's son, of whom she had grown extremely fond.

Upon arriving in the border town, Whitlock made his next move: he took the baby to a nearby mission and had him christened under the name of Christopher Pitt Nielson. Whitlock was never sure exactly why he had named the baby Christopher. It had been his own father's name; perhaps he felt something more than the Pitt was necessary. To the good padre of the mission he gave himself as the father of the child, saying the mother had died, thus getting on the christening certificate the padre gave him not only the birth date of Nielson's son but Nielson's name as well. Fortunately he had heard the name of the child's mother, the day she was buried, so that part was taken care of too. Perhaps the padre had never heard of Hawk Nielson; if he had, it never occurred to him to connect that name with the name Pitt.

" I'm damned if I can get what you're drivin' at," Gabe

Houston had complained a few nights later. He and Whitlock were seated at a table in one of the border town's *cantinas*, a bottle of tequila between them. " We've got Nielson's kid. When you goin' to ask him for the ransom? Sure, sure, he thinks now he's got a girl, but you could make him see otherwise. I want to see him hurt—— "

" No more than I do," Whitlock said bitterly. " But I got a better plan now, Gabe. We'll not only get our money back from Nielson, but we'll hurt him too—hurt him bad."

" How you meanin'? " Gabe frowned.

" The longer we wait, the bigger the shock will be to Nielson. Nielson is going to be a right big man in the Cascabel Mesa country someday—far bigger than he is now. He'll be known far and wide. And he'll want a respectable name—all men do when they've acquired a great deal of money. These days, when folks hate him, he'll want forgotten—but all his life he'll be regretting the son he thought he had at first. And when the time comes, we'll produce that son."

Houston looked blank. " I don't get what you're drivin' at."

" Keep still and you will. We're going to wound Nielson where it will hurt most—in his pride. Oh yes "—Whitlock laughed harshly—" we'll produce that son, but it won't be a son to be proud of. Look, Gabe, when that kid gets big enough so he can work, I'm going to take him in hand. I'm going to train him in the use of a six-gun. I'm going to teach him to steal cattle and money. Then we're going to set him on Hawk Nielson. He's going to steal all he can from Nielson, then when the time comes we'll arrange a put-up job so he'll be caught stealing from Nielson. And then "—Whitlock's eyes glowed fanatically—" when he's arrested, Nielson will learn that it's his own son in prison. That'll hurt, Gabe, hurt like the devil."

"By Gawd! You've got an idea, Vard! Only—only that's going to take some years. I'd like to get back my 13-Bar right soon."

"Forget your 13-Bar, Gabe. You'll have more money than the outfit will ever bring you. What is best, we'll be hurting Hawk Nielson."

"As he should be hurt! I hate him. Like a plague of locusts he is, always devourin', always devourin'——" Gabe broke off and reached for the bottle.

"You've had enough for to-night, Gabe," Whitlock said sharply. "You drink more'n is good for you. Sometime you'll get drunk and talk too much."

"No, I won't. You can trust me, Vard." Houston laughed. "Yep, that plan will work. We'll make Hawk Nielson regret he ever picked on you'n me."

"Meanwhile," Whitlock said, "you and I are going to leave the kid with our Mexican friends. We can't loaf forever. We'll travel around for a while and get jobs, save our money. It's going to take money to handle this thing. Later we'll come back here and get the kid. . . ."

And thus the two warped minds planned, while time passed on and the tequila grew lower in the bottle.

The following morning Whitlock and Houston saddled their horses and rode to another range, leaving behind them the small boy baby who was to grow up under the name of Christopher Whitlock. . . .

Back on the Forked Lightning, Hawk Nielson nursed his disappointment in silence. Josefa and Guadalopa were still paid to look after the small girl baby, but otherwise Nielson paid the child no attention. He still felt, somehow, that he had been swindled, but couldn't figure out just how it had been accomplished. In his heart he felt certain he was the father of a boy—but there, in his own house, was a daughter. Had Sanford Gallatin tricked him in some manner, or had the drunken doctor, through fear, lied about the sex of the child?

In an effort to get to the bottom of the matter, Nielson paid out thousands of dollars trying to locate Gallatin, but all the private detectives he hired failed in their search for the missing doctor. The same detectives had questioned Josefa and Guadalopa and had got exactly nowhere. Finally Nielson gave up.

No more did people in Ordway ask after the welfare of Nielson's boy—or his daughter either. They remembered what had happened to Vard Whitlock. It was known there was a girl baby on the Nielson ranch, but there was no telling when Hawk might decide to change his mind again. In time the whole matter came to be ignored.

Nielson himself ignored the child for the first five years of her life. When he saw her about the house, he scowled and hurried past. Guadalopa and Josefa had named her Dorada, the Golden One. The child was unusually large for her age and lived, most of the time, at the Moqui-Mexican settlement, with either one or the other of her nurses. She played with the Indian children and grew up to be much like them.

In an effort to forget his disappointment Hawk once more plunged into the business of making money, and in this he was more than successful. And then one day when he was riding across the range he spied a brown-faced youngster with long braids the colour of red gold beneath a tattered sombrero, sizes too large. The child was mounted on a moth-eaten, saddleless burro, which was trotting sleepily towards a small bunch of Forked Lightning cows. Hawk eyed the long bare legs hanging on either side of the burro's ribs, and at first took the rider for a boy. Then he noticed the braids and the voluminous skirt gathered about the burro's shaggy back. Even then he didn't recognize his child.

DELTA PUBLIC LIBRARY

He watched half carelessly while the youngster drew near the cows and commenced shaking out a frayed lariat. The loop whirled through the air and then sped true to drop about the neck of the nearest cow. " Damned good cast," Hawk grunted admiringly, and then swore.

The instant the rope tightened, the cow was off in a scattering of dust and gravel. Hawk had a brief glimpse of a pair of long brown legs sailing through mid-air at the end of a rope, while the cow ran one way and the burro moved the other to stop after a moment and start cropping grass, while its rider, prone on her belly but still clutching the rope, was hauled with considerable speed across the waving grasslands.

" These fool Indian kids," Hawk grunted. " Probably break his neck. . . ." And then he paused. The kid was still hanging tightly to the rope, too game to let go. One thing Hawk Nielson did admire was gameness, courage. And then another thought struck him : those braids weren't plaited from Indian hair. This was no child of the Mexican-Moqui settlement. Furthermore, that rider wore skirts. Quite abruptly the fact dawned on Hawk. This was his own child being dragged across the terrain.

Nielson whirled his pony and started shaking out his loop to stop the running cow. Plunging in his spurs, he started swiftly in pursuit of the rapidly moving animal and child, but before he could reach them the child's rope broke, and she came to a sudden stop while the cow went madly galloping over the first rise of land.

He reached the child's side and dismounted from his pony just as the youngster was scrambling to her feet. She swayed groggily a moment, eyeing the broken length of old rotten rope she still gripped in one grimy fist. Tears of exasperation, rather than pain, stood in her bluish-green eyes.

" This here is one hell of a rope, mister," she declared in

a childish treble. " Ain't no man can do his job if you don't give him a good rope."

Hawk's eyes widened. " My God! What a precocious brat!" he exclaimed involuntarily. Then, " Do you know who I am?"

" Sure, you're Hawk."

" What else?"

" Somebody said you were my old man. You never acted like it. That's all right too. If you don't want me, I don't want you. I make out—— "

And then she slumped suddenly to earth, her face white, eyes closed. It was then Nielson realized she was hurt. He stopped over the small form and made a quick examination. One leg was skinned from ankle to hip. There was an ugly gash across the child's right ribs and a nasty purple bruise on one shoulder. None of it was serious, but the girl needed immediate care.

Hawk gathered her in his arms and remounted, heading for the Forked Lightning ranch house. Before he reached there the child regained partial consciousness and, eyes still closed, commenced talking a half-delirious mixture of bunk-house slang, Spanish, and Moqui Indian.

" Oh, my God!" Nielson muttered. " What thoughts for a kid to pick up! Maybe I've been a fool. After all, she's mine. I owe her something. Sure, I wanted a son. If a man can't have what he wants he'd better want what he can have. She's my blood. I can raise her my way. I can send her to school—hell's bells, no! I'll educate her myself. Schools don't teach what a man ought to know, sometimes. She'll take the place of a son before I'm through with her."

He arrived at the house. Fortunately Guadalopa was there, cleaning up. The Indian woman looked startled as Hawk came striding in, carrying the frail bundle in his arms.

Then she gave a short scream and rushed towards Nielson. " My Dorado—w'at is happen to the little *niña* ? "

" She's not hurt bad." Nielson surrendered the child. " Bruised and scratched some. Fix her up. And don't waste time. We've put off that christening long enough."

" So ! " With the familiarity of an old servant, Guadalopa allowed a certain trace of sarcasm to creep into her words. " At las' you are ready to take the interes' in your young daughtair, eh ? "

" Take an interest ! " Hawk roared, his tones shaking the rafters of the room. " By God ! I've always taken an interest in her. You thought I didn't know what was doing when you let her run wild. I was just waiting to see what sort of a mess you and Josefa would make of things. From now on you turn over a new leaf. And if you let her go near that bunkhouse again I'll flay you alive. Understand ? "

He swung round, leaving Guadalopa to minister to Dorada's hurts, and stamped angrily down to the bunkhouse. It was late afternoon now, and the punchers were just preparing to sit down to their supper. They glanced up as Hawk stood suddenly framed in the doorway, noting the angry look in his eyes.

" I've got one or two things to tell you hands," Hawk growled. " One of you bustards gave my daughter a rotten rope to play with. Next time that happens, somebody's neck will get broken along with the rope. From now on I'll tend to her cow training. And another thing, if she should happen to come in here, you foul-mouthed stupid bunch of two-legged cow nurses had better watch your language. My God ! Don't you realize there's a *lady* living on the Forked Lightning ? "

He turned, heading back towards the house, leaving behind him a bewildered, slack-jawed group of cow-punchers.

And thus Hawk Nielson found a new interest in life, though his hard exterior changed but little. Men still feared and hated him, while his wealth increased faster than ever. Now, at long last, he felt he really had someone to build for. He no longer felt entirely alone.

9

THE SON OF THE HAWK

NEARLY twenty-five years passed while the son of Hawk Nielson developed into manhood, going under the name of Christopher Whitlock. Chris knew he was no blood relation of Vard Whitlock's, but of his birth or the identity of his parents he knew nothing. Whitlock had given him some sort of tale about adopting him when he was an orphan, and the boy had never seriously questioned it until he had reached the age of twenty-one. Then such questions as he put forth were evaded by Whitlock in one manner or another.

The three of them—Chris, Vard Whitlock, and old Gabe Houston—had spent the years wandering around the country, taking jobs wherever work offered. Long before he'd reached manhood, there wasn't a man in the cattle country who was Chris Whitlock's equal with gun, lariat, or on a horse's back. He knew stock raising from beginning to end; in any sort of brawl he had a pair of fists more than adequate to take care of himself. Other things Vard Whitlock had taught him too: how to burn fresh brands over old ones, thus changing the design; how to hair-brand calves that they might later be picked up and another symbol burned; how earmarks could be changed.

It didn't stop there. Whitlock had instructed the boy in throwing knives and in wrestling. Such things as Whitlock himself couldn't teach he left to hired instructors. Certain months out of each year were devoted to schooling. Chris learned as well the various schemes by which gamblers defraud their victims—loaded dice, shaved and marked cards, leaden frets on roulette wheels—that sort of thing. To Vard Whitlock's credit it must be said that, regarding such things as were dishonest, the matter was explained fully to the youth, Whitlock explaining that these things were being taught only for Chris's own protection. Vard had, in fact, turned young Chris into the sort of man who could take care of himself in any and all situations. Chris had developed into the sort of man who " knows the ropes." He'd yet to see the horse he couldn't ride, and his luck at gambling was prodigious.

No doubt about it, Vard Whitlock had trained Chris well, but in doing so had lost his own heart; he thought as much of Chris as he would have had he been the boy's real father. And when the thought of framing Chris in a robbery and then seeing him turned over to the authorities entered Whitlock's mind, the final phase of his long-planned revenge against Hawk Nielson lost its zest. But for the rest, Vard remained firm: the one thought uppermost in his mind was to make trouble for Nielson, and the passing years had in no wise alleviated that determination.

Chris and Vard were sitting on the top rail of a corral fence one evening after supper, on a ranch in Idaho where they'd been working for the past few months. Vard's dark hair was streaked with grey now, and he was somewhat stouter, but otherwise he looked much the same, with his closely shaven features and blue eyes and rather wide mouth. Chris had grown taller than most men and filled out. In many respects he was Hawk Nielson's son: there was the same deep chest, the same span of muscular shoulders, the same easy-moving, light-stepping gait. Chris's shock of tawny blond hair might have been Hawk Nielson's own. However, the features were different; here Chris had inherited from his mother. The nose, chin, and lips were finely chiselled and lacked that certain touch of brutality found in Nielson's face. Chris's eyes were a smoky grey, but more candid, more devil-may-care than his father's.

At the present moment his eyes were fixed on far-away points, but they weren't seeing the far-off afterglow of Idaho sunlight as it faded behind purple mountains across the rangeland. He straightened one overall-encased leg slightly, shifted his weighted holster to a more comfortable position, and drew from a vest pocket a sack of Durham and cigarette papers. Pushing back from his unruly locks a weather-beaten sombrero, he commenced to roll a smoke.

Scratching a match on the sole of one boot, he drew deeply on the cigarette for a moment, then exhaled a slow grey plume into the still air. " Vard," he commenced, " I've been doing considerable thinking lately."

Whitlock glanced sharply at his companion. He surmised what was coming: something relative to Chris's birth, no doubt. Well, the usual evasions would take care of the matter. Whitlock said, " Thinking? What you been thinking about now? "

" Wondering exactly what your game is, Vard. As far back as I can remember you've been teaching me things. As soon as I'd mastered one thing, you swung me into something else. You've always been anxious for me to be foremost in anything I tackled. Oh, sure, things like shooting and riding and roping are natural in a cow country; but I've noticed every so often that we change locality and we always seem to run across somebody else who's a topnotcher in *his* line—and then there's something new for me to learn."

Whitlock smiled. This questioning was a trifle different from what he'd been expecting. " Maybe, Chris," he replied, " I just happen to think enough of you to want you to be top man in as many ways as possible. Has that occurred to you? "

Chris nodded and studied the end of his cigarette. " Yes, it has, Vard. You've been mighty good to me. But what's back of all this? When do I start making use of all the things I've learned? All we do is ramble around the country and punch cows and ramble around the country some more."

"Someday," Whitlock said slowly, "you might go up against a pretty big man—someplace. When—if that happens, I want to make sure you're the master."

"Would the man's name be Nelson—or something like that?"

Whitlock glanced sharply at Chris. "Where'd you pick up that idea?"

"I've overheard you and Gabe talking once or twice. I gathered it was somebody you both had had trouble with years ago. I asked Gabe about it, but he just put me off and started to mutter something about a plague of locusts devouring the range. Couldn't make head nor tail of what he was hitting at. Sometimes, Vard, I wonder if Gabe's mind isn't slipping a trifle."

"Maybe so," Whitlock said quickly, glad to change the subject. "He's no good for punching any more—just for odd jobs around a ranch like he always manages to pick up. Gabe is——"

"Let's forget Gabe. I'm still asking why, Vard."

Whitlock didn't answer for fully three minutes. For years Chris had carried out without question any suggestion of Vard's, but the older man realized now the time had come to act. The matter could be put off no longer. He recognized now that the reluctance that had come over him when he considered carrying out his revenge was based on his love for Chris and his disinclination to get Chris into trouble. But it had to be sometime; of that, Whitlock had made up his mind.

"To tell the truth, Chris," Whitlock said at last, "this is a matter I've been intending to take up with you. Don't know why I've put it off as long as this. No, the name wasn't

Nelson—it's Nielson, Hawk Nielson. He's a big cattle baron down in the Cascabel Mesa country. He's rich, Lord only knows how rich, but I've been following him in the newspapers from time to time and I know he has plenty money—money that was made by ruining better men. He murdered two of the best pardners I ever had—just to get their holdings. Nielson's all bad, at least he was in the old days. I've never heard that he changed any."

"Did he ever do anything to you?" Chris broke in. "Personal, I mean?"

"Took my ranch away from me. Hit me over the head with a gun barrel, then challenged me to draw when I was so groggy I could scarcely stand." Slow fires blazed in Whitlock's eyes; his cheeks darkened. "Stole Gabe's outfit, too."

"But I don't see how he could steal——"

"Oh, he worked it legally, so as not to tangle with the law, but it was theft nevertheless. That shows you how smart he is. I'll tell you the story someday. There's no time for details now."

"But where do I come in?" Chris wanted to know.

"I'll explain in a minute. Nearly twenty-five years ago I swore I'd get even with Hawk Nielson someday, and I've been training you to that end. You're a better man than he is—that I know. With your help we'll steal him blind. You've got the ability to handle things. We'll clean him out proper. Nielson stole from poorer folks than himself. In spite of what any law might say, we won't be doing wrong if we take every cent Hawk Nielson ever made." As he talked, Whitlock's tones became more embittered; his eyes blazed fanatically.

Chris looked queerly at his companion. "This doesn't sound like you, Vard."

"Maybe it shows what Hawk Nielson's done to me. But

with your help I'm aiming to square that account, once and for all!"

Chris looked dubious. "I don't know," he said slowly. "Somehow or other, it doesn't seem right. Stealing is stealing, any way you look at it. You see, I don't know Hawk Nielson. I can't understand why I should plan to rob him——"

"Throwing me down, eh?" Whitlock flared.

"Don't talk like that, Vard," Chris said earnestly. "I don't want you to feel that way. I'm owing you more than I can repay, as it is. You've been like a father to me, and I've never yet wanted for anything. But try to see my side. Hawk Nielson never did anything to me. I can't see where it's my fight. You've always taught me to stand on my own two feet and handle my own troubles, and now you're asking that I handle yours. I'm finding it hard to understand you, Vard."

"Just a minute." Whitlock raised one hand to get attention. His mind was working swiftly now. He'd have to give Chris a mighty good reason, or his plans for revenge would go for nothing. "Suppose," he questioned, "that the bulk of the property and money that Nielson owns would be rightfully yours, if you could get it legally. In other words, except that something happened, Nielson's property would have someday belonged to you——"

"Do you mean," Chris asked sharply, "that I'd have a right to it?"

"Just that—exactly that, Chris."

Chris gazed steadily at Whitlock, then slowly slipped down from the corral rail to the earth and carefully extinguished his cigarette butt under one booted foot. Whitlock followed him to the ground. The two men faced each other again. Chris said, "I'm not quite getting it, Vard. Do you mean that this Nielson hombre did my folks out of what rightfully belonged to 'em?"

Whitlock side-stepped the issue. "We-ell, something like that," he replied lamely. "We'll not go into that part of it now."

Chris stiffened. "We will go into it, Vard. If you want me to go after Hawk Nielson, I intend to know just why! What did Nielson have to do with my folks anyway? Who is he? For that matter, who am I? There's been too damn much secrecy about my birth, Vard. You haven't come across with everything you know. You've been mighty good to me, and I appreciate everything you've done, but there's a limit. Don't you think it's about time I was told a few things?" Chris was doing his best to keep the angry tones from his voice.

"I'm not saying you're wrong, Chris," Whitlock admitted, much against his will, "but the time hasn't come yet for you to learn—well, learn certain things. There's too many other things involved——"

He broke off, then, "I tell you, Chris, you see this thing through with me, and one year from now I'll tell you anything you want to know—I'll even tell you things you haven't dreamed of asking me. Is it a go? We could start heading south to-morrow."

Still Chris hesitated. Vard's answer hadn't satisfied him. "I'm not saying you're wrong," he said at last. "Maybe Nielson is all that you say; maybe his money should belong to me. Just the same I'm not making war on strangers without a better reason than you've given me so far. I don't like to doubt your word, Vard, but it might be you're a little twisted where this Nielson is concerned. Could be you're not thinking as straight as usual. Something tells me there's a knot in the rope, someplace. If you'd only explain more clearly, maybe I could see things your own way, but . . ." Chris's voice trailed off into uncertainties.

Then Vard Whitlock played his trump card. He fumbled

within his shirt a moment, then his hand came out holding an old blue bandanna handkerchief, knotted at one corner. "I've never let this off my person, all these years," he commented, while Chris eyed him curiously. Slowly Whitlock untied the knot, and a small gold locket with thin chain attached was displayed to view.

He passed the locket to Chris, who examined it in silence. On one side a tiny rose was engraved. Otherwise it was smooth, no names, initials, or dates appearing upon either of its surfaces. Whitlock went on, "Nobody knows I have this—not even Gabe Houston. I never told him. I'm asking that you don't mention it to anybody."

He reached over and took the locket from Chris's hand, pressed a small spring, and the cover flew open to display a faded bit of photography. It was the picture of a sweet-faced woman with sorrowful eyes. The hair was done in the style of a generation back, and the clothing—the picture was cut off at the shoulders—was old-fashioned. Whitlock passed over the open locket for his companion's inspection.

Chris didn't have to be told who it was. He knew. There were certain features that were too much like his own for him to be mistaken. For a long time he gazed at the photograph in the fading light. "It's my mother," he said softly, something of reverence in the tones. "I've always wondered what she was like."

"Yes, I guess it's your mother, Chris." Whitlock was speaking the truth now. "I couldn't say for certain, though, because I never saw her in the life. All I know is the locket was fastened about your neck when I—when I got you. The chain is too long for the locket to ever have been bought just for you at that time, so I reckon it must have been hers. Probably some nurse, or somebody, took it from her and placed it about your neck."

Again Chris gave his attention to the locket. The sun's

last light deserted the range, twilight lingered but an instant, then darkness descended. One by one stars twinkled into the velvety blackness overhead. Neither man moved. Lights had long since leaped into being in the bunkhouse a short distance away. A voice lifted in a song of the range. Someone accompanied the singer on a broken-stringed guitar.

Abruptly Chris announced, " I'm keeping this." It wasn't a question, simply a statement of fact.

Whitlock heard the tiny spring snap shut. For Chris to keep the locket hadn't been Whitlock's idea at all; now, however, he knew it would do no good to demand it back. " Sure, hang on to it," he said easily. " That's why I gave it to you. Just keep it out of sight, that's all."

" Cripes, Vard," Chris protested. " Why all this tight lid on everything? We haven't done anything wrong—or have we?"

" Don't talk like a fool, Chris."

" I still want to know more about this locket."

" I'll tell you more—one year from to-day. Providing you throw in with me to settle Hawk Nielson."

" I'm asking for that information right now." Chris's voice was tinged with anger.

" One year from to-day, Chris, if you'll throw in with——"

Then came a quick soft rasping of metal against leather, and Whitlock felt the hard round muzzle of a six-shooter boring against his middle. In the light from the stars the eyes of the two men searched, locked. " Dammit, Vard "—the voice was strangely reminiscent of Hawk Nielson's now—" I can force you to tell me everything I want to know, right now."

Whitlock didn't move a muscle. He knew he was nearer death than he'd been in many years. It wasn't difficult to imagine this was Hawk, rather than Chris, holding the gun against his body. Did the son, after all, have the same brutal streak . . . ? Whitlock found his voice: " No, Chris, I don't reckon you can force me to talk before I'm ready. I've been through something like this before. I don't scare easy. . . ." Maybe it was about this stage the gun barrel had crashed against his head. . . . Whitlock finished, " Well, go ahead, Chris. I'm not talking."

" You're going to change your mind before I count three," Chris snapped. " Otherwise I'm going to let you have it, Vard, may God forgive me——"

" Go ahead with your counting," Whitlock said wearily. " Maybe that's the answer to this whole business." In that moment he could see his long years of planning going for nothing.

" One ! " came Chris's voice, tense with suppressed emotion.

" Save your breath, boy," Whitlock advised in a tired voice.

" Two ! " The gun muzzle bored harder against Whitlock's middle.

Whitlock only laughed this time, a cold, humourless laugh.

" Three ! "

Whitlock waited, expecting every instant to feel hot lead ripping through bone and muscle. He felt the gun quiver in Chris's hand, heard a short, sharp indrawn breath as Chris nerved himself to pull the trigger. . . . Then the weapon was deliberately withdrawn. Again came the soft scraping of metal against leather. Neither man spoke.

Silence for some minutes. Chris fumbled in his pockets, again seeking papers and tobacco. The scratch of the match as Chris lighted his cigarette showed a face pale and drawn. Then darkness again; only a dull glow that changed red now and then to bright showed through the gloom. Finally Chris spoke, something like a sob in his voice: " I couldn't do it, Vard. I owe you too much."

In that moment Whitlock came near to telling Chris everything. His heart went out to the younger man, but he steeled himself against the feeling. There ensued another silence.

Finally Chris's cigarette butt was dropped on the earth and stepped on. " I suppose she's dead ? " he inquired after a time.

" Yes. She died shortly after you were born. I attended the funeral."

" And my father—who was he ? "

" You'd better get your six-shooter out again, son," Whitlock said, flat-voiced. " That's one of the things I'm not telling until a year has passed. We'll just say he was no good and let it go at that. You wouldn't have had any use for him, Chris, if you'd known him the way I did."

" Not very pleasant, getting news like that—about my father," Chris said slowly. " I was hoping—oh hell ! Say, did this Nielson have anything to do concerning my mother ? "

" Some," Whitlock said brutally, and at the same time hating himself for what he was doing, added, " Maybe it was Nielson caused her death. I'm not the one to say that though. I do know he never treated her the way a man should treat his—the way a man should treat a woman. Certain things happened, and I'm pretty sure your mother didn't get a square deal from Hawk Nielson."

" Did Nielson know my father ? "

" Yeah, I think he did," Whitlock answered with a touch of grim humour.

" Were they friends or enemies ? "

" Friends—by all means." Whitlock laughed shortly.

The moon had pushed above the horizon by this time. Again Chris took the locket from his pocket and endeavoured to make out the features on the age-yellowed photograph. There was something of acute suffering in his face now, but he realized it would do no good to ask further questions. " There's just one thing I'd like to know," he said at last, replacing the locket in his pocket. " Does Hawk Nielson know about me ? "

" If you mean," Whitlock said cautiously, " does Nielson know your mother had a child, I'll say yes. But with you bearing my name, if we go ranging through Nielson's territory, he won't know who you are."

Chris considered the matter. Finally, reluctantly, he said, " All right, Vard, I'll throw in with you for a time anyway. I want to learn something about this Hawk Nielson. If I change my mind after I've seen him, I'll let you know. Otherwise I'm your man."

" Good." Whitlock nodded, but he felt no particular elation. He felt he'd played the part of a liar. Despite all he'd done, that wasn't easy for Vard Whitlock. It didn't seem square, somehow, to double-cross Chris in such fashion. Then, thought of Hawk Nielson steeled his mind. " I'll go see the foreman, tell him we're pulling out to-morrow, Chris. I'll have Gabe get our things ready to move on. He can pack some grub and so on."

" Yes, and he'll probably kick like the devil," Chris said. " Gabe's getting old and crabby."

" No doubt about it. Like you mentioned a spell back, he seems a bit queer in his mind sometimes. His brain gets to wandering and he thinks on the wrong Nielson did him and he nigh explodes the top off his head."

It was true. With the passing of years, old Gabe Houston had lost strength, both mental and physical. He could still sit a horse, but his days of hard work were past. Chris and Whitlock saw to it the old man accompanied them everywhere they went, but he could never pay his own way. Always they had to help him out. He worked doing odd chores. The past few months he had been helping the ranch cook wash dishes and peel potatoes; his had been the job to bring in the firewood.

"I'll go talk to Gabe right now," Whitlock said. He didn't add that he wanted to tell Gabe certain things that weren't for Chris's ears. Every so often Whitlock had found it necessary to remind Gabe not to let slip any information regarding Chris's parentage.

"Say, Vard," Chris called a last question after Whitlock, "is my—father—still alive?"

"I'll tell you that one year from now," Whitlock replied, and hurried on towards the bunkhouse.

Chris frowned, then reached once more for the locket containing his mother's portrait. The moon was brighter by this time.

10

THE FIRST ENCOUNTER

By this time Hawk Nielson was indeed master of the Cascabel Mesa country. His holdings stretched for hundreds of thousands of acres, and his Forked Lightning brand was one of the foremost in the cattle country. Other ranches there were, clinging precariously to the outskirts of Nielson's land, but he was only biding his time until they, too, could be gobbled up.

Even the town of Ordway—now known as Nielson City—had changed. The T. N. & A. S. trains made daily stops at the neat, red-painted station, and at the southern edge of town was a maze of whitewashed cattle-pens and spur track from which Nielson shipped great numbers of beef animals each fall. Many of the stores and saloons in Nielson City were Hawk's property. He held a controlling interest in the weekly newspaper. As for politics, Nielson saw to it that men of his own choosing were elected. In short, Hawk Nielson ran practically everything in his neck of the woods.

Naturally his affairs were now too large to be handled by himself alone. A two-storey structure of brick, known as the Nielson Building, housed on its lower floor an office where he and his assistants handled his business. The second floor of the building was given over to living quarters where Hawk and his daughter lived about half of the time, the other half being spent at the rebuilt Forked Lightning ranch house, now a large, rambling structure of Mexican-type architecture. But it was at the Nielson Building office that Hawk put through most of his business. Here his secretary—who was also his daughter, Dorado—handled matters, and

Hawk had only to sign papers, give orders, or pass judgment on the various deals that came up for his attention.

Nielson himself couldn't say offhand how wealthy he was. His interests were widely spread, much of his capital being invested in the East, and when he wanted information regarding the bulk of his various holdings a number of clerks spent many hours compiling figures before such information was forthcoming. Wall Street capitalists realized these days that Hawk Nielson could have become a power in the financial world had he cared to do so.

Nielson had also changed in many ways. He was still the great, arrogant, commanding figure as of yore, but these days he was careful to live more within the law. Where before he had seized ruthlessly practically anything he wanted, or used nefarious means to gain his ends, he now achieved his desires through shrewdness. People said his daughter was largely responsible for his "toning down." Perhaps that was so. At any rate, he had reached that stage in his career where he wanted a certain respect from the community. Respect of a sort he had, but there existed very little real liking.

Only his appearance remained the same. The years had dealt more than kindly with him. There wasn't a grey hair in his head, and he still rode round-up with a youthful figure that was envied by men half his age. In fact only the men who had been longest with him could believe that his years were in the vicinity of the half-century mark. His muscles were still supple, his step springy. It may be the lines of his face were a trifle tighter, but that was difficult to say where one of Hawk Nielson's disposition was concerned. Every ounce of his steel-muscled, big-framed body was in perfect commission.

It was mid-morning when Chris and Vard Whitlock rode into Nielson City. Old Gabe Houston, a withered, weazened bundle of skin and bones, lagged along in the rear, muttering to himself and brushing the snow-white hair from his rheumy eyes when a sudden movement of his pony jarred it down below his battered sombrero. What he was muttering about neither Chris nor Whitlock knew; they paid him small attention when he got this way; he was always muttering about something that didn't matter.

It was only after the three riders had entered the main street that Gabe awoke from his restless reverie. Then he spurred alongside Vard Whitlock's horse. "The old town's changed, eh?" he cackled. "'Tain't like it was twenty odd years back when my 13-Bar was the envy of this whole range. Nielson City! Bah!" he snorted his disgust.

And, indeed, the town had changed. Gone were the slovenly shacks of more than two decades ago, and in their place were neat rows of brick or adobe and rock buildings. New hitch-racks had long ago replaced the old, and at two or three spots stood what was known in those days as "horseless carriages"—and again, in those days, they usually "just stood," much to the amusement of the populace in the Cascabel Mesa country, which didn't take readily to automobiles.

Nielson himself had imported a Hispano-Avispa, a great brute of a machine, which after a few thundering trips had been unable to withstand certain chuckholes on the road to the Forked Lightning. Thereupon Nielson, somewhat regretfully, it is true, had decided it lacked the durability of a horse and had it hauled to one of the local blacksmith shops, where it stood, defiant of the attempts of any and all mechanics to put it back on a running basis. Though it was noticed thereafter that Nielson commenced to promote legislation for paved roads.

Hawk Nielson, say what you will, was progressive in his ideas. Cement sidewalks lined either side of Butterfield

Street, and it was rumoured that within another year or so there'd be pavements and natural gas piped in. And that modern spirit had caught hold in other quarters: there were shops for ladies where the styles weren't more than five years behind those worn in New York. Nielson had leased for agricultural purposes a large number of acres of land. Each year an exhibition of produce and stock was held at the county fair-grounds—donated by Nielson—just north of town. But much of the old remained, too, and in many ways Nielson City retained more cow-country flavour than most towns of that period.

What surprised Chris, Whitlock, and Gabe most was the festive air that seemed to pervade the streets. Evidently there was a gala occasion of some sort under way. The windows of the stores were decorated, and at various points tie-rail posts were wound with coloured bunting. Then the riders caught sight of a bulletin board which read:

BIG ANNUAL RODEO

For the Benefit of the Survivors

of the

Silver King Disaster

Open to All $10,000 in Prizes

July 10, 11, 12

Below in smaller letters was given a list of purses, day prizes, and events. The three riders drew rein and perused the bulletin with interest.

"By cripes!" Whitlock exclaimed. "We're in luck, Chris. You might almost think they knew we were coming."

Chris nodded. "I think I'll give it a whirl at that. Starts to-morrow, eh? Let me see"—reading more of the bulletin—"I've got until to-night to make my entries. Plenty of time. Just now I've got something more important to think about."

"What do you mean?"

"I want to sashay around town and see if I can get a look at—at this hombre we came here to—well"—with a quick look at Gabe—"you know what I mean."

Gabe was still looking up and down the street, his old eyes wide. "Rodeo, eh? No wonder they's so many folks passin' back and forth. Crickey! If this ain't a boom town, I never see one. Let's all go get a drink."

"Drinks can wait," Whitlock said. "We'd better find a place to stay, right off. This rodeo has brought a lot of visitors to town, and probably more will arrive. Let's look up a hotel."

The first hotel they approached was full up, but the clerk at the desk directed them to a smaller hostelry, called the Cascabel House, farther along Butterfield Street. Here they secured two rooms—Gabe was to sleep with Whitlock—in a neat two-storey brick building, cleaned up a bit, had their ponies taken to a nearby livery, and then sauntered out to see the town.

Old Gabe was eager to see if the Brown Jug Saloon still existed; he'd missed it on his way through town. They made inquiries. Yes, the Brown Jug was just a block farther on, at the corner of Butterfield and Cibola streets. But to Gabe's great disappointment, only the name Brown Jug remained. The building was gone, and in its place stood a much larger saloon of rock-and-adobe construction.

"Might be Herb's inside, anyway," Gabe said hopefully. "Now that we're here, we might as well get a drink."

They pushed through the entrance, and saw instantly that the interior had changed also. There was a new, longer bar, with pyramids of gleaming glasses and bottles stacked behind it and reflected in the back mirror. There were pictures of prize-fighters and burlesque queens and race-horses framed on the walls. Several men were ranged drinking along the bar, but all were strangers to Whitlock and Gabe. So far they'd seen none of their old acquaintances.

"What'll it be, gents?" inquired a bar-tender with slicked-down black hair and white apron and shirt.

Whitlock and Houston took whisky. Chris ordered a bottle of beer. The drinks were served and paid for.

Whitlock asked, "Is Herb Brown around?"

The bar-keep frowned. "Herb Brown? Can't say I know him."

"He used to own the Brown Jug."

"Must have been some years back," the bar-keep replied. "Come to think of it, I seem to remember hearing that Hawk Nielson took over this property—must be nearly twenty years ago—closed a mortgage on it or something of the sort—— What's the matter, Dad?" to old Gabe, who had suddenly choked on his drink and was in the throes of a violent coughing spell. "That liquor go down the wrong way?" He poured the little old man's glass full again. "Take it slow next time, Dad."

"We were hoping to see Herb Brown," Whitlock said a trifle wistfully. "I noted the name is the same."

"Yeah—Brown Jug—good name," the bar-tender returned. "My boss just leases this property from Mr. Nielson. You got friends here in town?"

"Might have at that," Whitlock evaded. "I used to—to live near here."

The bar-tender left them to serve fresh customers, and returned a few minutes later. "Better have one on the house," he invited. The glasses were filled again. Old Gabe commenced to look more hopeful. "You three come in for our big doings?" the bar-keep asked genially.

"One of us will enter, maybe," Whitlock returned.

The man's eyes shifted to Chris. "You, I reckon," he surmised, his gaze taking in with appreciation Chris's well-knit body.

"I'll probably enter a couple of events." Chris smiled. "Have a pretty good show here, do you?"

"Best in the country," the man replied, with true civic pride. "Take that Pendleton affair, up north. Well, that got a lot of advertising last year, but I think we're just as good. Smaller maybe, but just as good. Mr. Nielson spends a lot of money advertising this show, and it's become right well known. It's a good thing for the town: brings people here. This is the third show we've held. The other two were big successes. We get entries from four or five States around. This year we're donating the proceeds to the victims of the Silver King disaster."

"I noticed that on one of your signs," Whitlock commented. "What is this disaster? I haven't heard anything about it."

"The old Silver King Mine, up-State, caved in," the bar-keep explained. "You know, up there near Freeore. It happened while they were changing shifts. Good many fellers killed outright. They ain't got all the bodies out yet. Some of them that were saved will be crippled for life. On top of that some sort of epidemic broke out. Freeore's in a bad way, I guess, and can use all the money we send up there. Better put in your entry. It's in a good cause."

"Sounds like it." Chris nodded. "I'll get in all right. Who's been in the habit of grabbing all your prizes? Anybody in particular?"

The bar-keep scratched his chin thoughtfully. "We-ell, the prizes will probably be pretty well divided this year. You see, Hawk Nielson's took the all-round championship the past two years——"

"Hawk Nielson got a son?" Whitlock asked quickly.

"Nope—just a daughter——"

"But you said," Whitlock interrupted, "that Hawk Nielson took the championship prize——"

"Hawk Nielson ridin' rodeo contests!" old Gabe exclaimed.

"That's what I said." The bar-tender nodded, looking curiously at Gabe and Whitlock. "You act like you knew him."

Gabe nodded as Whitlock continued in puzzled tones, "Yes, we used to know a hombre by that name. However, it can't be the same man. Must be some relation. The man we know is around fifty now, and probably in no shape for the roughing a rodeo contest hands out——"

"It's the same man," the bar-tender cut in. "I've heard he was about fifty, but you'd never think it to look at him. He pretty much runs things in this country. It was him that built our rodeo arena out at the fair-grounds. He's got plenty of money and is as active as a yearling bull."

Whitlock shook his head dubiously. "I'm still not understanding how he could win the all-round championship."

The man behind the bar laughed. "He fooled a lot of fellers the first year our show was put on, and last year too. This year he decided to just enter two events, so some of the other waddies would have a chance at prize money. Oh, I tell you, Hawk Nielson is good, he is—I mean at riding and such." He lowered his voice a trifle and leaned across the bar. "Just the same, in spite of what Nielson has done to build up this town, folks say he done it for his own benefit. In some ways he's a mighty hard man. He's the sort of feller you maybe don't like—but just the same you got to respect his ability."

Chris had been listening closely to the conversation and, his curiosity becoming aroused, he was more than ever eager to meet Hawk Nielson. He had consented at first to throw in with Whitlock's schemes to learn what was possible about the secrets of his parentage; now he felt his very manhood was challenged. His mind was already made up. It would be a contest of youth against experience.

The drinks were finally finished, and the three men started for the street. On the saloon wall, near the door, was another poster advertising the rodeo. Chris fell behind a moment to check over the list of events. Several items captured his interest. Whitlock and Gabe continued on their way through the entrance.

Just as Whitlock and Gabe reached the sidewalk, they spied a familiar figure approaching the Brown Jug Saloon. It was Hawk Nielson. Then and there Whitlock agreed that the bar-tender had been correct in his statements. Except for his clothing, Hawk Nielson looked exactly the same as he had the night he killed Tod Ranson and Steve Taylor. He now wore corduroys instead of overalls; hat and boots were of a more expensive make; there was a white shirt under his open vest, and now he wore a black string necktie. Otherwise his appearance was practically the same, even to the gun hanging at his hip.

The big man swung easily along the sidewalk, and was just about to enter the saloon when he noticed Gabe and Whitlock gazing at him. He paused suddenly; his piercing grey eyes swept their forms and lighted instantly with a look of recognition. Then a short, contemptuous laugh broke from his thin lips.

" So you two come back, did you ? "

" You see us here, don't you ? " Whitlock replied quietly as he faced his old enemy. He was fighting down the surge of hot anger that welled in his breast.

" We wouldn't be here if we hadn't come back, would we ? " old Gabe croaked in defiance. " Any fool could see that."

"Easy on the lip, Gabe," Whitlock warned. "There's no use stirring up old trouble."

"That's good advice, Houston," Nielson growled. "I'm not holding anything against you fellows, so if you mind your own business there isn't any reason why you shouldn't come here."

"Exactly what we've done," Whitlock said calmly, "and maybe we'll stay a spell. So far as I know this is a free country."

"Free, yes," Nielson snapped. "However, my word carries a lot of weight here, so don't get any wrong ideas. What are you doing back? There's none of your friends here any more."

"What we're doing is our business," Whitlock said steadily. "We might buy some cows and start operating——"

"You won't find land near Nielson City."

"You own everything, eh?" Whitlock laughed shortly.

"What I don't own I can control."

"Yaah!" Gabe could restrain his anger no longer. "Just like a plague of locusts ruinin' the country——"

"Shut up, Gabe!" Whitlock ordered sharply. The old man shut up, but his lined features continued to work with emotion. Whitlock continued, "It's this way, Nielson: we've done pretty well. We're not looking to any man for our money. Maybe we'll buy in this vicinity and maybe we won't. We might just stay a day or so and then drift. What we came here for was your rodeo."

Nielson gave him an amused smile. "*You* weren't figuring to enter, I hope."

Whitlock shook his head. "I've got a boy that figures to enter, though." It had already been decided that Chris was to pass as Whitlock's own son. "He's done all right in some other shows."

" Son, eh ? " Nielson said. " You must have got married after you left here."

" It's usually the case." Whitlock smiled drily. " By the way, is it all right to say, ' How's your daughter ? ' these days, Hawk ? "

Nielson reddened slightly. " These days a great many folks ask that question. I'm always glad to tell them she's well."

" Take it better than you did once, don't you ? "

Nielson shrugged his ponderous shoulders. " Some people had a habit of riling me those days. Maybe you don't know how lucky you were to get off the way you did, Whitlock. And I still don't like to be riled. So it might be a good thing not to get an idea you can slip anything over on me. You had your chance once and lacked the nerve to draw. You might not get another——"

It was Whitlock's turn to crimson. " Maybe I had too much sense to draw that day, Hawk."

" Too much sense ? Bah ? You were yellow then, and I'm betting you're still yellow. Just keep out from under my feet if you want to avoid trouble. I wouldn't stay here too long if I were you." Abruptly Nielson swung away and started for the saloon entrance again.

Whitlock had turned white with anger, but he held his tongue.

Old Gabe could restrain his rage no longer. " It was you," he quavered, shaking his bony, gnarled fist at Nielson's back, " that robbed honest folks of their land. Just like a plague of locusts you was, always devourin', always devourin'——"

Nielson disregarded the words, but he paused to turn in the saloon entrance. " Whitlock, if that son of yours figures to enter our rodeo, I advise him to find out what events I'm entering and keep out of them. He'll lose sure if he bucks me—just like you did ! "

A knot of passers-by had paused at old Gabe's voice, and now heard Nielson's words as well. The people viewed with some awe these strangers who had had the temerity to cross Hawk Nielson.

By this time Chris had concluded reading the rodeo poster describing rules and events and started to leave the saloon just in time to hear Hawk Nielson's last words. At the same instant Hawk, on his way through the entrance, collided with Chris.

There was considerable shock in the meeting as something like four hundred pounds of bone and muscle was involved in this first contact of father and son. Both men staggered back a step from the impact. Nielson's Stetson had been on the back of his head, and was jarred off when he so abruptly crashed into Chris.

Chris was first to recover. " Excuse me." He smiled, stepping to one side. " I didn't see you coming."

Nielson stooped, recovered his sombrero, and again started through the entrance, his features flushed with anger. The door was a narrow one, but had Nielson turned sidewise there would have been sufficient space to allow him to pass. This he refused to do. Hawk Nielson turned sidewise for no man. His injured pride demanded that Chris leave the doorway completely and step out of his path. This Chris declined to do. It was the old problem of an irresistible force meeting an immovable object.

Instead of replying to Chris's courteous apology, Nielson swung forward, trying to brush Chris from the doorway. Chris, sensing the manœuvre, tightened his lips in a cold smile and stood firm. Much to Hawk's surprise, the younger man refused to give an inch.

" Step aside, cowhand," Nielson growled, trying to push his way through. He was compelled to step back; not one particle would Chris budge.

"I've already given you plenty of room," Chris quietly pointed out. "Do you have to have the whole doorway?"

Nielson's face darkened with anger. "I've got no time for foolishness, young fellow. Get out of my way. I'm Hawk Nielson."

"Never heard of you in my life," Chris said blandly. "Do you own this saloon, or are you in the habit of displaying bad manners wherever you go?"

From the sidewalk beyond came Vard Whitlock's mocking tones: "Hawk, you've met your match. Allow me to introduce you to Chris Whitlock. You'll see a lot of him before we leave here."

And thus father and son met for the first time after a separation of more than two decades.

II

"HE'S A REAL MAN!"

FOR a brief interval the two men stood facing each other like statues graven from living granite, measuring each other inch for inch and eye for eye. Hawk Nielson knew, in that moment, he was facing a *man*. Something in the other's eyes made him uneasy; too, there was something vaguely familiar about the face that met his own with so much defiance.

For Chris's part, he saw an individual as big as himself, fully as broad-shouldered; he remembered the shock of tawny hair when Hawk Nielson's sombrero had tumbled off; he had caught a glimpse of strong white teeth when Hawk snarled certain words. A man must be in prime condition to have teeth like that. Something in Nielson repelled and at the same time attracted Chris. Of one thing there was no doubt: an instant antagonism had risen between the two.

Chris felt Hawk's eyes blazing into his own, heard the snarled curse as the man again stepped forward. He felt Hawk's powerful forefingers sink into his biceps as the older man grasped him by the arms and lifted him bodily to one side!

Chris's feet left the floor, then he steeled his muscles, his arms darted out and seized Hawk around the back. He put into that grip all the strength at his command. In another moment, Hawk realized, his ribs would crack unless he could break this young fellow's hold. Hastily he released his grip on Chris's arms and quickly lowered his antagonist to the floor on the same spot from which he'd lifted him.

In that moment Hawk Nielson knew he had met his equal—perhaps his better.

"Damn it, you're strong!" The grudging words of admiration were torn from Hawk's lips.

"You're not so bad yourself," Chris admitted coolly, "but I think I can give you odds and still come out on the long end."

Nielson stepped back a pace, his eyes still riveted on Chris's face. Something in those eyes troubled Nielson, stirring vague memories. He said impulsively, "Where have I seen you before?"

"That's something I wouldn't know. I've been a lot of places. Maybe you've been there too."

"Where?" Nielson snapped the single word.

"A lot of places." Chris smiled. "And I've seen a lot of men. I don't ever remember seeing you. You're strong enough though," he conceded, "so I might remember you next time."

Nielson grunted. "Maybe you're a mite stronger, but that's not saying much." Even as he said the words, he was unable to understand his admission. "After all, it's brains that count."

"You should have used yours, then," Chris laughed easily. "I was strong enough to beat you with sheer muscle. I can beat you in other things too."

Nielson struggled to keep his tones steady. "That remains to be proved." Then, arrogantly, "You don't know who you're bucking. I'm a sort of king in this country."

"Kings have been known to lose their thrones," Chris laughed shortly. "I've a hunch your time has nearly come. That's something that can be proved within the next few days."

"In what way?" Hawk fairly spat the challenging words.

"They tell me," Chris said quietly, "that you're right good in the rodeo events. I'm figuring to enter. That clear? Now we've wasted enough time charging each other like a pair of bulls at this doorway. I offered you half the doorway once; I'm willing to do it again. Any difference that lies between us can be settled later." As the words left his lips he swung to one side.

For a moment Hawk Nielson just stared at Chris. Usually it was Nielson who terminated arguments; once more this brash young man had taken the play out of his hands. Hawk cursed once, shortly and violently, then, dropping his eyes, he turned sidewise and pushed on through to the bar-room.

Chris, a slight smile playing about his lips, turned and noted Hawk's advance towards the bar, watched him unceremoniously shove aside two of the patrons as though they were flies, while the rest of the customers looked on, wide-eyed. Then Chris laughed, threw back his head and laughed as though the whole proceeding had been one of intense merriment. But down underneath Chris wasn't laughing. He'd caught the glare of hate in Hawk Nielson's eyes, and knew he was in for a battle to a finish.

Then he stepped out to the sidewalk where Whitlock and old Gabe awaited him.

"Looks as though you won the first round," Whitlock commented cautiously, "but don't let yourself get too confident. Hawk Nielson has never yet been licked in a long fight—or for that matter in a short fracas, until now. This is just a beginning."

"I'm in this thing with both feet now, Vard," Chris said seriously as the three walked along the sidewalk. "To me it looks like a finish fight. We'll clean Nielson proper or—he'll finish me." Then, more enthusiastically, "But, holy mackerel! Hawk Nielson's a real man! He may be bad clear through, but I'm stating here and now, there's nothing small about him."

"You're correct on that point," Whitlock conceded grudgingly.

"Except when he takes folks' outfits away and don't treat his wife——" Gabe commenced in a whine.

"You hush that, Gabe," Whitlock said quickly.

Chris hadn't heard the remark. He was still thinking about Hawk Nielson. "There's one thing certain," Chris said. "I'm a lot better man than I think I am, if I can best Hawk Nielson. Matter of fact"—rather ruefully—"I'm wondering if I'm going to be good enough."

"Don't you worry about that," Whitlock said confidently. "I know Hawk Nielson. I haven't trained you all these years for nothing."

The three pushed their way along the crowded sidewalk. Fresh arrivals in town continually swelled the flow of traffic. Many came on the train, some in wagons and buggies, leading horses behind them; others arrived on ponies that had the appearance of having covered many miles. By this time Butterfield Street was swarming with people from all points of the compass. Runners passed—small boys—shouting loudly the accommodations to be had at various boarding-houses. A man drove a covered wagon down the road, the sides of which bore signs attesting the excellent care given horses left at a certain livery stable. All the restaurants were full, though it was mid-afternoon. Cowboys strode past, carrying saddles on their shoulders, their high heels clicking sharply on the cement walk.

At the far end of the town Chris sighted a straggling queue of men in puncher togs, lined along one side of the street, the far end of the queue disappearing gradually into the doorway of a building farther on. Fastened to the front of the building was a huge canvas sign on which were painted the letters:

NIELSON CITY RODEO
HEADQUARTERS

Chris gestured towards the sign. "Vard, I reckon I might as well get in line now and hand in my entries."

Whitlock nodded. "Gabe and I will mosey around and look the town over. We might see somebody we know—though I'm commencing to doubt it. You can pick us up on the street someplace. If you don't, we'll see you at the hotel whenever you get there."

Chris said so long and cut diagonally across the street towards the queue, stepped to the sidewalk, and fell into line behind a good-natured-looking, stocky-bodied, red-haired cow-puncher in a plaid shirt and levis.

"You're in for a long wait, pardner," the sorrel-topped one greeted Chris. "This line is moving like sorghum in December—it's plumb bogged down, seems like. If I'm not mistaken we're due to break last year's record for entries. I never saw so many folks here. Course the fact that Nielson advertised that he was going to give the proceeds to the Silver King victims has brought in folks that otherwise probably wouldn't have come."

Chris nodded. Further conversation brought out the fact that the puncher's name was Dusty Snow—at least, that's what he was called. A heavy dusting of freckles across his bronzed features may have had something to do with that. He was bow-legged, with a carefree, laughing manner that instantly attracted Chris. Chris shook hands and mentioned his own name.

They talked a few minutes, then Dusty asked, "Where you from?"

Chris waved his hand in a wide arc to indicate any point in the country.

Dusty nodded understandingly. "Me, too, until just recent. I've been peelin' broncs for Stan Farrel's outfit, about seventy miles east of here. Stan played in hard luck and is giving up his place until he can get some fresh capital. Hawk Nielson offered to lend, but Stan wouldn't take Nielson's money. He's seen too many men get caught in that web. Anyway, Stan paid me off last night. I figure to add to my bank roll in this rodeo, then drift some more."

"Why didn't your boss want to borrow from Nielson?" Chris asked.

Dusty shrugged, then lowered his voice. "Nielson asks too much interest, and Stan just hates to play into Hawk's hands, like others have. That's an old stunt of Nielson's—squeezing the fellers that can't help themselves."

The line of men moved nearer the door to rodeo headquarters. Chris said, "Nielson isn't very popular around here, is he?"

Dusty shook his head. "Not with anybody that has any money or property to lose. Other folks think he's all right. In one way, I reckon he is. He's sure made a right town out of this burg. Howsomever, most people never stop to think that Nielson's money grows with Nielson City. But he sure rides roughshod over folks when the urge hits him and he wants something." Dusty said, "Oh hell," and changed the subject: "What events you entering?"

"I'm not sure yet," Chris replied. "I want to see first what ones Nielson picks."

The other laughed. "Maybe we're both smart. I'm doing the same thing. Any man that's hoping to draw down first money had better steer clear of Nielson's entries. Most of us are thanking our stars that he's not going in for the all-around stuff this year. He always has things too much his own way——"

"You've got me wrong, cowboy," Chris interrupted. "I just figure to enter the same events Nielson does."

For a moment Dusty couldn't comprehend. His eyes widened in astonishment. "You don't—don't mean to tell me you're out to beat Hawk Nielson's time?"

"Nothing else. Somebody's got to enter the same events he does or you couldn't call it a contest——"

"Sure, those fellows that are satisfied with second or third place—but cripes! I didn't figure you were that type——"

"Against Nielson I'm after first place."

"I'll be everlastingly damned!" Dusty looked at Chris with fresh interest. "You're sure a glutton for punishment. Don't you know Hawk Nielson hasn't his equal in these parts?"

"So I've heard. But I'm aiming to change that." There was no boasting in Chris's tones, just a world of confidence in his own ability.

"Well," Dusty said dubiously, "I'm wishing you a run of luck. And I won't be the only one congratulating you if you come out topside." Then, a few minutes later, "Sa-a-ay, did you say your name was Whitlock?"

"That's right, Chris Whitlock."

"Not the feller who's been doing things at the Pendleton show, and the Cheyenne Frontier Days, the last coupla years? Then there's that rodeo in Las Vegas. There was a Chris Whitlock walked right through the events and——"

"I was there, copping down a few first prizes at those shows," Chris admitted modestly, "but I had a lot of luck. There's lots better than I am."

"Cowboy!" Dusty exclaimed enthusiastically. "Let me shake your hand again. I guess maybe you will stand a show against Nielson, at that. . . . Say, do me a favour and don't tell anybody who you are. I'm out to get down some long-odds bets on you against Hawk."

"Don't risk too much," Chris laughed. "I understand Nielson is a right good contender."

The sun was swinging farther to the west while they talked. Chris and his friend had nearly reached the headquarters door by this time, as the line of men had gradually commenced to move a trifle faster. At last they were inside the building and within a short time had reached the entry-fees desk.

After some conversation with the man at the desk, Dusty Snow entered himself in the bronc-riding, steer-riding, and fancy-roping events. Then it was Chris's turn. He moved along to the desk and asked:

"What events is Hawk Nielson entered in?"

A look of disgust crept slowly over the desk man's features as he laid down his pen and straightened in his chair. "You too," he groaned. "What in the poppin' hell is the matter with so many of you waddies?"

Chris said placidly, "Nothing wrong with my question so far as I can see. Do I get the information or don't I?"

"Oh hell, you do," the man said wearily. "Nielson's entered for the calf-roping and steer bull-dogging. That being the case"—sarcastically—"I suppose I can write down your name for the cow-milking contest."

Chris chuckled. "There's been too much spilt milk as it is for you to cry that way, mister. Nope, just put me down for the steer bull-dogging and calf-roping. I'm sorry Nielson didn't enter more events."

Men within hearing distance of the desk craned their heads to see who this brash young speaker might be. Evidently someone was out to try and break Hawk Nielson's record.

For a moment the man behind the desk just stared, then he stuck out his hand, " Shake, cowboy," he exclaimed. " You've got guts, anyway. You're the only man that has asked that question to-day that didn't sidetrack the idea of bucking Hawk. Of course there's fellows in the same events as Hawk, but some of 'em never expect to win top money, and others entered without thinking."

He quickly filled out two blank forms when he had Chris's name. " There you are, Whitlock. That'll be twenty-five dollars—fifteen for roping and ten for bull-dogging. Yes, I know these entries are high, but we raised 'em this year, account of the Silver King disaster. It's in a good cause whether you win or lose."

Chris paid his entry fees and then, with Dusty Snow at his heels, made his way to the street, followed by the admiring glance of more than one man in the big room.

12

CHRIS MAKES A PROMISE

WHEN Chris and Dusty once more stood on the sidewalk, Dusty said, " A man can get mighty dry standing in a line like that."

" I could use a beer. Where'll we go—Brown Jug ? "

" Brown Jug's all right—but I always sort of favoured the Silver Star when I wanted beer. They carry several brands. I've always been partial to that San Antonio brew—you know, ' The Beer That Made Milwaukee Jealous,' as they call it."

" Silver Star's fine with me."

The two started off along the sidewalk, and were walking parallel with the queue of men still waiting to enter the rodeo events, when Chris noticed the approach of a girl who stopped frequently to speak to the men standing in line. Invariably the conversation was concluded when the man to whom she was talking handed her a bill or piece of metal money.

Chris slowed down to watch her actions, taking in her shoulder-length abundance of reddish-gold hair, at the present moment tied back from her forehead with a white silk ribbon. She didn't wear a hat, but a mannish flannel shirt, open at the throat, a divided riding skirt, and riding boots displayed her slim, boyish form to some advantage. Her breasts were small and high beneath the flannel shirt, her arms bared to the elbow A plain silver bracelet of Navajo workmanship adorned her left wrist. Deep pockets on either side of the divided shirt bulged with the money she'd been receiving.

" Decidedly pretty," Chris mused, watching her draw nearer. No, there was something more than mere prettiness there. There was a lot of character, strength, in her face as well. Chris came to a full stop now. Dusty glanced inquiringly at him. Chris said, " Who's the girl ? "

" Dorada Nielson—Hawk's daughter."

" Cripes ! I didn't know he had a daughter—for that matter, I guess I never gave it any thought. Is there a Mrs. Hawk too ? "

Dusty shook his head. " I understand Hawk's wife died years ago. Dorada acts as Hawk's secretary. I've heard Hawk claims he couldn't get by without her—and that's a lot of admission for a man like Hawk Nielson to make. I've a hunch if it wasn't for Dorada, Hawk would be a lot harsher with folks than he is. She keeps him toned down some."

" Secretary, eh ? She must have brains as well as good looks."

Dusty laughed. " She has. Dorada sure knows stock-raising and finance. Until she took over, Hawk used to get him a man secretary about every six months——"

" Gosh ! " Chris interrupted. " I've got a feeling I could be friendly with that girl. Without ever talking to her, I know I like her." He frowned. " I can't understand a man like Nielson having a daughter like—— "

" You, too, eh ? " Dusty laughed. " Well, you're not the only one. Half the town's sweet on Dorada. She's one square shooter and straight as a string. Nothing like Hawk a-tall. Hawk spends half his time, I reckon, trying to keep fellows from courting Dorada. If you ask me, though, I'd say it was wasted time."

" Why ? "

" She's never been more than just friendly with any young fellow around Nielson City. She's too well educated for most. It's said that Hawk did the educating himself. I don't know. Maybe so."

"I sure hope he didn't educate her along his own lines of philosophy," Chris said shortly. "Say, what's she doing? Looks like she's collecting money from various hombres."

"Yeah—she is. You heard about the Silver King disaster, didn't you? Well, Dorada is doing a little charity gathering on her own for the widows and orphans. I gave her a five spot this morning."

Chris said fervently, "If she applies to me, she can have my whole roll."

And apply to him she did, about five minutes later. She approached the two men with an easy, swinging stride. Chris saw now she was taller than average; her skin was deeply tanned, and there were tiny greenish flecks in her blue eyes to complement the reddish tint in her luxuriant hair. Chris considered her eyes—level and very honest, he concluded—with their long, dark lashes. Her voice, when she spoke, had a sort of husky, contralto quality.

"Did I get you yet?" she asked Chris, after a friendly nod to Dusty.

"Nope, but you can have me any time you like." Chris smiled.

The girl's colour heightened a trifle, but she answered Chris's smile with a quick flash of even white teeth, as Dusty broke in with, "This is a friend of mine, Chris Whitlock, Miss Nielson. I've just been telling him about the collection you've been taking up."

"I'm glad to know you, Mr. Whitlock."

Chris, feeling her cool, firm grasp in his hand, was lost—lost for the first time in his life, where girls were concerned. Strangely enough, something had happened to Dorada Nielson too. For the moment Dusty, all Nielson City, was forgotten as the two stood gazing at each other. Even then the man and girl knew there could never be anyone else. . . .

Dorada was first to recover herself, and released the hand Chris was still holding. She said with a sort of breathless catch in her voice, " You here for the rodeo, Mr. Whitlock ? "

" I thought I was until just now," Chris replied. " Now I'm commencing to wonder if something, somebody else, didn't draw me here."

" Let's just say it was the rodeo," Dorada laughed. " And now, can I persuade you to subscribe to my Silver King fund ? "

" I don't think I could be stopped from subscribing," Chris replied. " What's the ante ? "

" That's up to you," the girl answered. " Anything you care to spare. I've taken as little as twenty-five cents, and I've twice received a hundred dollars."

Chris was only half listening. If he gave the girl what he had in his pockets, she'd probably go on her way and forget him. He had to do something special, something that would keep him in her memory. What could it be ?

" Well ? " Dorada hinted, smiling. " Are you trying to remember where you left your wallet ? "

" Excuse me." Chris chuckled. " What's the biggest donation you've received so far ? "

" I'm not asking you to match that," Dorada said. " Dad —you know, Hawk Nielson—is my biggest contributor, as he should be. I talked him out of a cheque for three thousand dollars this morning. Maybe it wasn't quite fair to him, after all he's put in already, but—well, I knew he could afford it."

" Three thousand, eh ? " Then Chris said impulsively, " You can put me down on your list for four thousand, Miss Dorada Nielson."

The girl stared at him, startled beyond belief, then turned

to Dusty. Dusty returned her gaze with one as fully devoid of comprehension. Then both turned to look questioningly at Chris.

" Do—you mean it ? " the girl gasped at last.

" Sufferin' rattler's puppies ! " Dusty exploded. " I've been trailing around with a millionaire and didn't know it ! "

" Of course I mean it," Chris laughed. " Naturally, I haven't got that amount on me right now, but I'll get a cheque for you by night." He stopped, a blush mounting to his temples. " I—I wonder if I could give it to you at supper-time—and if you'd have supper with me at the hotel, say around seven o'clock ? "

The look of astonishment fled from Dorada Nielson's features. " Why, I——" she began.

" Oh, I'm throwing a straight rope," Chris said, his face reddening as he surmised the thought in her mind. " I'm not just talking to see if I could get a date with you. Whether you're interested in having supper with me or not, I'm donating four thousand. Gosh ! I'll give you a cheque first, or you don't even need to consider my invitation—better still, I'll bring you cash ! "

The girl saw now he was sincere and regretted her first suspicions. " I'll be very pleased to have supper with you," she said simply, " whether you succeed in bringing the money or not. And—a cheque will do perfectly."

" That's fine." Chris was beaming widely. " Shall we make it at the Nielson City Hotel, at seven o'clock ? Good ! I'll be expecting you."

Dorada nodded, shook hands with the two men once more, and continued on her way, trying to determine in her own mind exactly what had prompted her to accept an invitation from this big stranger. She paused a minute, turning to look after him as he strode along the street with Dusty Snow. A small frown creased her brow. " I almost feel that

I've met him before someplace. He looks like somebody I know. Now who can it be?"

She shook off the thought. By this time the last of the queue was nearing the doorway to rodeo headquarters and she hurried to solicit more donations to the cause she was furthering.

A block farther on Chris and Dusty encountered Whitlock and Gabe Houston. Chris introduced his new-found friend, then drew Vard to one side while Dusty talked to Gabe.

"Vard, you got the cheque-book with you, or is it at the hotel?"

Whitlock reached to his hip pocket. "Shucks! It's in my other clothes. I've got some cash, though. How much do you want?"

"Four thousand bucks."

Vard's jaw dropped. "Sounded just like you said four thousand bucks," he laughed after a moment.

"That's what I said."

"Huh! What for? What you want four thousand dollars for?"

"Hawk Nielson's daughter. You see . . ." Chris told Vard of his promise.

Whitlock's face darkened while he talked. When he had finished, Whitlock said angrily:

"Sucker! What's the idea? We came here to trim Nielson, not to add to his wealth."

"This isn't for Nielson," Chris said exasperatedly. "Dorada's giving the money——"

"Dorada, eh? Seems to me you got right chummy in a hurry."

"That's neither here nor there," Chris said, trying to keep the impatience out of his tones. "You don't understand, Vard. She's nothing like Hawk Nielson——"

"Hell! She's pulled the wool over your eyes," Vard said disgustedly.

"Have it that way if you like," Chris said shortly. "You've always handled our money, and given me what I wanted when I wanted it. Right now I want a cheque for four thousand. If you don't want to sign a cheque to Nielson's daughter, that's all right. I have the right to sign cheques. I'll go to the hotel and get the cheque-book——"

"Won't do you any good," Whitlock said angrily.

"Why not?"

"We haven't got that much in our bank," Whitlock lied. He wasn't meeting Chris's eyes now.

"What? Hell's bells, Vard! We should have that much and more. We've always saved our wages pretty regularly. Any money I made gambling I turned over to you. And there's the rodeo money I've been picking up the past few years too. And how about that piece of property we bought in Oklahoma and sold a month later at a nice profit——"

"I know, I know, Chris. But we've spent a lot of money too. We haven't always travelled by horse. We've covered a lot of country. 'Way up in Canada, down to Mexico City. Shucks, Chris, travelling costs money. You've always left the spending to me; I guess you haven't realized how fast money goes."

"Just the same," Chris said tersely, "I've an idea of what we've spent. One thing you taught me when I was just a kid was always to keep track of where my money went."

Vard swallowed hard and told another lie. "I know, Chris. I reckon you'd better handle your own dough from now on. You see, I lost a bunch of money. Never said anything to you about it before. I was trying to double your cash, so I loaned a feller up in Wyoming some money last year. It looked like he had good security—he gave his ranch as security—but after he got the money he lit out and I learned he never owned the ranch. I was ashamed to say anything to you before." Vard looked miserable.

Chris grinned suddenly. "Holy mackerel! And the hombre took you for a ride, eh? Gosh, that's funny! I always thought you were too wise, Vard——"

"I'm a fool," Whitlock said.

"Forget it, Vard!" Chris laughed. "Easy come, easy go. I'd probably lost the money gambling someplace, anyway."

"You'll just have to tell that girl"—Whitlock breathed easier again—"that you couldn't raise the money. Here, I got about seventy-five dollars on me. Wait until we see what Gabe has. Probably won't be much, though——"

"Keep your dough. I'll think of something."

"I'm plumb sorry, Chris."

"I said to forget it." Chris chuckled. "All these years now you've had me wondering if you weren't ever going to make a slip someplace. Now I know you're not infallible." He swung around to Dusty. "Come on, I'm still thirsty."

Whitlock's gaze followed Chris's broad shoulders as they disappeared in the crowd thronging the street. "Christ! What a dog I am!" Whitlock muttered. "And a liar to boot. I should be booted. But I'm damned if I want to see a Nielson get that much money—or any money—from us. And this girl, now. I don't like the looks of it. If Chris gets tangled with the girl, God only knows how we'll end up. Maybe I'll have something to break up. We've got too much at stake——"

Old Gabe quavered, "What's thet? You say you made a mistake?"

Whitlock didn't speak for a minute. "Maybe I have at that," he conceded moodily.

Meanwhile Chris and Dusty Snow were pushing their way through the stream of people passing along the sidewalk. Chris was lost in thought.

Dusty said, " Don't get hoarse."

" What? Oh," Chris laughed. " Guess I wasn't saying much, was I? Had something on my mind. Where is this Silver Star we're heading for?"

" Down the street a piece in the way we're heading."

" Good. We pass the Cascabel House going this way. I'd like to stop in at the hotel a minute if you don't mind waiting. Got a few extra bucks in my other clothes I'd like to pick up."

" It's all right with me."

They went on, until they'd reached Chris's hotel. Dusty waited on the sidewalk while Chris went upstairs. He got some money from his room, then on a sudden impulse entered Vard's room and found their cheque-book. A look of perplexity crossed his face as he consulted the stubs. " Either Vard made a mistake," he muttered, " or else he hasn't jotted down all withdrawals. I'll have to ask him later." On the spur of the moment he tore out a couple of cheques and then thrust them in his pocket. A minute later he had rejoined Dusty on the street.

" Don't tell me," Dusty said, " that you went up to your room to get that four thousand."

Chris shook his head. " It's not that easy."

" Cripes!" Dusty went on. " When I took up with you I never dreamed you could lay your hands on that much money. Twistin' side-winders! That's a fortune for some folks."

The words completed the process of snapping Chris back to reality. He looked thoughtful, then laughed a bit uneasily. " To tell the truth, Dusty, it's a fortune for me right now."

The cow-puncher eyed him sharply. " You mean you ain't got that much?"

Chris plunged one hand in a pants pocket, withdrew it,

and contemplated the pile of gold and silver in his palm. "I have," he announced somewhat sheepishly, "just sixty-three dollars and ninety cents."

Dusty seized Chris by the sleeve and gazed earnestly into his face. "How in the name of the seven bald steers are you going to give Dorada Nielson four thousand dollars by seven o'clock?"

"I'm sort of wondering that myself."

"That way, eh?" Something of disgust tinged Dusty's words. "You were just running a whizzer on her to get a date, eh? Oh hell! She's a blame nice girl too." He heaved a long sigh. "I've got about twenty bucks left you can have."

Chris grinned suddenly. "Back me up even if you have lost faith in me, eh? You know, Dusty, I'm not going to forget that." There was an awkward pause between the two. "Don't worry, old wasp," Chris continued after a minute. "I passed my word to give her that money, and I've never yet broke a promise."

"I'm damned if I can see how you're going to keep it."

"We'll drink first and then give the matter some consideration. What sort of a place do you do your gambling in, in this town?"

Dusty looked aghast. "You figuring to luck your way into four thousand bucks?"

"I asked you a question."

"The Silver Star—right where we're headed."

"The games straight?"

"So far as I know. It runs pretty wide open, and you can get most any sort of game you want. Hawk Nielson controls it, of course. But with him back of it, the sky's the limit—just like the limit is off on a lot of things here. There's an ordinance in Nielson City that says you can't wear a gun on the street. Nielson gave out word to disregard it. Anyone who wants to wear a gun is welcome to, but he'd better not start any trouble."

"What's all this talk about guns! Do you figure I'm planning to hold up the Silver Star?"

"I'm blasted if I know how else you're going to get four thousand dollars in the next couple of hours."

Chris looked thoughtful. "I might have to at that. Are you with me?"

Dusty swallowed hard. "I don't like it, but I won't back out now."

A sudden gale of laughter left Chris's lips. "Holy mackerel! You are a loyal cuss, Dusty. Do you think I'd *steal* money for—for *her*?"

Dusty grinned with relief. "Come on, I'm still thirsty."

13

A BIT FASTER THAN FARO

THE Silver Star was housed in a big, barn-like building constructed of timber, rock, and adobe. Along the right side of the interior stretched a shining mahogany bar, lined with customers and presided over by three perspiring bar-tenders. The back bar glittered with polished glasses and bottles. The room was noisy with many voices; tobacco smoke swirled and drifted above the heads of the customers.

The remainder of the room was given over to tables for poker players and the equipment devoted to various other games of chance—faro layouts, chuck-a-luck, keno, blackjack, roulette—above which hovered the droning voices of the various operators and the soft *click-clicking* of poker chips.

Chris and Dusty shouldered their way to the bar and ordered drinks. That part of the business taken care of, Dusty was about to suggest an encore, but before he could speak Chirs turned his back to the bar.

" I've got to raise some money," he said. " Let's take a *pasear* around and look at the games."

" It's a slim chance you've got raising that money," Dusty voiced dismally, a doleful expression on his usually good-natured features. " I heard once of a feller that sold his soul to the devil for what cash he needed. You might—— "

" It's a question whether my soul would bring what I need." Chris smiled. " However, we might ask the devil—there he is over there."

Dusty's gaze followed Chris's pointing finger and saw, at one of the Silver Star's two roulette wheels, the bulky-framed figure of Hawk Nielson. Dusty nodded. "Yeah, Hawk plays here quite frequent. With him it's a sure thing, I reckon. He can't lose."

"You mean he owns the Silver Star, too?" Chris asked.

"Not the business. He built the building and fitted it up. He leases it to a fellow named Rod Blackburn for a percentage of the profits. He may lose at gambling here, but he gets it back in rental in the long run."

"In other words," Chris said thoughtfully, "it would take an outsider to really win Nielson's money. Maybe that's an idea, Dusty."

"What are you talking about?" Dusty frowned.

"I think I know where I'm going to get that four thousand."

"Oh, my Gawd!" Dusty exclaimed. "What'll you think of next?"

"I've got just room for one thought in my mind now."

"But, Chris, you can't expect to buck his kind of money."

"I can try, can't I?" Chris grinned. "Come on, let's go see what he has to offer."

He sauntered over to the roulette wheel, followed by the reluctant Dusty, and stood by, watching several spins before speaking. Hawk Nielson was winning on every turn. Finally, as the little ball clicked into a compartment bearing a number upon which Nielson had placed a bet, Chris spoke:

"You seem to be having a run of luck, Nielson."

Nielson raked in his winnings, then glanced around to learn the identity of the speaker. Recognition flashed into his eyes. There was a touch of anger there too. "You, eh?" Nielson said harshly.

"You're right." Chris smiled genially. He wanted to appear friendly, for a time at least. "I merely remarked that you seem to have the Indian sign on that little ivory ball."

" I got the Indian sign on anything I come in contact with, young fellow," he growled.

" Excepting . . ." Chris reminded gravely.

The big man drew himself to his full height, glowering at Chris from beneath his bushy brows. " We're ignoring that episode for the present, Whitlock," he said shortly. " Muscular strength isn't everything. That's just a matter of training. Had much of that ?"

Chris said non-committally, " Enough for my purposes."

" Had some training in games of chance, too, I suppose."

" I'll risk a few dollars now and then." Chris nodded carelessly.

Nielson grunted contemptuously. " A few dollars! Penny ante, I suppose. Or did Vard bring you up to play for matches ? "

Chris laughed softly. " I've played for matches. Once we even had poker chips. I didn't like that so well, though."

Nielson took the bait : " Why don't you like poker chips ? "

" Blame things kept piling up in front of me," Chris explained gravely. " After a few hands it got so I couldn't see the other players."

Nielson grew red. Several men who were listening near by snickered. Dusty let out an astonished guffaw.

" Phaugh ! " Nielson growled. " Is that supposed to be a joke ? "

" Not unless you have a sense of humour," Chris said. " I guess I made a mistake in judging you. You can't take it." He pretended to start away.

Nielson caught at his shoulder. " Wait a minute, Whitlock."

Chris turned. " What's on your mind ? "

" I'm wondering if you can take it—risking a few dollars and losing them ? "

" I might be able to." Chris shrugged carelessly. " But

if you're suggesting a little game, I'm warning you that I feel luck is riding my shoulder to-day. You feeling in the mood for a few hands of draw?"

"Too slow," Hawk refused. "How do you click on faro?"

Chris laughed scornfully. "Maybe poker's too slow, but I'm used to something a bit faster than faro too."

Hawk Nielson's mouth tightened. He didn't realize that Chris was doing his best to irritate him. Nielson considered himself "quite some shucks" at dealing faro; as a matter of fact, there wasn't a man in Nielson City to compare with him at the game. To Hawk's mind, Chris's words were almost an insult: faro was Hawk's favourite game. With an effort he choked down his wrath. Despite himself, he found himself liking certain qualities in this big stranger.

"I'm waiting to hear what your game is," he hinted.

Chris had been engaged in manufacturing a brown-paper cigarette. He kept Nielson waiting while he moistened the edge of the paper, struck a match, and lighted up. "Where I come from," he said finally, "we like quick action on our bets. Perhaps"—there was just a touch of insolence in the words—"perhaps my game will be too fast for you."

Tiny bulges of white appeared at the corners of Nielson's tightened mouth, his eyes narrowed, burning into Chris's frank gaze. "I'm still waiting," Nielson said, "to hear what your game is."

"It's simple," Chris explained. "We take a deck of cards, lay our bets, and cut. High man wins. Do you feel like giving it a whirl?"

A deck of cards lay on a nearby poker table. Nielson moved over to the table, slipped the cards from their cardboard case, and swiftly examined them, counting as he did so. Chris and Dusty had followed him, as had several other men in the room. Nielson looked up from the cards.

" Full deck here," he announced. " Do you want to look it over ? "

" I'll take your word it's a straight deck. I'm ready any time you are. Aces high, eh ? "

" That's good with me," Nielson snapped. " How much are you laying on the first turn ? "

Chris drew out his sixty-three dollars. " There's my pile. I'll shoot the whole thing on the first cut."

" Good God ! " Nielson sneered. " And you're the man who's been talking about fast action. And then when I offer you fast action, all you produce is sixty-three dollars. Maybe, little boy "—sarcastically—" if you look real good you could find a few pennies in your pockets. Sixty-three dollars ! Chicken-feed ! "

" No good for a hawk, eh ? " Chris said good-naturedly. He added pointedly, " Not being a professional, I'm not in the habit of carrying large amounts of cash. However, if you're willing to accept my cheque, maybe I can make it interesting for you."

Nielson hesitated, then placed the cards on the table. " I don't know," he commenced dubiously. " I don't know you——"

" I don't know you either," Chris cut in sharply, assuming a look of indignation. " I've heard you had plenty of money, but it appears to me you're acting like a tinhorn——"

" Damned if I am," Nielson rasped. " Let's see your cheque. How much is it good for ? "

Without replying at once, Chris drew from his pocket one of the cheques he had got from Whitlock's room. If he lost, he was warning himself, he'd been in a tight spot. Cripes ! He couldn't lose. Of that he felt certain. He searched in another pocket and found a stub of indelible pencil, quickly drew and signed a cheque for five hundred dollars.

" Suppose we use this for a starter," he proposed easily, handing the cheque to Nielson. " Cover it with one of your own cheques. That will make us even."

Nielson took the cheque and examined it. His jaw dropped a little. Who was this stranger who could so coolly write a cheque for five hundred dollars ? Something more than an ordinary cow-puncher, that was certain. To cover his surprise, he grunted, " El Paso National, eh ? That's a good bank."

" That's one of the reasons I keep my money there," Chris said gravely.

Nielson abruptly dropped all pretence. " Say, who in hell are you ? "

" My name's on the cheque." Chris smiled. " Do we play, or is five hundred too much for you to risk ? "

The taunt accomplished what Chris had been working towards. " We'll play," Nielson growled angrily. He jerked from one trousers' pocket a roll of bills large enough to choke the proverbial ox, peeled off five one-hundred-dollar notes and tossed them on the table together with Chris's cheque. " You want first shuffle ? "

" You take it," Chris said whimsically. " I'll give you all the breaks to start. You're going to need 'em. I'll shuffle next time."

Nielson swore under his breath, shuffled the cards, then placed the deck, face down, on the table. " Start the ball rolling," he growled.

Chris reached to the deck, removed a few cards from the top and turned them face up. His card was the seven of diamonds.

Nielson grunted scornfully. " That should be a cinch to beat." He cut and turned over—the trey of spades ! " Hell's bells," he snapped and slammed the paste-boards down on the table.

Chris laughed softly. No one heard the long breath of relief that escaped his lips. Now he had a stake to play with. " Looks as though your luck deserted you, Nielson," he commented coolly. Reaching for his cheque, he quickly tore it in small pieces, which he dropped to the floor. " Seeing you don't feel quite safe about my cheques," he added, " we'll use cash from now on—providing you feel like covering that money on the table."

Hawk's eyes were thin slits now, his face a mask of hard lines. He nodded shortly, again produced his roll, and once more stripped off five century notes, dropping them beside the money Chris had won. " Don't talk so much," he muttered tersely.

Chris picked up the cards and shuffled them with a dexterity born of long hours of practice. Nielson's eyes widened a trifle as he noticed the flying cards manipulated by Chris's long, strong fingers, but he made no comment. Chris felt sure of himself now ; luck had been with him from the start, apparently. He placed the shuffled deck on the table beside the ten one-hundred-dollar bills.

" I'll give you a chance to pull out now, before it's too late," Chris said carelessly. " I'm warning you again, luck's riding my shoulder to-day."

Nielson swore a short oath. His hand darted to the cards. He turned up an ace of spades.

" Oh, my Gawd ! " Dusty Snow gasped. It was almost a moan.

Nielson's eyes gleamed triumphantly. " Beat that, you bustard ! " he challenged.

His laugh of exultation was cut short when Chris turned up an ace of hearts !

There came a choking sound from Dusty ; nothing more. A certain tenseness had gripped the ring of onlookers gathered about the two big men.

"I matched you," Chris said placidly. "We'll cut again, Nielson."

The look of triumph had faded from Nielson's face. He reached over and turned up a nine of clubs. Chris beat it with a jack of diamonds!

Something ugly crept into Nielson's tones. "That kind of luck can't stay with you long," he rasped. "Are you game to stay for some more?"

Dusty whispered frantically in Chris's ear: "For cripe's sake, cowboy! Pull out now while you can. She'll be satisfied with a thousand——"

Nielson interrupted with, "I asked if you were staying."

Chris assumed a look of surprise. "Have I said anything about quitting? I just thought maybe you'd had enough. No, I'm letting that money lay. Want to cover all of it?"

Nielson glanced sharply at Chris. This big young stranger was altogether too confident. Something warned him to move with caution. By this time quite a crowd had gathered about the two men. Realizing something unusual was afoot, men had left the bar and other games and were clotted closely around Chris and Nielson. Nielson whirled angrily on the onlookers. "Give us some room here, will you? Get back, damn your hides!" The suspicion had entered his mind that Chris might have a confederate in the crowd who, somehow, was passing him winning cards.

A soft laugh parted Chris's lips. "High stakes make a man edgy sometimes, boys. Better stay well back."

Nielson cursed, picked up the cards, and examined them closely, back and front.

Chris watched the inspection with humorous eyes. "Looking for thumbnail marks or shaved edges?" he queried lightly. "You won't find any of mine on those cards. Remember it was you chose them from this table yourself——"

"But I don't know how they got on this table in the first

place," Nielson snapped. He finished his scrutiny, with no more words. A baffled expression crept into his face. Abruptly he grasped the deck in his powerful fingers and with one terrific twist of his hands tore the deck in halves and dropped the torn paste-boards on the floor!

"Those cards may be all right; again they may not," he half snarled above the comments of the lookers-on. "I'm calling for a fresh deck. You're having too much luck with that deck."

A smile played about the corners of Chris's mouth. He nodded agreement as Hawk raised his voice to call to one of the other gambling tables: "Hey, Nick, shoot a fresh deck over this way."

The man known as Nick, who had stayed at his table to watch the sum of money that he kept on hand to play with, reached down, then came up holding an unbroken packet of cards. His arm raised and he sent it whizzing through the air, over the heads of the crowd.

Hawk put up one hand, deftly picked the flying pack from space, and then broke the seal. "We'll see now if my luck doesn't change," he muttered, taking the cards from the case and dropping the empty case on the table. Now he gave the cards a thorough shuffling, after first examining them carefully. Then, laying them down before Chris, he again produced his roll and reduced it to the extent of one thousand dollars, which were thrown down on top of the thousand Chris had already won.

"Suffering rattlesnake's puppies!" Dusty exclaimed. "Two thousand in the pot!" Small beads of perspiration stood on his forehead. He glanced at Chris, and wondered how he could remain so cool and collected.

The result of the next draw was swift and sure, Chris drawing a king of spades and Nielson not even coming close when his turn brought up a deuce of spades.

A sudden silence descended on the scene, only the breathing of the spectators breaking the quiet. Abruptly, as Nielson had turned over his losing card, he had broken into a fit of cursing that turned the atmosphere a vivid purple. Someone laughed and, realizing he was making a fool of himself, Nielson quieted down and held himself in check.

"You'd better pull out while you're ahead, cowboy," a man shouted at Chris.

Nielson looked expectantly at Chris. He had a feeling that the luck was all against him this day. "That's damned good advice, Whitlock," he blazed. "Do you want to pull out?" Nielson didn't so much mind losing the money as he did the fact that the big stranger was making him look foolish.

"No, I don't want to pull out," Chris replied, laughing confidently. "That is—say, maybe you've had all you can stand."

That stung. Nielson turned white with rage. He tried to speak, but words wouldn't come. Only an angry spluttering sound left his lips.

Chris's smile broadened. He pulled out his watch and consulted it. "I tell you what we can do, Nielson. I've got an appointment for seven o'clock. If we hurry we've got time for one more cut—that is, if you haven't lost your nerve." There was a hint of a sneer in the last words that got under Nielson's skin.

"I'll show you if I've lost my nerve," he flared, jerking his rapidly diminishing roll from his pocket. Then he paused suddenly, his features crimsoning. "Nothing but small bills left here now," he explained. "You'll have to wait a few minutes while I get some more money or"—he finished lamely—"take my cheque."

Chris chuckled at Nielson's discomfiture. "I wouldn't think of doubting your cheque," he said gravely. "Come on, let's get busy. You can make out the cheque later. Your word, as well as your cheque, is good with me."

Nielson just stared at him now. Hawk had the feeling he was beaten even before they started. Common sense told him to draw out before he lost another two thousand dollars, but the man was game, if nothing else. It wasn't that he minded losing the money; it was the condition under which it was being lost. He watched narrowly while the cards rippled through Chris's hands, but could discern no crooked manipulation of the deck in any way.

"There you are, Nielson." Chris placed the deck face down on the table. "This is the last one. Do your damnedest!"

There wasn't a tremor in Hawk's muscular fingers as they reached to the cards and turned over a king of hearts. For a brief moment he felt his luck had changed, and a smile tugged at his thin lips.

And then Chris cut the ace of clubs. It was all over. Hawk Nielson had lost four thousand dollars!

Flames of fury leaped in Hawk Nielson's eyes, then slowly died down to prove there was still something of the white man in his make-up. Abruptly he stretched out one hand to Chris. "Your luck's better than mine, boy," he said, level-voiced. "It's been a pleasure to meet a man like you."

Without thinking, Chris's hand shot out to meet Nielson's. For a moment all trace of exultation left him. Then he thought of the things Vard had told him, and of his mother, and Chris steeled himself against the feelings of friendliness that welled in his breast. He remembered only that Hawk Nielson was a hard man.

In that moment something passed between the two, something that neither understood. "I still got the feeling," Nielson said slowly, "that we've met before. Your face is familiar."

Chris nodded coldly. " I don't think you'll ever forget it now, Nielson."

Slowly he gathered the scattered cards, replaced them in the empty cardboard case that Nielson had dropped on the table. There was something of frigid scorn in the look he bent on Nielson—then there came a swift motion of his muscular hands, a sudden wrenching—and cards and case lay on the table ripped across by Chris's sinewy fingers. " You see, Nielson," he said cuttingly, " I can even go you one better at that trick. It's the third time to-day I've licked you."

Instantly he was sorry for the words and action. Both smacked too much of showing off, of humiliating a fallen enemy.

Nielson's eyes were narrow slits once more. " I've admitted once before to-day that you were strong, Whitlock," he said quietly. " There's no use my repeating that statement. Just don't get too cocky. I take just so much crowding and no more. You'd better keep that in mind."

Chris changed the subject. " Keep that money on the table, if you like," he said, " and make out a cheque for me."

" Thanks," Nielson said shortly. " I need that cash to pay off some workers out at the rodeo grounds to-night. How you want the cheque made out—to cash or in your name ? "

" Make it out to the order of Miss Dorada Nielson," he said quietly.

Nielson's head jerked up. " That's my daughter." His tones were sharp. " What's the idea ? "

" I'm turning this money over to Miss Nielson's Silver King fund, Nielson."

A sudden cheer from the onlookers broke the silence. It was followed by more cheering until the voices of the crowd nearly raised the roof. Chris had instantly become popular.

He had shown he could dispense money as easily as he won it.

" In case Miss Nielson should ask how you happened to give me this cheque," Chris said mockingly, " I'm relying on you, Nielson, to explain it was in return for some education I gave you in manipulating the paste-board market."

In silence Nielson made out the cheque, handed it to Chris, then without another word lost himself in the crowd, his face set in a heavy, perplexed frown.

14

"LET 'ER BUCK!"

" DUSTY SNOW coming out on Hell-and-Gone ! " came a strident, carrying voice through a megaphone.

The announcer's further words were lost in the applause and shouts that burst from the packed arena grandstand, as Nielson City's Cowboy Rodeo Band crashed into a stirring march.

" Ride 'um, cowboy ! "

" Let 'er buck-k-k ! "

" Stay with 'im, Dusty boy-y-y ! "

" Cowboy, knock on that hawss-s-s ! "

The stands were in an uproar, brought about by the megaphoned announcement. Dusty Snow was doing some top " bronc twisting " these days of the rodeo, and his infectious grin had found favour with all who witnessed his riding. Furthermore, he was a favourite in the betting that had caught Nielson City like a fever.

Things commenced to happen : a gate at one end of the arena was thrown open, and out of the chute flashed a twisting, squirming, squealing, kicking devil disguised in roan horse-flesh, doing its damnedest to unseat the sorrel-topped rider astride its back.

Another wild cheer rose from the grandstand :

" Shake 'em down, Dusty ! "

" Fan that hawss, cow-punch ! "

" Yip-yip-yip-ee-ee-e-e-e-e ! "

The din was terrific. Six-shooters were jerked from holsters and their contents exploded skyward. The audience was on its feet, breathless with excitement as it stared intently at the tremendous struggle taking place between Dusty Snow and the bucking devil that wore his saddle. Dust floated towards the turquoise sky to be caught by the breeze and lifted to the rolling hills beyond the arena.

There was nothing fancy about Dusty's riding. Serious work there. Just a good, workmanlike job of bronc-forking. It was his last ride of the rodeo, and it simply had to be good. He came tearing through space like the proverbial bat out of hell, unchapped legs high, spurred boots against the horse's shoulders.

Suddenly the bronc stopped dead still, bunched its muscles wickedly . . . its nose dived! Up . . . up . . . up it went!

Then down!

All four hoofs, close together, struck the earth with a thud that jarred Dusty from his toes to the flying tips of his tossing red hair. He rose a trifle from the saddle, then settled again. The horse was bucking like mad, twisting, turning, sun-fishing. Dusty's head was snapping back and forth on his shoulders as though it might leave his body. A thin trickle of crimson traced a narrow thread from one nostril. Dirt, dust, and gravel flew in all directions from beneath the flying hoofs of the plunging animal.

Then Dusty commenced to scratch his mount! Fore and aft he raked the vicious foaming brute. The grandstand went mad with joy, all eyes centred on the cyclone taking place in the arena. Suddenly a shrill whistle sounded from one of the mounted judges, signifying it was over. Dusty had made his ride. Again the crowd thundered its approval as the event was concluded.

It was the third and last day of the Nielson City Rodeo. The various events had been run off in smooth succession and to the vast satisfaction of the rodeo committee. Mostly the usual winners in that part of the South-west had been running true to form, but one upset had taken place: Hawk Nielson was finding himself running second to Chris Whitlock in the calf-roping and steer-wrestling—Hawk's own favourite events. However, he was a close second.

The first day Chris had roped and tied his calf in twenty-four seconds flat. Nielson had accomplished the same trick in twenty-four and three-fifths seconds—losing out by a scant three-fifths of a second. And that was a new record for Hawk Nielson.

Chris had had more of an edge in the steer-wrestling—or bull-dogging, as it is more generally known—having required but nineteen seconds to Hawk's twenty-three seconds, to down his animal. Compared to records to be made in the rodeos of future years, there was nothing startling about the time set by Chris and Hawk in their events, but in that early day such time seemed nothing short of unbelievable.

The second day of the rodeo Chris had taken twenty-six and one-fifth seconds to finish off his calf, while Hawk required twenty-seven seconds flat to tie his animal. The bull-dogging had again been not so close: Chris had downed his animal in twenty seconds, compared to the twenty-six seconds clicked off for Hawk's time in the same event.

Interest was unusually keen, now, in the bull-dogging and calf-roping, in which Chris and Hawk were running a close first and second. Other contestants there were, but even third time was considerably behind the time set by Nielson.

Dusty Snow and a few other reckless ones had cleaned up big in the betting on Chris the first day, having secured long odds from the many Nielson supporters. The second day people commenced to realize that the contest was narrowing down to Chris and Hawk, and the betting was even. Now the third day's contest opened with the odds on Chris, although there was still the chance that Hawk might make a better showing the final day, and thus grab the prizes offered for the best average time for three days' contests.

Speculation was rife as to who would be the winner of the two events. All other contests were lost sight of in the terrific struggle between Hawk and Chris, each trying to prove supremacy over the other. It was Chris's youthful vigour and strength against Hawk's muscles and experience.

So keen was the interest in these two men on the morning of the third day that it was decided by the directors of the rodeo, with Hawk grimly concurring, to change the steer-wrestling and calf-roping events from fourth and eighth place on the programme to fourteenth and fifteenth, thus making these two events the final ones to be staged. The bronc-riding was third last on the list, the wild-horse roping, racing, relays, fancy riding and roping, chuck-wagon race, et cetera, having been run off first.

Chris was standing down near the chutes when Dusty arrived after his ride. He smiled response in answer to the sorrel-topped one's weary grin. "Congratulations, cowboy!" Chris stretched out his hand. "That was a *muy elegante* ride you made."

"I've just been telling myself how lucky I was," Dusty panted happily. "That Hell-and-Gone horse sure come apart in all directions. I was expecting to eat gravel any minute."

Chris looked surprised. "You were? I didn't suspect you were having any trouble a-tall. That gives you first place, doesn't it, in the bronc-riding?"

"That's what one of the judges was telling me on the way back here." Dusty nodded nonchalantly, as though winning first place was an everyday occurrence. "That will give me six hundred lovely dollars, about, with my day money."

"You'll be getting rich, Dusty," Chris laughed, "what with the cash you picked up on fancy roping and steer-riding."

Dusty tilted his sombrero over one ear and gravely scratched his head. " Shucks! I wish you hadn't gone and reminded me of those two events. I haven't been showing up so pretty——"

" All out for the steer wrestling-g-g!" came a bawled announcement at that moment.

" That includes me!" Chris exclaimed. " I've got to go look at my pony. You're hazing for me to-day, aren't you?"

" You couldn't lose me." Dusty nodded. " I owe you that much for what I've snagged betting on your little old horn-twistin' and doggie-tyin' stunts. I'll be ready when you are."

In addition to Hawk Nielson and Chris, there were five contestants in the steer-wrestling. These five were run off first, none of them producing anything startling in the way of fast time. One of the men lost his steer altogether and failed to qualify; another was badly injured and had to be carried from the field.

A few minutes later came the voice of the announcer: " Chris Whitlock-k-k next-t-t! Whitlock has best time to date-e-e-e——" Further words were lost in the thunder of applause that greeted Chris's name.

Chris was in the saddle, waiting, when the words " Ready, Chris!" sounded in his ears. The gate of the chute swung back and a big, wide-horned steer lumbered out, gathering momentum as it got under way. Despite its clumsy gait, the animal was moving fast, heading towards the open, away from the yelling punchers at its rear.

Chris kicked his pony in the ribs and was almost instantly alongside the animal. As he approached the deadline tape he reined back an instant that daylight might show between his horse and the flying steer, then he shot forward again, drawing up on the wide-horned beast in a fraction of a second.

Opposite Chris, on the other side of the running steer, rode Dusty Snow, acting as " hazer " to keep the steer running straight, in case it should decide suddenly to turn off its course.

Both horses and steer were running like the wind now. Chris ranged closer to the steer, until he could almost touch it. Then, loosening his feet from the stirrups, he dived forward, timing his leap to the steer's motion. At the same instant both horses swerved wide to one side to give Chris a clear field.

The leap was perfect! Chris shot through the air, his hands reached for and grasped the spreading pair of horns. The sudden impact of his weight threw down the steer's head momentarily and slowed its flight. Then its head came up, carrying Chris with it. In mid-air Chris shifted his grip until his right arm passed under the steer's right horn and around its head. His left hand was already bearing down on the beast's left horn. Again the steer lowered its head, bellowing madly. Chris dug in his heels as they struck the earth, felt himself raised once more, came down again, braced himself and dug in, striving with might and main to stop the impetus of the steer as his boot heels dug twin furrows in the dusty sod.

This time it was accomplished. The steer halted and started to shake its head in an effort to loosen Chris's grip. In that moment Chris commenced twisting—hard! For just a fraction of a second the big animal resisted his efforts, then quite suddenly the front quarters dropped. An instant later the steer was thrown flat on its side, head twisted to the proper position, all four feet out!

Chris's arm came up like a flash to signal the fall.

" Got you, cowboy!" came the voice of the field judge. " You made good time, too."

Dusty came loping up. " Gosh, that was sure pretty,

Chris." He grinned as Chris was climbing to his feet. "Never saw anything sweeter. Here, jump up behind me. Your pony was picked up and taken to the far end of the field."

Chris climbed to the back of Dusty's horse and clutched the cowboy about the waist. The steer was getting slowly to its feet, and started away, after a moment, half dazed. Chris generally brought 'em down pretty hard! Two punchers with swinging ropes started after the animal and brought it back to the corrals a few minutes later.

Half-way back to the chutes, Chris heard the announcer's voice: "Chris Whitlock—sixteen and three-fifths seconds——" A mighty roar greeted the news. Men were on their feet, yelling like maniacs. It was the best time yet turned in. For fully five minutes the cheering continued.

"Hear that, feller." Dusty spoke over his shoulder. "That's for you!"

"It's all a lot of foolishness," Chris protested. "I've just been right lucky so far."

His eyes were searching the lower rows in the grandstand. At last they found what he sought—a slim golden-haired girl in a bright red silk sweater and plaid skirt. He waved, and in answer saw a handkerchief flutter in the air. Chris had been seeing considerable of Dorada Nielson the past few days. The cowboy band broke suddenly into "My Lulu Gal" and the cheering died down.

Dusty hadn't missed that movement in the stands. "I wonder why Miss Dorada didn't enter any of the events this year? That girl rates high when it comes to riding and roping—cleaned all the prizes the last two years."

"That's why she didn't enter this year," Chris said. "She told me she thought she'd stay out in the hope of getting more girl entries. It was getting so there wasn't hardly anyone in the women's events. This year, she says, it's better——"

A megaphoned announcement broke in on Chris's words. "Hawk Nielson coming out of——"

There were further words, but Chris didn't hear them as Dusty said, "Let's get over to one side out of the way, and watch Hawk. This should be something to watch——"

"Any particular reason?"

Dusty nodded as he reined his horse off at a tangent. "Hawk had the bad luck to draw that Old Dynamite steer that nobody's been able to handle yet. You know, that brute of an animal that nearly killed Slim Wilson yesterday and broke Jim Fleetwood's leg the first day. Old Dynamite's got a Brahma strain in him that keeps him on the prod all the time, seems like. He's vicious!"

Chris's eyes narrowed thoughtfully. "So that's what Hawk drew. I told you I've been lucky, Dusty——" He broke off, noting the commotion over near the chutes. A deathly silence had descended over the grandstand.

Then Chris saw Old Dynamite. The big red steer was just being hazed across the deadline tape, moving with all the force of a hurricane. Hawk was living up to his name, though. Like some great predatory bird of prey, he was swooping on his swift-moving horse alongside the great plunging red animal. An instant later he shook his stirrups and made his dive! It was as pretty a leap as had been made during the three days of rodeo events, Hawk's hands meeting Old Dynamite's horns true and firm.

What happened next no one was quite sure. The dust clouds were so dense much of the action was obscured from view. Hawk's feet were seen to leave the earth, but before he could force down the red steer's head Old Dynamite gave a sudden vicious twist of his powerful neck, shaking loose Hawk's grasp. Hawk's body was flung up, up, then he crashed to earth thirty feet away.

The next instant the maddened steer had started, horns

down, for Hawk, who was sprawled on the ground, dazed by the fall. It looked as though he'd be gored to death, but half a dozen alert horsemen had already spurred forward, half a dozen ropes hissed through the air to drop on various portions of the steer's anatomy. Old Dynamite was thrown heavily to the earth a split second later.

Immediately a small knot of men gathered about the fallen man, but Nielson was already struggling to his feet, smiling grimly. Fortunately he was uninjured, but he was realizing, right then, that Chris had won first place in the steer wrestling.

The arena was again cleared and fifteen minutes later the calf-roping events were announced. Chris remained back near the chutes until his turn had come. None of the participants who had preceded him came anywhere near equalling his time for the two previous days, nor did they turn in, now, better than ordinary time. Left were only Chris and Hawk and then the rodeo would come to an end.

Chris was in the saddle ready to go when his turn arrived. The word was given, the gate swung open, and a russet-coloured calf came tearing out. Chris waited until the small animal had had a thirty-foot running start to the deadline, then threw spurs to his pony. The horse darted forward, eager for the work at hand, covering the ground in swift, distance-devouring strides. Three timekeepers rode closely behind.

Chris was already shaking out his loop. Nearer and nearer he approached the fast-running calf. His noose soared through the air, flying true, then dropped gracefully over the little beast's head. Instantly the wise little cow pony slowed pace and, without throwing the calf, brought it to a stop, holding the rope taut. Leaping from his saddle, Chris ran hand over hand down the rope until he reached the calf. Lifting it bodily in his arms, he threw it on its side, produced his " piggin' string " and—it seemed—in no time at all had tethered three of the little beast's legs together!

" Right, judge! " he called.

" We got it," one of the three timekeepers answered. " Twenty-three seconds flat. Nice time!"

By the time Chris got back to the chutes Hawk Nielson was already in pursuit of *his* calf. Hawk was riding easily, but was evidently still somewhat unsettled by his failure in steer wrestling. He was a trifle hasty in making his cast and the rope loop missed completely its mark. The calf swerved to one side. Hawk swung his pony savagely around, guiding it with his knees, while he retrieved and again coiled his lariat.

Once more the loop sailed through the air. This time the calf was caught. Hawk slipped from the saddle like a flash, ran down the rope, and threw his animal. In an instant he had it tied, his hand rose in the air for time. Even considering his first miss, it was fast work—probably a record but for that.

Chris awaited the result with keen interest. Then it came through the announcer's megaphone:

" Hawk Nielson-n-n-n! Twenty-four and two-fifths seconds-s-s! "

A deafening roar ascended from the grandstand. The announcer drew his six-shooter and emptied it rapidly into the air. The crowd quieted to hear his next remarks:

" Chris Whitlock takes first money in the calf-roping! Hawk Nielson second! Cotton Vaile third-d-d-d! Breezy Thompson——"

The rest of the sentence was lost in the pandemonium that broke loose. Six-shooters were yanked from holsters and triggered towards the sky. For several minutes the din was terrific with the rattle of gunfire and cheering of the crowd. The Third Annual Nielson City Rodeo had come to a rip-snorting, hell-banging close!

15

THE BEST MAN

THE crowd from the grandstand came surging down on the field. For a time all was confusion, with everyone yelling, calling to friends, slapping contestants, when they came across any, on the back. Colt guns were emptied and re-loaded—emptied again in the exuberance of the minute.

"There's a new champ in Nielson City!" a man bawled wildly.

Chris glanced around to see a knot of men pushing towards him through the crowd. They were led by a widely grinning Dusty Snow. The next moment Chris was torn from his saddle and hoisted to the shoulders of Dusty and his followers.

Chris fought to get down. "Come on, fellows, cut it out," he protested, colouring with mixed pride and embarrassment. "I was only in two events. You can't make a champ out of me on that count."

"Hell, cowboy! We know what you could do if you wanted to!" roared a burly puncher in dust-stained overalls. "Anyway, Hawk Nielson knows what's what. Beat him and you beat anybody——"

"I'm not sure yet," Chris returned, "that I'm a better man than Hawk at bull-dogging. He had the bad luck to pull that Old Dynamite animal out of the hat. In three days I had the good luck not to draw that red devil. Maybe if I'd got 'im, instead of Nielson, things would have been different."

He finally prevailed upon the men to put him down. Then they picked up Dusty Snow and carried him off, hailing

Dusty as " King of the Bronc Snappers." Chris watched them a moment, laughing, then turned around to find himself facing Vard Whitlock and Gabe Houston.

" Nice work all through, Chris," Vard congratulated.

" I guess ye showed Hawk Nielson a thing or two," old Gabe cackled gleefully.

Chris shook hands with the pair. " He put up a damned fine fight, though," Chris said, " and I'm looking for him to tell him so."

Houston looked his disgust and turned away. Vard said slowly, " You believe in giving an enemy all the credit that's coming to him, don't you ? " There was a queer, baffled expression on Vard's features. " Well, maybe it's not a bad policy. It'll keep you popular with folks, now that you're wearing Hawk's crown. Folk's like to see rivals shaking hands. But you and me know, don't we, that the friendliness is just put on for appearances ? "

" I'm not so sure." Chris frowned. " Under different circumstances Hawk Nielson and I might have got along fine."

" Now don't you go turning soft on me, boy," Vard said sharply. " We came here to do a job. This rodeo business is done now, and we can get down to serious business. You passed your word to me, and you can't go back on it."

" Maybe I could, but I won't," Chris said ruefully. " I'm just not liking it, though, Vard."

" Bosh ! It's that girl that's making you this way."

" Let's not talk about it," Chris said shortly. He borrowed the " makin's " from Whitlock, rolled and lighted a cigarette.

Old Gabe said, " Well, Chris, what say we get out of here and sluice down our gullets ? I want a drink."

Chris shook his head. " I'll see you both at the hotel later. My horse is over near the chutes and I want to get him. So long." With that he turned away and was quickly lost amid the jam of people scattered over the field.

From his seat on the horse, a few minutes later, Chris craned his head in all directions, but of Hawk Nielson he could see nothing. He asked two or three men if they knew where Hawk was, but they couldn't give him any information as to Nielson's whereabouts.

Slowly Chris urged his pony through the milling crowd until he was half-way up the field. Still there was no sign of his defeated rival. Then his eyes caught sight of a tall, slim girl in a red silk sweater, some short distance to his left.

A minute later he was receiving congratulations from Dorada Nielson, as he alighted from his horse and grasped her hand.

"Shucks!" Chris protested. "I can't see where I did so much. Sure, I won a couple of events, but no matter how much a man wins, there's always somebody a little better comes along in time. It seems to me Hawk Nielson deserves a heap of credit for the showing he made. He's better than any other of these fellows half his age, and I've been looking for your dad to tell him so. Do you know where he went?"

"Why, he's down near the chutes," Dorada said. "I was talking to him not ten minutes ago. I came out here to give him a couple of telegrams that arrived this morning, regarding some investments back East. I wasn't able to get to him before."

"I'll go look him up right away," Chris said. "Say, maybe you and I could have supper together to-night. And the rodeo committee is giving a dance later. . . ."

Dorada looked dubious. "We've had supper together for three nights running now," she protested.

"Do you think I've forgotten?" He smiled. "But let's make it four. Isn't a top-place hand entitled to some reward?"

There was a pleading note in his tones that the girl couldn't resist, but her lovely, long-lashed eyes clouded. "I don't know, Chris," she said slowly. "I don't think Dad takes to the idea of us being together so much."

"Has he said so?"

"Not in so many words—exactly," Dorada evaded, "but——" She laughed suddenly. "All right, four nights running it is. You go and find Dad. I'll wait here for you, then we can pick up my horse. I left it outside the arena."

He looked uncertainly at the crowd moving all around them. "Think you'll be able to stay in one spot until I get back?"

"I'll be here, or hereabouts," she said.

"That's fine—and thanks a heap."

"Thanks my eye." Dorada smiled. "You're not the only one getting fun out of these suppers, you know. Now hurry and get along, or Dad will be leaving."

Climbing back into his saddle, Chris wheeled his pony back in the direction from which he'd come. The crowd was thinning out but slightly, and it was a slow procedure progressing through the masses of milling humanity. He was but half-way to the chutes when he noticed, above the sea of moving heads surrounding him, a sort of commotion up ahead.

There came sudden yells of excitement and fright, and an abrupt dispersing of the crowd moving about the field. The agitation became more intense. For a moment Chris was at a loss to understand what was happening, then frantic voices from near the chutes enlightened him:

"He's loose!"

"Old Dynamite's broke away!"

"Stop that stee-e-e-er!"

A sort of mass hysteria overtook the crowd. Women screamed; men cursed and scrambled awkwardly for safety. Like magic the field commenced to clear as people took to their heels to avoid being overtaken by the big steer that had so thoroughly wrecked Hawk Nielson's chances in the bull-dogging event.

Suddenly a path opened straight to the chutes. Chris caught a confused glimpse of a sagging, broken corral gate, the bright yellow of splintered pine-boards ; rearing horses, dust ; excited punchers, sweat streaming down their red faces, swinging ropes. Through the thick haze of dust rising from the hoof-chopped earth, Chris saw Old Dynamite pawing the ground, plunging, dodging hempen loops.

A noose sailed out, settled about Dynamite's rear quarters. The next instant it had tightened, stretched taut. Abruptly it snapped like a piece of thread, the tightly strained hemp springing back and whipping across the face of the rider who had thrown it ! Then Dynamite plunged on, doing his best to get his wicked horns into a target, any target. The brute had worked itself into a sort of insane frenzy, having fear for neither man nor beast.

One rider was a fraction of a second slow in getting out of the big steer's path. Chris saw horse and man bowled over as though struck by a cyclone ! The rider shook his feet loose from the stirrups as he was flung off balance and quickly managed to scramble out of harm's way. The horse didn't have a chance : Old Dynamite's head was down, the horns doing their work. The horse screamed, flailed helpless hoofs in agony, its underbody a mass of crimson.

In that moment, when cool heads were so necessary, something of awe overcame the men who were doing their best to capture the wild steer. Many mad beasts they had encountered on the range, time and again, but never one with the strength and maniacal fury of Old Dynamite. It wasn't that the men lacked nerve ; every one of them was doing his best. Their best wasn't quite good enough, that was all.

Dynamite whirled again, faced his would-be captors, bellowed madly, and charged, head down. Horses and men scattered like chaff before a hurricane. The animal stopped short, swung about, then started in Chris's direction, just as he was approaching to give a helping hand. Dynamite's abrupt movement was almost too fast for Chris to comprehend. For a brief instant it looked as though he'd be struck, but in the nick of time he made good use of his reins: his pony reared on hind hoofs, swerved to one side, and Dynamite went flashing past like a runaway express train.

As his pony settled once more to four feet, Chris saw a picture that was to remain vivid in his memory for years, every detail standing out clear: a foam-flecked, flying red mass, hurtling hoofs; bloodshot eyes, long sharp horns. Instead of wheeling and turning back on Chris, Dynamite continued on across the field.

Farther up the arena people were scattering for cover. Men and women both were knocked down in the rush, but gained their feet and fled on, stricken with terror. The field was nearly clear, and it looked as though everyone would escape, when suddenly Chris saw someone in a red silk sweater just rising from the earth. Dorada Nielson had been swept from her feet in the mad dash for safety, but was now again up, running towards the grandstand.

By this time that fleeing red sweater had attracted Dynamite's attention. The big steer whirled towards the running girl, its head down, tail in air, horns ready for business. The distance between Dorada and the big red beast was narrowing rapidly.

It required but an instant for Chris to get into action. With one jerk of the reins he swung the pony about, threw it headlong in pursuit of the maddened steer. Seemingly the faithful little horse knew what was needed. It asked no urging from Chris as it flashed over the green-brown sod. Spurring wasn't necessary. By this time Chris was standing in his stirrups, tensing his body for the leap!

Like a broadhead shot from a bow, he gained on Dynamite. Now only ten yards separated horse and steer—now five. Dorada was directly in the maddened beast's path. In a few moments more Dynamite would strike her. Chris gained another yard. Through it all, above the sound of pounding hoofs, he could hear Dynamite's insane bellowing. . . .

Suddenly Chris crouched a little, then leaped from the saddle, his body shooting through space like a rocket, arms flung wide towards Dynamite's head. The horns were too low for bull-dogging technique. He was forced to take chances on grasping the big red brute where he could. His hurtling weight struck the red steer with a terrific impact.

Chris felt one arm go around Dynamite's neck, then his hold was loosened. After that it was all a blur of dust and flying gravel. But his weight and the savage twist he gave before his grasp had been torn loose had done their work. Dynamite's head struck the earth, driven hard by the force of his own impetus. There came a sudden sickening, snapping sound, a wrenching of bone and muscle. The great beast slid a few feet on head and shoulders, its horns ploughing up the earth, then it crashed down and lay still, except for the slight quivering that ran through its steaming form.

Chris, too, had by this time struck the ground. He had recoiled from the big steer as though made of rubber, sailed head over heels through the air and dropped, sprawling, in the dust. Then a velvety black curtain had enfolded his consciousness.

When Chris again opened his eyes, after some short time, he saw a circle of anxious faces bending above him, heard voices: ". . . yeah . . . Dynamite . . . fast work . . ." He realized quite suddenly that his head was pillowed in Dorada's Nielson's lap and that the girl's anxious blue-green eyes were very close to his own. A wave of her tousled thick reddish-gold hair dropped across his forehead, carrying a certain fragrance to his nostrils. Dorada impatiently brushed it aside.

" Don't take it away," he muttered a groggy protest. Then his head cleared somewhat. " Did—did I stop that steer ? "

" Just in time." Dorada nodded. Her tones sounded a bit shaky.

" You certainly did, cowboy," spoke an enthusiastic cow-puncher at Chris's side. Other voices answered as well :

" You not only stopped him, you finished him for good."

" Dynamite's stopped forever ! "

" You hit that steer so blamed hard you drove his head into the ground——"

" —broke his neck ! "

" Nerviest thing I ever saw. . . ."

Chris's head was throbbing as though about to split. He raised one tentative hand and felt gingerly of a lump the size of a pigeon's egg just above one ear.

" You're all right, Chris," a man said. " No bones broke. Just got a hard bump on the conk, that's all. Course I don't blame you for layin' there——"

Laughter broke out. Dorada's cheeks went crimson.

Chris struggled to his feet. Everyone, it seemed, wanted to shake his hand. A big crowd was gathered about him. He was still dizzy. It felt good to hold on to Dorada's arm in such fashion. The whole field, the people, were swimming in circles about him, making a confused blur of faces and forms and voices. And, near by, a red silk sweater that afforded him much-needed support.

The dizzy mist cleared after a few moments and he was able to make out Hawk Nielson's features. Hawk was standing before him, one hand outstretched.

" I'm not trying to say thanks for saving Dorada from that steer," Hawk was voicing somewhat grimly. " I haven't enough words for that, Chris Whitlock." He paused a second. "Dorada says you were looking for me, after the contests." The words were coming hard. "Two or three others said the same. Well, I—I didn't want to see you then —didn't want to shake your hand. But now—now, after what you did, I'm—I'm admitting you're the best man."

It was difficult for Hawk Nielson to make that admission with so many people looking on. But he did it with good grace and an air of sincerity that won him the approval of everyone near.

Chris's hand came out to meet Hawk's, his fingers closed about Hawk's palm, as they stood gazing into each other's eyes. Even then it wasn't a handclasp of friendship; rather one of respect for the other man's ability and dawning manhood.

A sudden cheer arose. . . . Then another and another.

16

HAWK'S SCHEME

THREE months slipped past. Dorada Nielson sat in her secretarial office in the two-storey building on Butterfield Street. On the second floor were living quarters where she'd been staying the past month while Hawk Nielson had been out of town. Hawk had merely stated that he was going away on business, without mentioning any particular destination.

Mostly the lower floor of the building was given over to a battery of desks where clerks worked on the Nielson books, but at the rear of the building there were two offices, an outer one holding Dorada's desk and a second room which served as Hawk Nielson's private office. Beyond the partitioned-off offices a flight of stairs in one corner led to a small landing and closed door, beyond which were situated the second-floor living quarters, tastefully furnished according to Dorada's own ideas.

Dorada sat in her office chair, absent-mindedly drumming with a pencil against her desk. She wore a plain white shirtwaist and woollen skirt. Her smoothly brushed hair shone like burnished gold in the ray of sun that entered at one window. Mostly Dorada was thinking about Chris Whitlock. There was no doubt in her mind that Chris loved her, and Dorada would have married him in an instant, had he but asked her. There was the rub : Chris had never mentioned his love nor in any way spoken of marriage. He seemed satisfied to take her to dinner, or horseback riding, whenever she would consent to go.

Chris puzzled her : he wasn't running true to form, like other men she had known. She couldn't know, of course, that Chris had decided, in view of his reason for coming to Nielson City, not to say anything to her of his love until such time as he had carried out conclusively his promise to Vard Whitlock. Chris wasn't entirely easy in his mind about this war he was waging on Hawk, but, after all, a promise was a promise.

Abruptly Dorada voiced a small, bewildered " Damn ! " and somewhat impatiently threw down her pencil on the desk. " Chris," she half whispered, " you're one problem I just can't seem to solve."

Beyond her closed door, in the larger room, she could hear the click-clickety-click of a typewriter, and a buzz of voices calling figures—computing Hawk Nielson's great wealth. Dorada's own duties weren't heavy : a well-trained staff of clerks accomplished the greater part of the work, merely carrying out orders relayed through her from Hawk.

A step sounded at her door and it swung open. Dorada got to her feet. " Dad ! You're back ! "

" How've you been, girl ? " Never one to show great emotion, Hawk merely gave her a quick handclasp, man fashion. " You look well."

Which was somewhat more than could be said of Nielson. Not that he looked unwell ; it was simply that he had commenced to look his age. The years seemed to have piled up on him the past three months, as though his youth had fled that day Chris Whitlock took first place in the rodeo events. He crossed the room and sat heavily down on a chair across from Dorada's flat-topped desk, crossed his knees, and lighted a cigar. Dorada reseated herself opposite him.

There were deep lines in Hawk's face. Trail dust had settled in the folds of his clothing. There was a weariness in his eyes Dorada had never before seen there. " Everything going along all right ? " he asked after a moment.

Dorada nodded. " The K.C. Midland Bank met your terms. Their telegram just arrived this morning."

Nielson emitted a satisfied grunt. " I knew Krocker couldn't stall much longer. We'll make money on that deal."

" Is money all you ever think of, Dad ? "

" I think of you occasionally," he said with a slight smile.

" You know I didn't mean that."

" I know. . . . What price is listed in that Sierra Steel and Copper stock ? "

Dorada rummaged among some papers on her desk. " One thirty-six and a half. Up three points since last week. Want to sell ? "

" Hang on to it for a while," Hawk directed. He asked next, " What about C. M. & T. ? "

" That's down again—only two points above par now."

Hawk studied her from beneath shaggy eyebrows which were commencing to show traces of grey. " All right, I'll pull some wires and force the price up again. We'll be ready to peddle in two weeks—clean up a hundred thousand, or I miss my bets. Make a note to get some more of that Lake State Packing stock, if we can get it reasonable. Find out. I think it would be a good idea to buy another fifty thousand of Hartwick-Meadows bonds. Get me some information on them too."

Dorada had been jotting down notes on her memo pad. " Anything else ? "

" That's all," he grunted.

Instead of leaving, as he generally did after a conference of this kind, he settled back in his chair. Dorada watched him in silence. He wasn't happy, that she knew, in spite of his wealth, which he had rolled up from such a small beginning. At least, so she understood. Something was troubling Hawk Nielson. He looked tired and worn.

" Something worrying you ? " the girl asked at last.

Nielson shook his head. " Mite weary, maybe. Haven't had much sleep lately."

" Where've you been ? "

" In the saddle most of the time. Wanted to find out something that Ogden didn't seem to be making headway on."

Anse Ogden was Nielson's manager, his duties involving a sort of supervision over all of Nielson's various cattle outfits. The Forked Lightning was divided into seven sections, each section carrying its own foreman and crew, and each operating independently of the others, although all used the same brand in burning cattle.

" Now where did Ogden fall down ? " Dorada asked.

Nielson frowned. " You talk as though he was in the habit of falling down on jobs, and you know that's not so. It was just that—well, maybe I've had more experience in some things than Anse. Anyway, if you want a thing done right, do it yourself——"

" The thing being in this particular case ?" Dorada hinted.

Nielson explained. " There's been some rustlers operating around these parts. No, they weren't running off large amounts, but they have been taking prime stock. That sort of thing has been pretty well cleaned up around here, and Anse didn't just seem to know how to go at the business of learning who was responsible, so I took to the saddle myself."

" And . . . ? "

" I know how it's being done, anyway," Nielson said a bit evasively. " I had an idea my cows were being sold over the border someplace, so I did some riding. Finally located a man over there who's been buying stock from three men. No, the buyer is innocent. Fellow named Tracy Moore. He's been buying my cows at a dirt-cheap price and reselling them to some rancher in California. I looked over the last bunch of cows he'd bought, just a few days ago, and they were mine, sure enough. Moore had a bill of sale for 'em from somebody who signed his name, Kris Kringle——"

" Chris ! " Dorada said suddenly.

" Spelled Kris—K-r-i-s," Nielson said, eyeing the girl narrowly. " You know, Santa Claus. Moore hadn't got the point, but at the price he was getting my cows it was a Christmas gift."

Dorada breathed easier, and Nielson continued, " I bought back one of my cows, killed it, and peeled back the hide. Sure enough, you could see my Forked Lightning brand plain from the underside. The cow thief had done a mighty slick job of brand-blotting on the outside though, changing my Forked Lightning to a Z-Slash for which he gave the bill of sale. But whoever did that blotting was a real artist with a wet blanket and a running iron. It's years since I've seen anything like that around here."

" But you don't know who the rustlers are ? " Dorada asked.

" I'll locate 'em in time," Nielson said, side-stepping a direct reply. " It's not bothering me any."

" Something's bothering you," Dorada persisted.

" Maybe—a little. Dorada, how would you like to go to school in the East, some good college someplace ? " Nielson's words sounded a trifle lame.

" I—go to college ? " Dorada looked her amazement. " Dad, what's got into you ? Five years ago I might have been interested, but now . . ."

" It occurred to me, perhaps I hadn't given you a good education ? "

" Fiddlesticks ! You've taught me everything I know. We've had good books—history, philosophy, literature——"

" That's not like going to college."

" Just why," Dorada asked, " are you trying to get rid of me ? "

" You know better than say a thing like that, girl. Maybe

I'm just trying to suggest something for your own good. You've probably heard folks say I'm a hard man, Dorada. I'm not denying it. I had a purpose in view, all these years—money! Now I've got money, but it doesn't seem to be giving the satisfaction I thought it would. Lately I've been thinking I took the wrong way—anyway, I don't want you to ruin your life. I want you to have all the chance necessary——"

"Just what are you driving at, Dad? Come to the point."

Hawk came to the point: "Dorada, you're seeing quite a bit of young Whitlock."

"Chris? Why, Dad! Quite a bit—well, I don't know. I've had dinner with him several times. We went riding twice. But—quite a bit? There was more than a week passed once when I didn't see him——"

"Do you know where he was during that time?" Hawk interrupted.

"No, I can't say as I do. Why?"

"No matter. Anse tells me you even had him here one night—upstairs in the living quarters——"

"Anse Ogden? You've had him spying on me while you were away." Dorada's cheeks flushed angrily.

"Don't blame Anse. He only did what I told him to do. But you should know better than to bring him here. Folks might get to talking——"

Dorada's scornful laugh cut in on the words. "And who was it always taught me not to care what folks thought? Not to 'give a damn,' was the way you expressed it."

Hawk winced a trifle. "That's whatever, girl. I don't like——"

"But, Dad, he only came in a few minutes. There was a book I wanted to give him. He smoked one cigarette and left."

"That wasn't the impression I got from Anse."

" I don't care what Anse told you. Gosh, Dad, he's so narrow-minded his ears rub together. What else did he tell you ? "

" Nothing much," Hawk evaded. " Maybe I got the wrong impression. I saw him on Butterfield Street for a minute, just before I came here. He'll be in to see me in a few minutes. . . . Just how well do you like this Chris Whitlock ?"

" Pretty darn well, Dad," the girl replied frankly.

" Like to marry him, I suppose." Hawk glowered at her.

" He hasn't asked me." Her cheeks grew redder. " Nor even kissed me, if you want the truth."

Hawk frowned. This puzzled him, too. He said slowly, " You know, Anse Ogden wanted to marry you once."

Dorada looked surprised. " He never mentioned it to me."

" I told him not to. Figured you were entitled to—well, anyway, I need you to help me. But maybe I'm wrong. How do you feel about Anse ? "

" You should know better than to ask," Dorada said testily. " He may be a good manager, but he's not for me."

" And you won't go away to school ? "

" I'm not interested."

Hawk swore suddenly. Dorada listened placidly ; she was used to his outbursts. " Damn it," Hawk finished, " I should have had a son. Now that I've planned you could carry on when I'm gone, you'll probably get married to somebody who isn't worth——"

He paused at a knock on the door. Dorada called, " Come in."

Anse Ogden entered and closed the office door behind him. He was a tall, wiry man, all bone and muscle, with the reputation of being a rather tough customer when crowded. He carried a long-barrelled six-shooter at all times and was known to be able to get it into action with considerable speed, though no one had any proof he'd ever done any gun fighting. Nor did Hawk Nielson care about it. The only thing that interested Hawk was that Ogden was a good cattle-man and managed the Forked Lightning with complete efficiency.

Dorada had never liked him very well, though their relations were pleasant enough. By some women he might have been considered handsome, with his dark, wavy hair and small moustache he was forever fingering. His swarthy face was lean, with a long, muscular jaw and tight lips. Dorada gave him a cool nod when he entered, then Hawk rose and headed for his own office with a " Come on in here, Anse."

Ogden followed him in and closed the office door. Hawk indicated a chair and sat down, himself, at an old-fashioned roll-top desk. He said abruptly, " I learned who's stealing our cattle, Anse."

" The hell you say," Ogden said, somewhat surprised. " So that's where you've been. Who's doing that thieving ? "

" Vard Whitlock and his son, Chris, and that red-headed puncher, Dusty Snow."

Dusty had, indeed, thrown in his lot with Vard, Chris, and old Gabe. They hadn't told Dusty all the story, simply that they were picking up Forked Lightning cattle as a matter of revenge, and that they were out to " clean " Hawk Nielson. While Dusty didn't feel quite right in his own mind about it, he was inclined to consider the whole business as more or less of a prank. He fairly idolized Chris, and anything Chris did, Dusty considered, couldn't be too wrong. And, after all, most of the present-day cattle barons had got their start with a " sticky loop." And so when Chris had suggested the idea, Dusty had fallen in with the plan.

In tones tinged with anger Hawk Nielson told Ogden the story he had told Dorada a short time before. " They're damned clever all right," Hawk growled, " but this sort of business can't go on."

"You're sure it's the Whitlocks and Snow?"

Nielson nodded. "There wasn't any doubting the description Tracy Moore gave me—he's the fellow over the border who's been buying my stock. Snow and Vard Whitlock might fit the description fitting any two of a hundred other fellows, but there was no mistaking the line Moore gave me regarding Chris Whitlock. There's too few men who look like him for there to be any slip-up."

"What's the next move?" Ogden asked. "Turn what you know over to the sheriff and let the law take its course?"

Nielson shook his head. "This isn't a job for Sheriff Redfield, Anse. We'll handle this our own way."

Ogden's dark eyes took on an interested shine. "Now you're talking, Hawk. I've been thinking, the past few years, that there's been too much of leaving matters to the law-and-order boys. I've been fair hankering to cross guns with Chris Whitlock and——"

"You've got me wrong, Anse." Nielson cleared his throat. "I don't want any bloodshed—at least, not Chris Whitlock's blood. For the rest I don't too much care. You see, a good many years ago, Vard and Gabe Houston and I had some trouble. I've got a hunch they just came back here to get some revenge."

"Wasn't Houston in on the rustling?"

Nielson shook his head. "No, old Gabe is no good for that sort of work. I had a chance to talk to him. You know that old shack, about three miles out of town. Well, the two Whitlocks, Houston, and Snow have been living there——"

"I know that. I've been sort of keeping cases on 'em when I could——"

"Anyway, they rented the place, saying they might buy. That was all talk, of course. On my trip back to-day I dropped around that way, just to see if I could pick anything up. Nobody was there except Houston. I shot a lot of questions at him, but didn't get anyplace. The old codger is batty as a loco cow at times—his head just isn't right, mind about gone, I think. He didn't even recognize me at first. Then, when he did, he got plenty peeved about an old deal he and I had one time. He looked like he was ready to kill me, and all the time he was mumbling something about a plague of locusts eating up the range. I couldn't make head nor tail of his talk."

This was the truth. Old Gabe had undergone a serious illness the past month, and although he had recovered physically, his brain seemed affected somewhat. About all he was good for these days was to keep house for Vard, Chris, and Dusty, though at times he was as rational as he had ever been.

"Where do you suppose the other three were when you were talking to Houston?" Ogden asked.

"In town here. I saw them just coming out of the Brown Jug when I rode through."

"You worked up any sort of plan to take care of the business? If that Tracy Moore still has some of our cows, we should get 'em back."

"We'll let the cattle go," Nielson said shortly. "Moore can keep 'em to sell. He's just getting on his feet after a run of hard luck, and I reckon the loss of a few cows won't break me."

There was a hint of a sneer in Ogden's laugh. "Getting soft-hearted, aren't you, Hawk? I've been working for you about ten years now, and it strikes me you've changed a heap since I first went on your pay-roll. Sometimes, the last couple of years, I've wondered if you were getting ready to join the Church or something——"

"Anse," Hawk said coldly, "I don't remember asking you for your opinion. What I do, or don't do, is none of your damned business."

" All right, all right," Ogden said hastily. " Maybe I misspoke myself. You give orders and I'll carry 'em out."

Hawk drew out a couple of cigars and handed one to Ogden. The two men lighted up. " My plan centres on one man, Anse," Hawk said slowly. " I want Chris Whitlock out of this country. Once he's left, Vard, Gabe, and Snow will follow."

" You mean you want me to put a slug of lead through Chris——"

" Dammit, no! That would be the worst—you see, Dorada—well, look at it this way. Maybe I've sort of taken a liking to Chris Whitlock, but the Cascabel Mesa country isn't big enough for both of us. I was here first, and I aim to stay here. If it was just a matter of gun-play, I'd handle this myself. What I want you to do is is hire a couple of good gun-slingers, force Chris Whitlock into some sort of fight, then, without shooting him, persuade him that he's not wanted around here."

" Suppose he doesn't persuade easy? Do I use my own judgment then? "

Nielson pondered, frowned. " Hell's bells, Anse! If it looks like he doesn't scare easy, you just drop the matter, and *I'll* take care of it some other way. At the same time, I want you to protect yourself. This Chris hombre might be fast with a Colt gun."

Ogden laughed scornfully. " Don't you worry about me, Hawk. Chris may be good at some things, but you know there isn't a man around here that can match me throwing lead—unless it's yourself."

" Uh-huh," Nielson muttered non-committally. " Just the same, if he has to be shot up, remember it's my job."

" Oh sure, sure, I won't forget," Ogden replied.

At the same time Ogden had his own ideas on this point. For a long time a resentment had been growing within him:

there was Chris's growing popularity around Nielson City since the rodeo had ended and, something more, his friendship with Dorada Nielson. Ogden had sworn to himself that someday, if the time came, he'd take Chris Whitlock down a peg or two. And maybe more.

Right then Ogden was planning to shoot first and talk afterwards. Anything that happened could be explained away later, so far as Hawk was concerned, in the event Chris did get shot to death.

The two men talked a short time longer, then Ogden prepared to leave. He rose from his chair and opened the door.

Hawk said, " You won't have any trouble getting a couple of good men to help you, will you, Anse ? "

Ogden turned back, neglecting to close the door. " Hell, no ! I know half a dozen men around town who are good with their guns and not averse to picking up a little easy money for putting the work on Chris Whitlock. It'll be an easy matter to pick some sort of fight with him——"

" Close that door, you damned fool ! " Nielson thundered. " Do you want everybody within earshot learning what we're talking about ? "

The door was slammed shut with sudden violence.

Dorada was still seated at her desk and had heard Ogden's words while the door was open. Her face blanched, then she rose and on tiptoe left her office and ascended the stairway to the second floor to change to riding togs.

17

GUN-PLAY

THE following day Chris and Dusty were seated on the small porch that fronted the shack in which they'd been living. Gabe and Vard had gone into town to get some supplies; undoubtedly they would remain there for their dinner and spend the afternoon either at the Brown Jug playing seven-up, or at the Paris Poolroom chasing ivory balls around a green-covered table. It wasn't yet eleven o'clock.

Dusty started to get to his feet. "Guess I'd better go in and open some cans and build a fire to boil the coffee." Chris didn't answer, but sat smoking with his feet on the porch railing, his eyes fixed on the distant hills towards Mexico. The sun was bright, picking out details in every bit of brush and cactus growth that met his vision, though he was seeing neither. Dusty went on, "How'll it be if I open some canned peaches and sardines?"

"Huh?" Chris's head swivelled on his shoulders. "Getting near dinner already?"

"Hour or so to go yet, but I'm commencing to get hungry. There's some biscuits left from yesterday——"

"Sure, anything's all right with me. Wait a minute, I'll lend a hand."

Dusty laughed suddenly. "You've only heard about half what I said to you. What you thinking about?"

"Several things," Chris said moodily.

"Maybe about those Forked Lightning cows we've been picking off?" Dusty asked. "You know, Chris, I don't quite understand this cow-stealing. If you say it's all right, it's all right, but it doesn't seem that sort of game would interest you long. Sure, we've knocked off some easy money, and, from all I've heard, Hawk Nielson has grabbed off enough from other people so that we're no worse than he is. But to tell the truth, I don't like it."

"Maybe I don't either," Chris said moodily. "But Vard is running the show."

"Why?" Dusty demanded.

"That," Chris said evenly, "is something we won't go into right now, Dusty. You're free to quit any time you like, of course."

"Hell's bells! I'll back any game you play. Is that all that's bothering you?"

"Maybe we'd better not talk any more about it, waddie."

"Just as you say. . . . Hey, I know what you're thinking about. Miss Dorada, I'll bet. It's none of my business, but when she came out here yesterday I know she told you something mighty important. I couldn't know what she said, because you immediately took her down under that live oak yonder, and you talked mighty serious——"

"You were watching us?" Chris's face slowly crimsoned.

"Not intentionally, but I could tell the way you both acted when she started back to town that you'd reached some sort of agreement. You were so happy, you looked positively silly."

Chris grinned. "Let's just say we had an understanding. But that's not what she came out here for."

"Feel like talking?"

Chris nodded. "Dorada brought me a warning. She overheard Anse Ogden and Nielson making certain plans on my behalf. Hawk's got some sort of scheme cooked up, so Ogden is going to work me into a fight——"

"Six-shooters?" Dusty queried sharply.

"That's what I gathered."

"T'hell you say! Chris"—concernedly—"just how good are you with a gun?"

"I'm not worried."

"You've been doing a lot of thinking, though."

"Just trying to figure out how Ogden will work it." He repeated, "I'm not worried."

"Just the same, Chris, I'm aiming to stick mighty close to you from now on."

"No need, Dusty, thanks just the same. This is my fight."

"That's all right for you to say, but——" Dusty broke off suddenly. "Rider coming!"

Chris glanced down the road that ran towards Nielson City and spied a rapidly moving cloud of dust. After a few minutes he said, "That looks like that buckskin gelding Dorada rode out here yesterday. Yes, it's her horse all right, but—no, that's not Dorada. Don't know who it is."

The rider came nearer, and finally the horse was pulled to a halt in front of the house. A small Mexican boy slipped down from the saddle. "I'm look for the Señor Chrees Wheetlock."

"I'm Chris Whitlock, son. What's on your mind?"

"Is the note." The boy drew out of his shirt a folded sheet of note-book paper and handed it to Chris. Chris opened it and read:

CHRIS DEAR,

Will you please come in and see me right away? It's important.

Yours,
DORADA

A smile touched Chris's lips. He handed the note to Dusty for perusal and chucked a two-bit piece to the Mexican boy, who was already remounting Dorada's horse. Chris said, "Dusty, it looks as if you'd eat your dinner alone."

Dusty returned the note and said sadly, "Just my luck. Every time I find a pard to knock around with he goes and gets tangled with a girl."

Chris laughed as he folded the note and placed it in a pocket. "Maybe I'd better ask Dorada if she can't dig up a girl for you."

Dusty shook his head. "Nope, I'm aiming to save my money. One of these days I'm going to buy into a spread someplace, or start a small place of my own. But that's after I've seen what the rest of this country looks like."

By this time the Mexican boy was far down the road. Chris stepped inside the house, strapped on his belt and gun and donned his Stetson, then went to saddle up his pony, which stood in a small fenced-in enclosure at the rear of the house. Five minutes later he had said good-bye to Dusty and was loping easily along the road that led to Nielson City.

About a mile outside of Nielson City the road dipped through a small hollow and elbowed its way between two gigantic upthrusts of grey granite standing like irregularly formed towers on either side of the trail. The terrain being lower at this point, it retained more of the moisture furnished by the winter rains; consequently there was a considerable growth of brush, cottonwood trees, scrub oak, and piñno. No more suitable place along the trail could be found for ambushing purposes.

It was here, hidden among the brush, that Anse Ogden waited with two henchmen, Smoky Calvert and Ed Colton. All three men were mounted, ready instantly to ride out and bar the way when Chris slowed pace to make the bend between the two great rocks that flanked the trail.

Colton was a lantern-jawed individual with pale blue eyes and a ragged-brimmed sombrero. Calvert was dark, swarthy, with straight black hair and a shifty gaze. Both men liked to think of themselves as being in the tradition of the gun-fighters of the Old West; each was forever telling some wild tale of his exploits in the company of Wild Bill Hickok or Buffalo Bill or Texas Jack, though had their hearers paused to do a bit of calculating, they would have realized that Calvert and Colton were probably babes in arms in the days when those three stalwarts were making history.

Nevertheless, both Calvert and Colton had worked up quite a reputation as gun-slingers. It was the only work they ever did; how they lived depended on their luck with the cards or dice, and they weren't above doing a little stealing now and then. Mostly they spent their time reading the dime novels of the day, and thus gathered fresh material for the tales they related to gullible listeners. They did practise assiduously with their six-shooters against targets, and were better than average when it came to hitting a mark.

Anse Ogden hadn't been deceived in the pair's abilities. He figured he was capable of handling Chris by himself. Smoky Calvert and Ed Colton had been hired just in case Chris proved to be a tougher nut to crack than Ogden had anticipated. Despite Hawk Nielson's orders, Ogden was out to finish Chris; he cared little just how that event was to be brought about.

Calvert stirred impatiently in his saddle. "That Chris hombre should have been along here by this time. I wonder what's keepin' him?"

"Maybe he stopped to eat his dinner first," Colton suggested.

"I doubt it." Anse Ogden scowled. "When a fellow gets a note from a girl like Dorada Nielson, he don't stop to do any eating——"

"Where is he, then?" Calvert interrupted. "It's over

an hour since that Mex kid reported that he'd given the note to young Whitlock."

"Might be," Colton said hopefully, "that his bronc went lame, and he had to go back and get another horse."

"You two wait here," Ogden growled. "I'm going to move out of this brush and take a look along the road——"

"Hell! He might see you, if he's coming," Colton protested.

"What if he does?" Ogden snapped. "I came out here to see him. I just want you two along to prove that he pulled on me first and I didn't have any chance except to kill him."

He touched his pony with spurs and pushed through the brush to the edge of the road. Within a few minutes he returned, features clouded with disappointment. "There wasn't a soul in sight," he growled, backing his pony once more into line with his two confederates.

The three sat their saddles in silence for a few minutes, their gaze towards the road, their ears strained for the first sound of an approaching horse.

Ogden was growing angrier every minute. "By God!" he exclaimed. "I got a notion to head out to his shack and——"

"Listen!" Smoky Calvert interrupted. "I hear something."

The three listened intently. Faintly to their ears, and still some distance away, came the drumming of a pony's hoofs.

"Coming fast," Ed Colton jerked out. "Must be he was held up in gettin' started. How do you want us to handle our part, Anse?"

Ogden quickly drew his gun, as did the other two. "We'll move out to the road now," Ogden snapped, "and be waiting for him when he slows down to round that big rock. Let me handle——"

A new voice cut in on the words: "You aren't capable of handling anything, Ogden. You hombres hold those ponies right where they are and drop those guns pronto!"

That voice, coming from behind him, sent a shiver coursing along Ogden's spine. A startled exclamation left his lips. Colton gasped a frightened oath and hurriedly dropped his gun; his arms shot into the air and he cast a quick glance over one shoulder. "My Gawd! It's Chris Whitlock!"

Chris had arrived silently at a point a few yards behind the three mounted men. He was on foot, and stood there gazing at them, cold amusement lighting his eyes. "I take it you were waiting for me," he said, a certain touch of grimness tinging his tones.

Both Calvert and Ogden still retained their weapons. They shifted cautiously in saddles, then their eyes widened as they saw Chris hadn't even drawn his six-shooter. Ogden spurred abruptly to one side, whirling and shooting at the same instant, but he was moving too fast for accurate shooting. His eyes caught the swift blur of movement near Chris's hip, the flash of white fire, then something struck his shoulder a tremendous blow and he felt himself toppling from the saddle.

A second shot from Chris's six-shooter almost blended with the first, the leaden slug striking Smoky Calvert's gun and sending it spinning from his hand, even as Calvert was starting to throw down on Chris. Calvert gave a startled cry and commenced to shake his numbed fingers, then flung both arms in the air. "Don't shoot me—don't shoot me!" he half screamed.

Chris laughed scornfully. "Shut up, you scut!"

Powder-smoke drifted lazily in the air. The drumming hoofs heard along the road a few moments before were closer now. Chris tensed, ready, if need be, for further action.

Ogden was sprawled, groaning, on the earth. Calvert and Colton still sat their horses, arms high in the air, mingled fear and astonishment in their eyes.

"Look here, Whitlock," Colton commenced. "We didn't know what Ogden intended——"

"Shut up," Chris said shortly. "Lying won't help you. You three were waiting for me——" He broke off as the hoof-beats sounded nearer. "Who's that coming?" Before either of the mounted men could reply, Dusty Snow came bursting through the brush, then drew up short at the sight before him.

"You all right, Chris?" he cried anxiously.

"I'm all right." Chris nodded. "What brings you here?"

Dusty explained, "I got to thinking that Miss Dorada wouldn't be likely to write that note in lead pencil on a sheet torn from the sort of note-book a man generally carries. She'd have pen and ink and paper handy. I figured it might be a trap, so I saddled and came on as fast as this chunk of horseflesh could carry me. But what hap——"

"I figured the same way when I first saw that note," Chris cut in. "After I left the house I cut off the road, hid my horse in a hollow, and came here on foot—figured this was the most likely spot for an ambush. These bustards were waiting for me, all right——"

"Why didn't you tell me before you left?" Dusty asked.

"Figured I could handle this alone. No use pulling you in on my scraps. I didn't want anybody shot up on my account." Dusty's gun was out by this time, and Chris started reloading his depleted cylinder. He turned to Calvert: "Just how did you hombres get Miss Nielson's horse? That horse almost convinced me for a minute."

Calvert said sullenly, "Ogden got it from the livery stable."

"Naturally he didn't have any trouble," Colton put in, "him working for Nielson and all——"

"Ain't you going to get me to a doctor?" Ogden was whimpering from his prone position on the earth. "I'm bleeding to death——"

"Take a look at that scut, will you, Dusty?" Chris asked. Dusty got down from his horse and stooped over Ogden.

"Look here, Whitlock," Calvert proposed. "We know we're in wrong, but we didn't know exactly what Ogden's idea was. He told us he just intended to scare you into leaving town. We never did want any trouble with you. It was just that we needed money bad and—and—well, if you'll let us go, we'll get out of this country and you'll never see us again——"

"Cripes!" Chris said good-humouredly. "I don't want you to get out of the country. So long as Hawk Nielson has your kind to hire, I won't have any worries. It's never difficult to contend with stupidity. How much was Ogden to pay you for this job?"

"Fifty bucks each," Colton said.

Chris chuckled. "Had an idea my life might be worth more." He put one hand in his pocket and drew out two twenty-dollar gold pieces. "Here, catch!" he said, tossing the coins, one after another, to the startled Colton and Smoky Calvert. "Now get to hell out of here! Go back to Nielson City and tell folks just the sort of dirty deal Hawk Nielson tried to put over on me."

"Gesis!" Calvert exclaimed. "You're a white man, Whitlock!"

"Gosh, Chris," Colton said earnestly, "if there's ever anything we can do for you, you can count on our guns——"

"That's something I'd surely hate to do," Chris said fervently. "Go on, get out of my sight."

"Can—can we take our guns?" Calvert asked.

"Take 'em for all I care," Chris said carelessly. "Only don't ever turn 'em my way, or I might get mad and sure as hell somebody would get hurt." He added meaningly, "And it wouldn't be me."

Two minutes later Calvert and Colton were riding hard in the direction of Nielson City to tell all they expected to encounter in the various bars what a hell of a swell fellow Chris Whitlock was.

Dusty Snow had helped Anse Ogden to his feet by this time. The man's shoulder had been bandaged with bandannas. "Not hurt too bad," Dusty replied to Chris's question. "Shoulder smashed, but he can ride."

"You got anything to say for yourself, Ogden?" Chris asked.

"For God's sake get me to a doctor. I'm dying." Ogden swayed, eyes half closed. His face was the colour of dirty paper.

Chris eyed the man contemptuously, then said, "Take him in to the doctor, Dusty. I'll get my horse and meet you in town—in front of Nielson's office."

Together they helped the moaning Ogden into his saddle. Chris secured Ogden's six-shooter from the ground and jammed it into the man's holster. "Either learn how to use that Colt gun or throw it away, Ogden," Chris advised. "But don't ever cross my trail again when you've got it in your hand. Next time you won't get off so easy. Only that I hate killing—oh hell, on your way!"

Ogden didn't make any reply as, with one hand clutching the saddle-horn, he urged his pony towards the road, with Dusty riding closely at his side.

Something like an hour later Chris dismounted before Nielson's office, pushed open the door, and strode inside the building. Clerks looked up, somewhat startled at his entrance, but he paid them no attention as he paced down the long room and opened the door to Dorada's office. Dorada was absent at the moment, but through the open door to Hawk Nielson's office Chris could see the big man seated at his desk, studying some papers.

Nielson looked up, frowning, as his door was suddenly flung wide and Chris's broad-shouldered frame filled the opening.

"What do you want, Whitlock?" Hawk demanded coldly.

"Nothing that you can give me," Chris said contemptuously. He tossed a folded sheet of note-book paper on Hawk's desk.

Hawk picked it up, eyed the written words, then glanced sharply at Chris.

"This isn't Dorada's writing," he said.

"I knew that when I first saw it." Chris smiled coldly. "Your man Ogden wrote it. He and a couple of plug-uglies tried to corner me on the way here. Nielson, I'm disappointed in you. I thought you were man enough to do your own fighting, instead of hiring three ineffectual gun-toters to wipe me out. I don't know when I've witnessed such a feeble effort. And I thought all along you had brains. Hell! You don't even know enough to employ a first-rate manager." He added mockingly, "If I were you I'd fire the bustard before he ruins your business."

Hawk's jaw was sagging. "But . . . but . . . where . . . ?"

"Ogden's at the doctor's. He'll live. I paid off the other two myself. They weren't worth wasting lead on. But unless I miss my guess, those two are telling it all over town, Hawk Nielson, just what sort of methods you employ to get rid of a man. Before I get through with you, you'll be a laughing-stock in Nielson City——"

"By God!" Nielson thundered. "I didn't know Ogden planned anything like——"

"But you did give him the go-ahead to plan, didn't you?"

Chris snapped. " You're losing your grip, Hawk. You'll have to think faster—and better—than this, if you want me out of your way."

Nielson was on his feet now, eyes blazing. With an effort he held his rage in check. " All right, what's done is done, Whitlock. I'll admit you've won the first hand——"

" I've won all of 'em so far," Chris pointed out.

" I'll admit that too." Reluctant admiration shone in Nielson's eyes. " I believe in hiring the best men I can find. You've proved you're a better man than Ogden. Do you want his job ? "

Chris's eyes widened, then he laughed scornfully. " You can't buy me off that way, Nielson. I've a bigger job in view——"

" Buy you off ? Why, you damned fool, you don't know enough to realize I'm giving you a chance—the last chance you'll have from me. From now on it's war——"

" I've never considered it as anything else where you're concerned. All I ask is that you do your own fighting."

" I'll do that and gladly." Nielson's features were crimson with anger.

" When ? "

Hawk started to speak, then checked himself. It would never do to let Chris Whitlock rush him into a situation. He'd make his own time for a meeting. This was a matter that required thought. He sat down again. " When ? When it suits my purpose, Whitlock. The time may come much sooner than you expect—or want. Now get out of here."

Chris laughed coolly. " Don't want trouble right now, eh ? Stalling for time, Nielson ? I repeat, you're losing your grip. The longer you wait, the tougher it's going to be. *Adios*, Hawk Nielson."

Still laughing, he turned and sauntered from the office and out to the street, where he found Dusty waiting for him.

18

A STRING OF FIGURES

HAWK NIELSON sat at his desk, lost in thought. His prestige had dropped the past two days. Smoky Calvert and Ed Colton had lost no time telling how Chris Whitlock had put one over on Anse Ogden—on all three of them, in fact. Probably four, if Hawk Nielson was included, and he should be as he was more or less responsible for the business in the first place. That Chris Whitlock was one great hombre, and various toasts were drunk to Chris's all-around abilities. People had grinned openly when they met Hawk Nielson on the street. No one mentioned the matter to Hawk, however ; that wasn't necessary.

Hawk contained his fury in silence, after that first day. He had gone to the doctor's, learned that Anse Ogden's wound wasn't serious enough to completely incapacitate him. But few words had passed between Ogden and his employer—then Hawk was no longer his employer. He gave Ogden a certain sum of money, and saw to it that the man left town on the first train to pass through Nielson City. As for Colton and Smoky Calvert, they were more than glad to leave town after one encounter with Hawk. Hawk had spoken to them in no uncertain terms. " And," he had concluded, " if you two ever show your lousy carcases in Nielson City again, I'll use my Colt on you ! Get out and stay out ! "

Both had gone scurrying out of Nielson City five minutes later.

But all this hadn't helped much. Chris's stock was rising hourly, while Hawk's was nearing bottom at the same rate of speed. Hawk could still buy respect; no one gave it freely. It was Dorada's attitude that hurt most. There was a look in the girl's eyes that Hawk couldn't face. She hadn't said a good deal, but Hawk knew he was lowered in the girl's estimation.

"Goddammit," he growled bitterly, "I should have taken my gun and gone after Chris Whitlock myself. Damn Anse Ogden for a blundering fool!" He considered the matter. "I could still have things out with young Whitlock—face him, man to man, gun to gun." He sighed deeply. "And after I've killed him—what? Dorada is near hating me now. No, my hands are tied in that direction unless—unless I can think of some way to have him make the first move—hell, no! That won't do either. Dorada would be sure to lay the blame on me."

He had another thought: "Suppose I told her that Chris and his pards were the ones who were stealing my cattle. Would she believe me? Would it make any difference if she did? She's crazy about Chris Whitlock now. Even if I gave her proof, that means bringing Vard Whitlock into the business. Vard would tell things I did years ago. Dorada might see his side of the story and feel that Chris was entitled to any cattle that were taken."

At that moment the door to his office opened and Dorada came in to place some papers on his desk. "There're the figures you asked for on the Winchester Farm Machinery Company," she said, and started to leave.

Hawk caught at her sleeve. "Just a minute, girl."

Dorada eyed him questioningly.

Hawk's gaze fell, then he flushed angrily. "Look here," he jerked out, "there's no use you taking this attitude."

Dorada looked at him calmly. "What attitude?"

"You know what I mean. All right, I'm ready to admit I

bungled matters where Chris Whitlock is concerned. But I never figured Ogden would act the way he did——"

"You probably figured he'd shoot Chris. Is that what you mean?"

"No, dammit, it's not!" Hawk blustered. "You know better than that. I suppose Chris has been filling you full of some sort of fool story and——"

"I've not seen Chris since it happened. I didn't have to hear the story from his lips. The whole town is talking. Dad"—a trace of moisture entered her eyes—"you've been made out to be pretty much of a fool. And maybe a coward——"

"Coward?"

"People are saying you're afraid to face Chris Whitlock, that he's beaten you every time you've encountered him——"

"Do you know why I've hesitated?" Hawk flashed angrily. "It's on your account. Right now you're infatuated with him. You'll get over that, but—well, I don't want any trouble now." The words sounded a bit lame. He went on, "Good God! I even offered him Anse Ogden's job, didn't I? And he refused."

"Maybe he didn't like the idea of being bought off," Dorada said coldly.

"So you think that too, eh?" Hawk glowered at the girl. "By God, you should know me after all these years, but I guess you don't. I offered him that job because I thought he could handle it. Whether I like him or not has nothing to do with the matter. Sure, I'll buy brains any time—but I've never yet bought my own safety, and I never intend to."

In spite of herself, the girl was impressed by Hawk's earnest manner. "Perhaps you're right," she said more softly. "The fact remains, however, that if Chris was on your pay-roll, you know what people would think. Look, Dad, I've never crossed you before, but I don't like this business. Why are you so set against Chris——"

"Set against Chris!" Hawk exploded. "By the seven horned rattlers! Ask him why he's so set against me. He came in here—in my own town—with his fur rising. He's laughed at me, challenged me at every opportunity." Hawk pounded furiously on his desk. "I didn't start all this, but, by God, I aim to finish it! This town isn't big enough for Chris Whitlock and me. One of us is due to leave. I'll show him that . . . that . . . that . . ."

His voice died in silence as he suddenly realized that Dorada had left the office and closed the door behind her. Hawk sank back in his chair and slowly cooled down. "You fool, you utter fool," he told himself. "Losing your temper won't get you anyplace. It's the wrong way to handle that girl. I've simply got to think of something else."

At the end of a half-hour he had come to a definite conclusion. He rose and opened the door to Dorada's office. "Dorada, send a rider out to Whitlock's place, will you? Tell Vard Whitlock——"

"Vard?" The girl looked surprised.

"Yes, Vard. Tell him I'd like to see him first thing in the morning, if he can spare the time. On a matter of business. I want to see him alone—alone, mind you."

"I'll take care of it." Dorada wondered what move Hawk was making now.

Hawk said, "Thanks," and again closed his door.

Had Hawk but known it, Vard Whitlock had passed through Nielson City but a short time before. He arrived at the shack where he and the others had taken up occupation around four in the afternoon, left his horse out back, and entered the house, carrying a bundle wrapped in ancient newspapers.

Old Gabe Houston was seated on a box, staring into blank space, when Vard came in. The gnarled little man looked up with dull eyes and after a moment recognized Vard. " Oh, it's you, eh ? " he said in sour tones. " Where you been ? "

" Riding," Vard said shortly. " Dusty and Chris not back yet, eh ? "

" Nope. Don't know where they went. Everybody goes off and leaves me alone."

" For all the good you do around here you might as well be away," Vard growled. " Bunks not made, no fire in the stove. You should be starting supper. This place doesn't look like it had been swept out for a week. Darn you, Gabe, why don't you show a little get-up-and-go now and then ? "

Gabe eyed him a moment, his gaze focusing blankly, then abruptly the rheumy old eyes cleared, and Gabe said, " Oh, hello, Vard. I didn't see you come in. Cripes ! It must be getting close to supper-time. I'll have to stir my stumps." He moved up with considerable alacrity and commenced stuffing paper and kindling in the ancient range. That done, he seized a bucket and hurried outside to fill it with water.

Vard looked after the wizened figure as it disappeared through the doorway. " Damned if he isn't getting battier all the time," Vard muttered. " One minute his mind is clear as a bell, the next he's crazy as a locoed cow critter. I don't know what we're going to do with him. Probably have to place him in some sort of institution one of these days."

Gabe came bustling back, poured some water in a kettle, put coffee in a pot, and shoved more wood into the stove. " Where'd you go to-day, Vard ? " he asked as Vard settled to a straight-backed chair and started to manufacture a cigarette. " That something for me ? " Gabe asked suddenly, noticing the bundle that Vard had placed on the table.

"I'll tell you about that later," Whitlock said, rising and taking the bundle across to a bunk built against one wall. He wrapped the bundle in an old towel, then shoved it far under the bunk, out of sight. "Don't mention that to Dusty or Chris, Gabe," he warned.

Gabe was busying himself stirring a pot of beans and placing dishes on the table. "I don't reckon we'll see Dusty and Chris until late to-night," he observed. "They've gone to spy out a bunch of cows that they heard about—Forked Lightning cows——"

"Yeah, I know about that," Vard said impatiently. "The four of us talked it over last night. What's happened to your memory lately, Gabe?"

"Danged if I know." Gabe looked puzzled. "Seems like I'm always forgettin' things. My head gets to achin' and then—well, I dunno. Seems like ever' time I get to thinkin' on Hawk Nielson I get so mad that—that——" His features clouded with anger. "Thet damn Nielson. Just like a plague of locusts he is—jest like——"

Whitlock rose quickly, crossed the floor, and struck Gabe a sharp blow across one cheek. "Come on, old-timer," he said not unkindly, "snap out of it."

"Huh!" Gabe looked a bit dazed, surprised. "Sa-a-ay, how did you get clear over here? I could have swore that you were sittin' in that chair over yonder. Now you go back and set down, Vard. I can get this meal 'thout no help. You've had a long ride, mebbe. You jest rest yourself. Where'd you go to-day?"

Whitlock sighed and returned to his chair. "You remember that Moqui-Mex settlement on the Creaking River, Gabe?"

"Sure enough. You been way over there? What d'you go there for?"

"I've made several rides over there the past couple of

weeks," Whitlock said. "If you'll think back a good many years, you'll remember I used to know one or two of those Injuns. I had connections through those Mexicans who took care of Chris——" He broke off suddenly. "I guess maybe you don't remember, though. Ever hear me speak of a couple of women known as Guadalopa and Josefa?"

Gabe scowled. "Sort of seems like I do, but I don't just place 'em."

"It doesn't matter. They're both dead now. But there was another pair of Injuns there—a brother and sister named Rosa and Tony Tiguan. They aren't as young as they used to be either. Tony hits the booze too hard to be much good any more. He'll do anything to get money for whisky."

"Yeah, I 'member them names. You been talking to this —what's his name, Tony?"

"I've talked to him several times." Whitlock chuckled reminiscently. "And how he does talk when he's got a skinful of liquor. Give him some whisky and throw a little scare into him and he's ready to do anything I ask."

"I guess I never knowed him personal," Gabe said. He unwrapped a square of bacon and commenced cutting thick slices which he dropped into a frying-pan. "What did this Tony Tiguan talk about?"

"I was asking him some details about something that happened a long time ago. He didn't want to talk at first. Him and his sister were both plumb scared. But I threatened to tell what I knew about 'em to Hawk—to somebody they're both scared of. They sure wonder how I learned so much about 'em."

"Bet they do, too." Gabe seemed only partially interested. He shoved more wood in the fire and rattled knives and forks on the table.

"It's taken a mite of time to break Tony down," Whitlock continued, "but to-day he gave me a Bible and some papers he got out of a wrecked wagon, one time. The papers tell who some people are——"

"Anybody we know?" Gabe asked.

Whitlock shook his head. "No; a man and wife who died. They were expecting a baby, and the Bible had a note in it, telling what the baby was to be called if it was a girl, or if it was a boy. It had a lot of other birth dates and such in it, too. You know, relations of the man and wife and so on."

"What was the name?" Gabe asked. He was slicing cold boiled potatoes now.

"Their name was Blair. The little baby they were expecting was to be named Cynthia Blair."

"Now thet's what I call a real purty name," Gabe said. "And did these folks die before she was borned?"

"One of 'em did—the other later."

"What become of this purty little gal named Cynthia?"

Abruptly Whitlock changed the subject: "Y'know, the big trouble with this Tony Tiguan is, he can't let the booze alone. He had a good job working for Hawk Nielson"—Whitlock hurried over the name, but apparently old Gabe's thoughts weren't too closely concentrated on what Whitlock was saying—"but Hawk finally had to let him go. Tony was working as a janitor in the office building, but he got drunk so often they had to give him the sack. He was plenty sore about it, too, after Hawk fired him. He swears he'll get even someday. I guess Hawk—er—that is, Tony's boss had been ridin' him pretty hard, always a-cursin' him out for a no-good Injun——"

"What's thet?" Gabe showed momentary interest. "Somebody's been swearin' at Injuns, y'say?"

Whitlock nodded. "Yeah, this boss of Tony Tiguan's. You know how those Moquis are—mighty proud and resentful. Once when this boss was going to be away, he wrote out some numbers on a slip of paper for his daughter—er

—his secretary. Tony happened to be in the office, sweeping, the day that happened, and he heard the boss say something about the combination to the safe. Later, when the boss had returned, the secretary tore up the paper and threw the pieces in the waste-basket. Tony had just come in to empty it, and saw the girl throw the bits of paper in. It made him curious to see what they were, so he saved 'em out and made a copy of 'em——"

" 'Nother ten minutes to supper," Gabe cut in abruptly. He turned over the bacon with his fork; a sound of sputtering rose from the pan. "Y'know, it seems like the sun starts settin' earlier every evenin'. 'Twon't be long before we'll be eatin' by lamplight."

" I reckon so," Whitlock agreed, realizing that old Gabe had heard only about half what he'd been saying. But Whitlock felt he simply had to talk to somebody regarding the break in luck that had come his way that day. He continued, " Of course, to Tony that safe combination was just a string of figures. He never really expected to do anything about it. It cost me the price of two quarts, but I got those figures from him. Here they are." Whitlock produced a slip of paper and read off a list of numbers: " 93—R 68—L 87—R 42—L 73—R 29—L 51. . . . What you think of that, Gabe?"

" The L 51, eh?" Gabe frowned. " Don't know as I ever heard of thet brand afore. Used to know a waddie what punched for the L-slash-B. Where's the L 51 located, Vard?"

" In Nielson City, you addle-pate," Whitlock said impatiently. " I'm not talking about cattle brands. That that I read you is a safe combination. If we could get to—to the safe this fellow owns we could maybe get ourselves a nice chunk of money."

" 'Thout him knowing it?" Gabe asked, aghast.

" We'd be fools to tell him."

" I dunno," Gabe said righteously. " That sounds like stealin' to me. Who's the feller ?"

" Oh hell ! forget it," Whitlock growled. " You ain't the least idea what I've been talking about. And to get this information has cost me a good many quarts of liquor, too. On top of that I had to throw a scare into Tony Tiguan."

" Ain't nobody I want to throw a scare into, 'ceptin' Hawk Nielson," Gabe rasped.

" But don't you understand, Gabe," Whitlock commenced, " that's who I'm talking about ? It's his safe and——"

" Want I should throw these beans in a pan and brown 'em ?" Gabe cut in. " Or do you want 'em wet tonight ?"

" Oh hell !" Whitlock said wearily, " any way at all suits me."

" You gotta admit I serve up good meals."

" It's getting so that's your prime interest in life—cooking," Whitlock snapped impatiently. He added under his breath, " Even when you're sane—which same becomes less frequent all the time."

" Now if you'll just slice up this bread," Gabe was saying placidly, " we'll be ready to eat in a minute——"

Hoofbeats drummed outside the house and came to a stop near the porch. A voice bawled, " I'm lookin' for Vard Whitlock."

Whitlock went quickly to the door, flung it open. A man in overalls, mounted on a grey gelding, waited near the porch. Whitlock said, " I'm your man. What's up ?"

" Got a message for you." The rider handed Whitlock a sealed envelope.

Whitlock ripped open the envelope, drew out the folded sheet of paper, and read the written words. A frown crossed his face. After a minute he said, " All right, feller. Tell Hawk I'll be there."

" You don't want to write your answer ? "

" You heard me, didn't you ? Tell Hawk I'll be in to see him. Is that clear ? "

" Clear as a bell." The messenger nodded. Turning his pony, he spurred it back in the direction of town.

Old Gabe met Whitlock at the doorway. " 'Nother mouth to feed at supper ? " he queried.

Whitlock shook his head. " No—just a feller with a message for me."

" That right ? What's the message say ? "

" Hawk Nielson wants to see me to-morrow morning."

" Hawk Nielson ! That lousy no-good crook. Jest like a plague of locusts he is, always devourin' up the range. It's best you leave your money t'home, Vard. He'll rob ye blind ! I'm warnin'——"

" Forget it," Whitlock said roughly. " And don't mention this to Chris."

" Why not ? "

" I'm not sure yet, but it's best to keep things like this quiet. I can trust you, can't I, Gabe ? "

" Crickey, yes ! I won't say a thing 'bout you goin' to see—say, who did you say you were goin' to see in the mornin' ? "

" Just a feller I know, Gabe," Whitlock said. " Nothing for you to bother your head about. Supper must be nigh ready, isn't it ? "

" Sure is," the old man cackled. " Jest you listen, you can hear that bacon a-scurrilin' in the pan now. Come on in, we'll eat."

19

"DEAD LIPS CAN'T TALK"

IT was about nine o'clock the following morning when Vard Whitlock dismounted in front of the Nielson office on Butterfield Street and entered the building. He had a speaking acquaintance with Dorada Nielson, Chris having introduced him one day on the street shortly after the rodeo had ended. The girl gave him a brief smile as he paused in her office doorway.

" Hawk here yet ? " Vard inquired.

" He's waiting for you, Mr. Whitlock. Go right on in."

Vard crossed the floor, pulled open the door to Hawk's office, passed through, and closed the door behind him. Hawk was seated at his roll-top desk across the room and he swung round in his chair as Vard came in.

Vard stood just inside the closed door. " What's on your mind, Hawk ? " he asked coldly.

Hawk glowered at him, from beneath bushy eyebrows, jerked one thumb towards a chair, and snapped, " Pull up and sit."

Vard got the chair and sat down a few feet from Nielson. Nielson pulled out two black cigars and gave one to Vard. Vard Whitlock said, smiling a bit grimly, " Peace pipe, Hawk ? "

" Call it what you like." Hawk scratched a match and held the flame to Whitlock's cigar, then lighted his own. He drew steadily on the smoke a few moments, trying to organize his thoughts.

Whitlock waited impatiently. Finally, " I'm waiting, Hawk. You got some sort of deal to propose to us ? It just struck me"—he laughed coolly—"that perhaps you've seen enough of the Whitlocks around here. You've had bad luck since we arrived, Hawk. Chris has proved he's more than a match for you—and that business with Anse Ogden, three days back—Gawd, Hawk, my boy made you fellers look foolish. Well, if it makes you uncomfortable for us to be in these parts, we might make some sort of deal——"

"You utter, witless fool," Hawk cut in scathingly. "Have you ever known me to compromise with anybody? Don't get big notions, Vard. You'll still dance to any tune I'll play in these parts——"

"You can't talk that way to me, Hawk." Whitlock started to rise from his chair.

"Sit down!" Hawk thrust out one mighty hand and shoved Whitlock back into the chair so hard that Whitlock's whole frame was jarred and the cigar fell from his fingers to the floor. "Pick up that cigar," Hawk rasped. "And listen to me. I'm going to do the talking. And when you answer, keep your voice normal. I don't want my daughter, out there, to hear what's being said. D'you understand?"

Whitlock looked rather pale. "I understand," he said and, stooping over, retrieved his cigar. He drew on it once, choked on the smoke, eyed the long black weed distastefully, and tossed it into a cuspidor at the side of Nielson's desk.

"Too rich for your blood, eh?" Nielson said with a touch of grim humour.

"Too rich," Whitlock said defiantly. "I could never bleed enough money out of other folks to pay for that kind of tobacco."

"You never could because you lacked the guts to try," Hawk rumbled contemptuously. He changed the subject abruptly: "Whitlock, how'd you like to spend the next few years in the penitentiary—you and that son of yours and Gabe Houston and Dusty Snow?"

"What do you mean?" Whitlock looked startled. "You figuring to frame us on something?"

"I don't have to frame you, Whitlock. I've got you dead to rights."

"We haven't broken any laws."

"Don't lie to me, Vard. You've been stealing my cows. It took me a little while to run it down, but I've got all the proof I need."

The words came as a shock to Whitlock: he thought their tracks had been thoroughly covered. Nor had he expected that the stolen cows would so soon be missed from the Forked Lightning's vast herds. Whitlock swallowed hard. One glance at Nielson's hard-eyed gaze told Vard it would be useless to try to bluff. Hawk Nielson knew! There was just one course to take, Whitlock decided: he'd brazen it out.

He forced a thin smile. "All right, so you know, Hawk. We've been taking Forked Lightning beef. But don't say we stole it. What we took I figure rightfully belonged to Gabe and me. You took our outfits away, years ago. Any beef we took and sold doesn't begin to make up the money we lost."

"You forget," Nielson said grimly, "that I never got back the money I loaned you on those outfits either. My part of it was legal."

"Even to the killing of Steve Taylor and Tod Ranson, I suppose," Whitlock said nastily.

"Even that." Nielson's tones were steady. "Those two drew on me first, if you'll remember back that far—but that's ancient history. We won't go into it."

"Sort of like to forget those old days, don't you, Hawk?"

Nielson looked at Vard sharply. "Just what do you mean by that?"

Whitlock shrugged his shoulders. He realized now that

he was treading on dangerous ground. Did Nielson still suspect there'd been a son born to him? Certain ideas commenced to churn in Whitlock's brain. He said easily after a minute, "Maybe we'd better forget the past and come down to the present. What are you aiming to do about those cows?"

"I could have Sheriff Redfield round you all up and throw you in a cell for trial."

Whitlock shook his head. "You won't, though."

"Why won't I?"

"Your daughter might not like it. She and Chris—my son—well, you know what I mean, Hawk. Think quite a lot of Miss Dorada, don't you, Hawk?"

"It's natural for a man to love his own daughter," Nielson said testily. "That's why I can't quite understand the thing you're doing——"

"Meaning just what?"

The words came a bit awkward for Nielson. "It's this way, Vard. Whether or not I like Chris is beside the point. I'm admitting, though, that he's pretty much of a man. Do you think you've given him a square deal in bringing him up a cow-thief?"

Whitlock squirmed. "That's neither here nor there," he said sullenly. "There's other things as bad as picking up a few cattle."

"I know what you mean," Nielson said promptly. "I've lived hard in the past. I had to live hard or be ground under the heel of somebody else. But anything I took, I risked my life to get."

Whitlock said, "Oh hell, I'm sick of this palaver. If you've got something to get off your chest, get talking. You had some particular idea in asking me to come here to-day. What is it?"

Nielson nodded. "I'll come down to cases. Whitlock,

this Cascabel Mesa country isn't big enough for me and you and your boy to live in at the same time. You're going to get out."

"You don't say so," Whitlock smiled thinly. "I'll admit you'd breathe freer if we were gone, but what do we get out of it? What's your offer, Hawk? I'll listen to reason. How much money you putting on the line that says we're going to move on?"

"Not one goddamn cent," Nielson growled. "You move on within the week and nothing will be said. Stay here and I'll swear out a warrant for Sheriff Redfield to serve. I'll put you all behind bars."

Whitlock looked surprised. "Is that your best offer?"

"My best and last. Don't think you can hold me up for any money. I don't buy off my enemies, Vard. You should know that after all these years. Now are you going to get out, or aren't you?"

"That's something I'll have to talk over with Gabe and Chris," Whitlock said evasively. He was sparring for time. He realized there was no use bargaining for money now; he could see Hawk Nielson was adamant on that point.

"Talk over hell!" Hawk growled. "Gabe doesn't count. Your own son will do as you wish, won't he?"

"I'm not so sure," Whitlock said slowly. "There's this matter of him and your daughter. Suppose they choose to get married?"

"That I will not consider for one minute!" Hawk pounded his clenched fist on the desk.

"How you going to stop it, if they decide to call in a parson?"

"I'll tell Dorada who stole my cows. I'll point out your son is a thief. Hell's bells, Whitlock! That's the main reason I want your son away from this country. Are you fool enough to think I'm afraid of him? Haven't you realized that if I wanted him killed I have power enough to accomplish even that? I'm trying to give him a break that you—his own father—won't give him. Go away from here. Make a new start. Make him see it's wrong to steal. Dorada means a lot to me. I'm not going to stand by and see her making a mistake—not when I have the strength to stop it."

"Look here, Hawk"—Whitlock was aroused now—"what have you really got against Chris? He's all man. Sure, he's beaten you in various ways, but look at things fairly. You're not as young as you once were. It's natural that a younger man——"

"Goddammit!" Again Hawk's fist came down on the desk; his eyes blazed hotly. "I'm not blaming the boy for what his father taught him. But I don't want my daughter mixed up with anyone of your blood—your thieving, cowardly Whitlock blood——"

Hawk halted suddenly. He had said more than he intended to say, but his temper had gotten away with him. He caught himself abruptly and concluded, "That's all, Whitlock. Are you leaving or aren't you?"

"Thieving, cowardly Whitlock blood," Vard repeated slowly, his face pale with anger. A minute ago he had been on the point of accepting Nielson's offer and getting out, but those four words had brought back all the old resentment, all the old grievance. Now he was once more determined to hurt Hawk Nielson, to make him pay dearly for the things he had said and done.

Abruptly Whitlock got himself in hand. He was thinking fast now, the plan was forming in his mind. For a minute he didn't speak while he strove to get his feelings under control. Quite suddenly he laughed harshly.

Nielson looked queerly at him. "Does this strike you funny, Whitlock?"

"I wouldn't say funny exactly," Whitlock commenced

slowly. "Hawk, did it ever occur to you to wonder just why I came back here?"

"More than once," Nielson snapped. "The only thing I could figure out was that you figured to steal enough cows to make up for your land I foreclosed on that time."

"Those few cows!" Whitlock spat scornfully. "You should know better than to accuse me of playing for small stakes, Hawk. Those cows just furnished us good living expenses. No, the fact is, I got in touch with some information that I figured you might buy."

Nielson's bushy eyebrows went up questioningly. "What sort of information?" he demanded.

Whitlock laughed softly. He was playing a part now, more sure of his ground. "Just through sheer luck, a short time back," he fabricated, "I happened to get in touch with an old acquaintance of yours—a man you hired once."

"Who's that?"

"A man named Sanford Gallatin."

"Sanford Gallatin!" Nielson's features sharpened. "Why—why, he's that no-good doctor I had when—when—— Almighty God! I tried to find that man—spent thousands trying to locate him." Nielson was on his feet now, towering over Whitlock. "You know where he is? Answer me, Whitlock. Don't stall!"

"Sit down, Hawk, sit down," Whitlock suggested softly, more sure than ever of his ground. "And now it's your turn to pick up your cigar. No need of you getting excited this way."

Impatiently Nielson ground his cigar under his foot, but still remained standing. "What about Gallatin?" he rasped. "Where is he?"

"Right at this very moment I couldn't say," Whitlock returned coolly. "Someplace between here and California. He had some bad luck out there——"

" What sort of bad luck ? "

Whitlock smiled. This lie was building up easier than he had thought. It sounded convincing, too. Almost Whitlock was inclined to believe it himself. Perhaps that is the reason the falsehood came so glibly to his lips. " The sort of hard luck a no-good doctor often runs into," Whitlock improvised lightly. " He performed an operation on a woman. The woman died. The authorities got after Dr. Gallatin and he had to hide out for a time, until he could get a train East. Now he's on his way here. Never mind how I got in touch with him. I'll just say that Gallatin needs money—you see, Hawk, I arranged to meet him here three months ago, but until recently he couldn't shake off the law hounds that were trailing him——"

" Goddammit ! Come to the point, Whitlock."

Whitlock eyed the big man standing over him and again laughed. " Interested, eh, Hawk ? Like I say, Gallatin is badly in need of money. He thinks he might be able to sell you a little information."

" What sort of information ? "

" Don't rush me, Hawk," Whitlock said mockingly.

" By God ! I'll choke some talk out of you——"

" Don't try it, Hawk." Whitlock smiled confidently. " I haven't any information to give you. But I can put you in touch with the man who has. But don't shove me around any. I think I'll take another of those fine cigars now, if you have one."

Impatiently Hawk produced a cigar and handed it to Whitlock. Whitlock lighted up and drew a deep breath of smoke with evident enjoyment. He was enjoying this ; it was nice to see the great Hawk Nielson squirm for a change.

" You'd better start talking, Whitlock." Nielson's voice shook with anger as he once more settled to his chair.

Whitlock realized he couldn't push the man too far. He

was treading dangerous ground now. Nielson's temper was something that had to be handled with care. He drew once more on the cigar, then, "Hawk, did it ever occur to you there was anything queer about the way Dr. Sanford Gallatin disappeared that night your baby was born?"

"There was something damnably queer about it," Nielson growled. "I've sometimes wondered if, after all——" He broke off suddenly. Beads of perspiration stood out on his forehead. Old memories rushed to mind with startling clarity; old doubts were renewed. He tried to hold his voice steady: "You and I, Vard, once had a certain disagreement as to whether that baby was a boy or a girl. Do you remember?"

Did he remember? Whitlock felt his face flushing hotly as he once again recollected how Hawk's gun-barrel had crashed against his head and the big man had challenged him to draw his six-shooter. It was an effort to keep the rage out of his tones as he replied dryly, "Do I remember? You don't think I'd be likely to forget, do you, Hawk? Oh yes, you had your way. I admitted it was a daughter was born—as you wanted me to."

"But in your own mind you still thought it was a son," Hawk flashed. "Why? What do you know that I don't know?"

"Me?" Whitlock assumed a look of surprise. "I don't know anything—not one damned thing."

"I think you're lying, Whitlock."

Whitlock shrugged his shoulders. "Think as you like."

Disappointment crept into Nielson's features. "But you do know something you think I should know."

Again that shrugging of the shoulders. It was a sort of cat-and-mouse game for Whitlock now. He became over-confident, forgetting Nielson could be pushed too far. "I might surmise certain things," he conceded carelessly.

"What exactly?" Hawk snapped.

"Several things might have happened," Whitlock said carelessly. "I know nothing for a certainty, you understand, though Gallatin once dropped me certain hints——"

"Will you come to the point!" Nielson's fist crashed down on his desk. He was on his feet once more.

Whitlock glanced up at the huge frame towering above him. Something of fear entered Whitlock's being now. But it was too late to turn back; he'd have to see through to the end this business he'd started. It was difficult to keep the tremor out of his voice: "Suppose, just suppose, Hawk, that it was a boy that was born that night——"

"By God! I knew it!"

"Wait a minute. We're just supposing. I know nothing, remember. But you had Gallatin scared out of his wits that night. Suppose that boy baby died, and Gallatin cooked up another plan, then fled, fearing your anger when you learned——" Tantalizingly, Whitlock broke off.

"You mean," Nielson demanded hoarsely, "you mean that Dorada—that Dorada isn't my . . . ?"

"I *know* nothing, remember. You keep insisting that I tell you something. Hell, Hawk, I was just doing some supposing——"

"You lie!"

Again that taunting shrug of the shoulders; that mocking smile. "I can't lie when I've made no definite statement."

"You've said too much to stop now. Talk!" Nielson ordered, his lined face working with emotion.

"I've nothing to tell. You'll have to talk to——"

Nielson whipped the gun from his holster and jammed it hard against Whitlock's middle. "I told you to talk, you bustard, or I'll blow you to hell!"

Too late, Whitlock realized his mistake. Yes, he could talk; he could talk plenty. But any talking he did would only put him in that much deeper. Hawk would never forgive him. He took a deep breath. There was still a chance to carry this thing through. Whitlock even forced a cool laugh. " Now you're acting the fool, Hawk," he said, and his voice was shaking like a leaf in the wind. " I've told you I know nothing for certainty. Even if I had information, how would you get it if you killed me ? Dead lips can't talk. Go ahead, shoot ! And be damned to you ! "

Slowly the truth of Whitlock's words penetrated Nielson's brain. Reluctantly he replaced his six-shooter in holster. And then—maybe it was a sort of hysteria that overcame Whitlock, or sudden relief that the tension was eased—Whitlock made the mistake of laughing in Hawk Nielson's face.

Blood rushed to Nielson's features, then they slowly paled to the white of murdering fury. " By God ! " he thundered. " You are lying. I'll choke the truth out of you, here and now."

One muscular hand darted to Whitlock's neck, fingers like steel bands tightened relentlessly about the man's throat. Whitlock's own hands came up clawing, tearing, but couldn't wrench loose Hawk Nielson's terrible grip. Nielson raised Whitlock bodily from the chair and shook him as some great mastiff might shake a lesser animal. Whitlock's legs flailed futilely at the air ; strangled gurgling sounds left his open mouth. Then his eyes bulged ; his tongue started to protrude. Both arms fell limply at his sides ; his face took on a dense purplish tinge as Neilson vented a berserk-like rage on his helpless enemy.

Some remnants of reason still remained in Nielson's make-up and finally brought him to his senses before it was too late. Abruptly he released his hold and Whitlock dropped into the chair, gasping frantically for air. " Damn me for a fool," Nielson cursed himself. " That'd be as bad as a bullet." He strode to the door, flung it open.

Dorada looked up questioningly from her desk. " Whatever are you doing in there——" she commenced.

" Get me some water, quick, Dorada. Whitlock has—has had a fainting spell of some sort. He's ill. Maybe it's his heart."

" Want me to get a doctor ? "

" Not right now. Get that water. Hurry ! "

The girl whirled and ran from her office. In an instant she was back, bearing a pitcher and tumbler. She tried to see within Hawk's office, but Nielson's huge frame barred her vision as he took the water from her hands.

She could hear plainly terrible gasping sounds from beyond the doorway. " Can I do anything to help, Dad ? " Her eyes looked curiously at him, reading in his face that he had lied to her, that something was horribly wrong.

" No," he said dully, " no, you can't do anything to help. Maybe you're all through helping me."

Before she could ask the reason for the words he had closed the door in her face.

An hour passed before Hawk spoke again. Every minute of that time he had spent gazing at Whitlock making a slow recovery. And in that hour Hawk Nielson had aged terrifically. Old memories had tortured his mind. He remembered now many things he shouldn't have done in the past. He looked at the man in the chair across from him. Had he wronged Vard Whitlock ? He didn't know. Legally, no. But was the law always right ? But there were certain things he had to discover. And to learn those things, Nielson was now prepared to pay a price.

He said finally, " Feel able to talk now, Whitlock ? "

Whitlock fingered his throat. " You damn nigh finished me, Hawk," he croaked. " The more fool you. I told you once I had nothing to tell you for a certainty." The very fact that Nielson hadn't throttled him to death now gave

Whitlock the requisite courage to carry out his plan. " All I tried to do was arrange a meeting with Sanford Gallatin. He can tell you things."

" When ? "

" It'll cost you a price. Gallatin needs money."

" You said that before. I'm ready to pay money."

" Fifty thousand dollars, Hawk ? "

" I'll pay fifty thousand."

" Do you have that much on hand ? "

Impatiently, " I can get it from the bank, any time."

" The bank won't be open on Sunday. Gallatin will be here for only a short time Sunday morning—no, never mind when he'll arrive. I'm not sure of that myself yet. But he plans to get out of Nielson City on the nine-thirteen train that passes through here. Remember, I told you the law was on his trail and he's moving fast."

" I can give him a cheque."

Whitlock shook his head. " Gallatin don't want to fool with cheques. He wants cash, in bills not larger than fifties——"

" You want to make sure of getting your cut, eh ? " Nielson said with a brief flash of temper.

" Leave me out of it," Whitlock rasped. " There's my proposition. I'll bring Gallatin here eight o'clock Sunday morning. You ask questions and he'll talk. When you're done you'll give him fifty thousand dollars—and your promise not to have him arrested or tell any law authority any place that you've seen him."

Nielson scowled. " How do I know this isn't a put-up job to take the money away from me ? You come here with Gallatin, your son, Dusty Snow, and God knows who else and hold me up——"

" Now you're talking like a fool," Whitlock said scornfully. " If you like you can have your whole front office filled with Forked Lightning hands, Sunday morning. If I don't come here alone with Gallatin, the whole deal's off, if you say so. You can take our guns away, if you like. For that matter, I doubt Gallatin carries a gun."

"It sounds all right," Hawk said slowly. "But how am I to know that Gallatin will have anything concrete to offer?"

Whitlock forced a raspy sort of laugh. "I'm so sure that you'll learn something you've wondered about, Hawk, that we'll leave it to your judgment as to whether the information is worth the money. That's how sure I am that you'll be willing to pay."

"It's a go," Hawk said suddenly.

"You'll have the fifty thousand here in bills at eight o'clock Sunday morning?"

"I'll be waiting for you." Hawk nodded. And added, hating himself for the weakness, "For God's sake, Vard, don't disappoint me." The gnawing doubts of years were finally commencing to break down Hawk Nielson's steel reserve.

Five minutes later Vard Whitlock had moved stiffly out to his horse. "Gawd A'mighty," he told himself in some awe. "He took the bait, hook, line, and sinker. But it damn nigh cost me my life." And then, with a trace of grim humour as he hauled himself into his saddle, "I wonder where Doc Gallatin is, these days, or if he's dead by this time?"

20

A BARGAIN IS A BARGAIN

CHRIS and Dusty had returned by the time Whitlock got back to the shack.

Old Gabe Houston was sweeping industriously, but put down his broom when Whitlock arrived. " Lemme put your hawss up for you, Vard," he said. " You go on in and talk to Chris and Dusty. Place looks right slick, don't it ? I been reddin' up ever since you left."

The old man's eyes looked clear and sane.

Vard nodded. " I noticed you disposed of all those old tin cans that were laying around on the ground. What got into you, Gabe ? "

" Damned if I know," Gabe said cheerfully. " I got up this mornin' feelin' right prancy, and it just struck me this place ain't been cleaned in a right long spell. So I got busy."

" Feeling pretty good, eh ? "

" Just like I never had a sick day in my life."

Chris hailed Vard from within the house and, leaving his horse in Gabe's hands, Vard entered the building. Dusty sat in one corner looking at an old magazine. Chris was rolling a cigarette. Both men greeted Whitlock when he came in. He hung his sombrero on a hook and drew up a chair near Chris's seat.

" You seem to have got back all right," Whitlock said. " No trouble of any sort, I suppose ? "

" None whatever," Chris said. " We spied out the land pretty thoroughly. There's a bunch of about seventy-five or eighty Polled Angus cows being held in a pole corral——"

" Trouble is," Dusty interrupted, " there's three Forked

Lightning cow-hands 'tending 'em—sort of guarding 'em, you might say. It might not be too easy to run off those cows without trouble."

"Shucks," Chris chuckled, "we can work out some plan to draw those fellows off whilst we drive away the cows. That part's easy enough——"

"I'm not so sure," Dusty said.

"I am," Chris laughed. He paused, then, "The thing that's got me wondering is why Nielson has put a guard on those cows. Do you suppose he's maybe missed those other cattle we took, and is getting suspicious?"

"That could be," Whitlock replied non-committally. "Anyway, we can forget those cows. Let Nielson keep 'em."

"Forget 'em?" Chris said, surprised. "After Dusty and I have put in two days spying out the lay of the land?"

"That's what I said, forget 'em. I've got something better in mind."

"Anything to do with where you've been this morning?" Chris asked.

"What do you know about that?" Whitlock said sharply.

"Nothing," Chris replied. "Only when we got back, old Gabe said somebody had come riding with a message for you and you'd told him you had to go to town on business this morning. Who did you have to see? And what for?"

Whitlock breathed easier. At that moment Gabe entered the shack, found a smelly old brier pipe, crammed it full of evil-smelling tobacco, and found a seat on an old wooden crate. Clouds of smoke rose around his head of stringy grey hair.

"To tell the truth, Chris," Whitlock said slowly, "I had word from—from somebody that Hawk Nielson is suspicious of us but hasn't any actual proof yet."

"Who told you?" Chris asked bluntly.

"I'm not saying—right now," Whitlock replied. "I promised not to reveal this fellow's name. It's nobody you know. I knew him long ago. Oh, I haven't been idle the past few weeks. I've been working on a scheme that is a scheme. No more of this small-time cow-rustling business. We make a killing, all in one pile, then we get out of this country as fast as our broncs, or a train, will carry us."

"What do you mean by a killing?" Chris asked slowly.

"Fifty thousand dollars."

Chris's smoky-grey eyes narrowed. "I don't know as I like the sound of this, Vard," he said slowly. "The fifty thousand belongs to Hawk Nielson, I suppose."

Whitlock nodded. "Want to do anything you can to hurt him, don't you?"

"I'm not so sure, Vard—any more. Still, when I think of that stunt he had Anse Ogden try on me—well, get on with your story."

Dusty, Chris, and old Gabe listened intently while Whitlock talked. "I happen to know—no, never mind how I learned this—that Hawk Nielson will have fifty thousand dollars in his office on Saturday night, Chris. He expects to use it—use it in handling a deal Sunday. The deal comes up on Sunday, because the bank won't be open then, and the fellow he's making the deal with don't want to have any time wasted dealing with a bank. Nor he doesn't want a cheque. The fifty thousand will be in bills——"

"In other words," Chris said shrewdly, "somehow you've convinced Nielson he should have the money on hand Sunday morning——"

"I didn't say that," Whitlock interrupted.

"I can do a mite of guessing, can't I? And the bank not being open, he'll have to get the money from the bank Saturday—so you think it will be in his office Saturday night. Is that it?"

"That's it," Whitlock said a bit sulkily.

" What makes you so sure he'll keep it in his office ?" Chris wanted to know.

" Where else would he keep it ? " Whitlock pointed out. " He's got a big safe in his office and——"

" When were you in his office ? " Chris asked.

" I didn't say I was, but—but—well, I know a feller that used to work there."

" And I suppose "—Chris's smile was mocking—" that this fellow even had the combination to the safe to give you."

" That "—Whitlock nodded—" is exactly what happened. I've got the combination in my pocket, written down on a slip of paper."

" I'll be damned ! " The smile left Chris's face. " You don't leave much to chance, do you ? "

" I told you I'd been working on this for some time."

" All right, you've got the combination to a safe that holds fifty thousand dollars," Chris conceded. " But whoever opens that safe has to get into the office first. I seem to remember there's a right good lock on the front door of that office. Got the key to fit that too, I suppose."

" I've got the key." Whitlock smiled.

Dusty swore suddenly in astonishment. " By cripes ! You have been working, haven't you, Vard ? "

Whitlock explained : " The fellow that gave me the combination used to be a janitor for the office. They gave him a key so he could get in there early, mornings. They fired him a long while back, but neglected to ask for the key. I guess Nielson just plain forgot it."

" What price did the fellow put on the key and combination ? " Chris wanted to know.

" Not enough for you to bother your head over, Chris," Whitlock replied. " That's all taken care of. The fellow was—well, he was sort of under obligations to give me the key."

" Crickey ! " old Gabe cackled gleefully. " If we could get fifty thousand of Hawk Nielson's money, that would sure put a crimp in him—take all the starch outten him."

" There's a train comes through Nielson City about three o'clock Sunday morning," Whitlock continued. " We'd have the fifty thousand before that, then we'd hop the train and get out. Just to be on the safe side, we could have our broncs waiting in the brush at the edge of town. In case something prevented our catching the train, we'd make our getaway on horses. The scheme is airtight."

Dusty said abruptly, " I don't want any part of your scheme, Vard."

Whitlock's eyebrows came up. " What's got into you, Dusty ? "

" I don't like it." Dusty scowled. " Running off a few cows from a man who's got so many it doesn't matter is one thing. Stealing his money is another. I didn't mind taking the cows—that was sort of fun in a way—and nobody was harmed, but——"

" You turned yellow ? " Whitlock snapped.

" No, he hasn't turned yellow," Chris said defensively. " I know how he feels. I feel the same way——"

" But look, boy," old Gabe put in, " it ain't like stealing to take from Hawk Nielson. He owes us that much and more——"

" He don't owe me anything," Chris said shortly. " Whatever you and Vard have against Nielson is your business. Any disagreements I have with him is my business, and I'll settle it my way——"

" You going back on your bargain, Chris ? " Whitlock said angrily.

Chris started to reply, then paused. " We-ell, dammit, Vard, I never dreamed you'd propose this sort of thing——"

" What's all this about a bargain ? " Dusty Snow asked.

"It's nothing that concerns you, Dusty," Chris said. "It's between Vard and me." Dusty fell silent. Chris continued, "You see, Vard, I just can't go for downright stealing——"

"A bargain is a bargain. You made me a promise, you know. You going back on that?"

"No, but——"

"I can't see where you're doing anything else," Whitlock said testily.

They wrangled for some time, old Gabe putting in a few words whenever he could make himself heard. Dusty took no part in the talk.

". . . and it's the last thing I'll ask of you, Chris." Whitlock's tones were pleading. "We've gone too far to quit now. You go through with this, and then I'll keep my part of the bargain. Tell you anything you want to know——"

"I still don't like it," Chris said steadily.

"Suppose I told you"—Whitlock chose his words carefully—"that that fifty thousand is practically owing to you, Chris."

"Can you give me proof of that?"

"I will when the job's done," Whitlock said promptly.

Chris said wearily, "Hell, Vard, let's forget it. The more you and I talk, the madder we get. I owe you too much to have a falling out now."

Whitlock considered. Then, "Would you get out of Nielson City if Hawk ordered you to?"

"Certainly not."

"Well, for your information, he ordered me to this morning. Called me into his office and told me to get out——"

"Vard, you don't mean that," Chris said unbelievingly.

"The hell I don't. And when I refused he practically killed me—damn near choked me to death. Look at my throat!"

Whitlock dramatically pulled back his shirt, disclosing the red, bruised skin. " Now will you believe me, Chris? Hawk's afraid of us. He remembers what he did to Gabe and me years ago. He wants us out of this part of the country. Are you going to let him run things to suit himself? He's afraid of you too—afraid you'll marry Dorada, and that is something he says he will not allow——"

" All right, Vard," Chris interrupted, " you've said enough. We'll get that money Saturday night. Someday I'll come back and make matters clear, though, with Dorada——"

" Good boy, Chris!" Whitlock exulted. " We'll teach Nielson a lesson he'll never forget."

" Maybe we will, maybe we won't," Chris said moodily. " The way I look at it, Vard, this is a one-man job—my job——"

" I'll be going with you, Chris," Dusty broke in.

" Thought you didn't like the idea, cowboy." Chris smiled faintly.

" I still don't, but if you go into it, so do I," Dusty said stubbornly.

Chris shook his head. " There's more people in town on a Saturday night than any other night," he pointed out. " One man can do the job, and I'm that man. If more than one man is seen entering that office building, it might look queer and someone might raise an alarm."

" Exactly as I figured, Chris." Whitlock nodded excitedly. " Gabe and Dusty and me can be waiting on the outskirts of town with our horses until you arrive with the money. Then we can catch the train out of town——"

" Whoopee!" Old Gabe gave a thin yell. " What won't we do with fifty thousand dollars? I can take me a trip clear East, far's Kansas City, even. I'll stay at a hotel and go to an opery house and see some gals a-dancin'. Maybe, seein' I'm still not so old——"

" Maybe you'd better start some dinner, Gabe." Chris smiled. " It's way past noon."

" Crackee ! So 'tis ! What say we open that bottle of Old Crow first and have a little nip to celebrate ? "

" Suit yourself," Chris said slowly, " but none for me. I don't exactly feel like celebrating."

21

GABE SETS A TRAP

DUSTY SNOW returned from town late Saturday afternoon. When he came into the house, Chris and Vard were seated at the table, talking and smoking. Old Gabe was busily engaged about the range, preparing food for supper. Chris and Vard looked up, questioningly.

Dusty nodded. " The money'll be there to-night, I reckon. I loafed around town, saw Nielson go to the bank with a small satchel. In a short time he returned with the satchel and entered his office again. If that satchel didn't contain the money, I don't know what he'd carry it to and from the bank for."

" He didn't see you, did he ? " Chris asked.

Dusty shook his head. " Not a chance. Being Saturday, there's more people in town than usual. I wouldn't be noticed among the people passing on the sidewalk."

" Saturday's a good night for a job like this," Whitlock said. " The town'll be noisier than usual."

Supper-time came and passed. Oil-lamps were lighted. Old Gabe washed the dishes, all the time muttering to himself. When the dishes were done, he busied himself over a small gunny-sack in which he'd started to pack a few belongings.

Whitlock cast a glance at the old man. " Don't try to take too much, Gabe," he advised. " Remember, we want to be travelling light when we step on that train to-morrow morning early. The rest of us aren't figuring to take much stuff with us. It'll be enough to have that fifty thousand."

Gabe nodded and went on with his puttering. After a

time he drifted out of the door, unnoticed by the others, who had started a three-handed game of seven-up to pass the time. A couple of more hours passed.

Vard said abruptly, " What time's it getting to be, I wonder ? " He pulled a large silver watch out and consulted it. " H'mm ! Dang near ten-thirty. The time's drawing close, Chris."

Chris tossed his cards on the table. " Yes." He nodded. " I ought to get started in another hour."

" You still got that combination, haven't you ? " Whitlock asked anxiously. " Don't want to lose that."

" I got it—and the key, too."

Dusty suddenly slammed down the deck of cards with which he'd been toying. " I still don't like this idea," he burst out. " Suppose Chris was to get caught or shot ? "

" Don't you worry about me, cowboy," Chris said. " I can handle myself."

" Can't see where you got any kick coming," Whitlock said testily to Dusty, " if Chris is for the plan. We took you in with us, and now you're trying to crab the job. You don't need to take your split of that fifty thousand, if you don't want it."

Dusty's eyes narrowed angrily. " I've never been in favour of your plan, Vard. Furthermore, I'm stating right now that I'm not taking any cut of the money—not unless Chris lets me run the same risk he'll be running. I'm not going to sponge on any man. This whole business makes me sick ! Chris does the dangerous work, while you and Gabe and me sit back and wait for him to bring us the money. Hell ! It's not square to Chris. That sort of plan may be fine for some folks, but I'm willing to risk my own hide for any money I get——"

" You hinting that I'm not ? " Whitlock demanded, straightening in his chair. He started to get up. Dusty did the same, as Whitlock continued, " Dusty, you just the same as stated I'm yellow."

" I'm not so sure you aren't," Dusty snapped belligerently. " I know there's something mighty queer about this whole setup."

The two men stood glaring at each other. Chris interfered just in time. He'd seen both men glancing towards their six-shooters hanging on one wall. " Cut it out, you two," Chris said sternly. " There's no use arguing at this late date. Come on, Dusty—you and Vard shake hands."

The two men suddenly relaxed. Whitlock put out his hand. " I'm sorry, Dusty. I sort of lost my temper for a minute. There's a lot of truth in what you said."

" Shucks, Vard, forget it," Dusty replied. " It was my fault as much as yours. I shouldn't have run off at the head that-a-way. You and Chris teamed together long before I knew you. You probably know what you're doing. It's just that I don't like to see Chris taking all the risk. I still think I should go with Chris to sort of act as look-out, if nothing else."

And that started another argument, albeit a more friendly one. They wrangled a half-hour or more. Finally Chris said, " This isn't getting any place, Dusty. My mind's made up——" He broke off suddenly. " Somebody mentioned Gabe a short time back. Where is the old codger anyway ? "

Whitlock didn't appear concerned. " Probably the same place he always goes on moonlight nights when he goes out for a ' view ' as he calls it."

" Where's that ? " Chris asked.

" You know that long ridge—regular hawgback it is—covered with brush, about half a mile east of here ? "

Both Chris and Dusty nodded.

Whitlock went on : " Gabe discovered that by climbing to the top of that hawgback he could look across the range and see a hill that was once part of his 13-Bar Ranch. He goes up there frequent and just looks at that hill and thinks about his old ranch. I don't like it too much, though; it always gets him brooding about Hawk Nielson and sort of throws his mind off balance. He was out there last night, and you notice when he came in he was muttering about locusts eating up the range—you know that old line of his."

"Yes, I know." For the first time Chris looked a bit concerned. "We should keep a close watch on him. He knows all our plans, and if he went sort of batty he might spill information to somebody. Dusty, will you duck out and pick him up? I don't like the idea of him wandering around when we've got this job on."

Glad of an opportunity to do something for Chris, Dusty seized his hat and started for the door. "I'll bring him back pronto." With that he departed.

Chris waited until he was out of earshot, then smiled. "That's one way of getting rid of Dusty. I'll be gone before he gets back, and there'll be no more argument about me going alone."

"I don't know," Whitlock said dubiously. "Maybe I'm wrong. Dusty thinks a heap of you. It never occurred to me that way before, but he sure spilled a lot of words that opened my eyes to-night. It isn't right, Chris, that you should take all this risk alone, while we wait for you to bring us the cash. Let's call this job off. We'll make a new start——"

"What?" Chris eyed the older man in amazement. "You going back on our plans? I haven't forgotten our bargain. I go through certain things for you; after that, you tell me things I want to know." He moved around the table, threw one arm around Vard's shoulders. "Shucks, don't *you* get to worrying now. We'll see this job through. I'm not worrying about risks. Just you be waiting at the edge of town for me with the horses when I show up with the money. I'll be there——"

"God, I hope so," Whitlock declared fervently. "I'm not meaning the money—it's you I'm thinking about. If anything was to happen to you to-night—hell, Chris, let's forget the job. You and me will have a long talk, now, about certain things."

Slowly Chris shook his head. "You save that talk until later. I've made a promise and I'm going to carry it out. You know, you're not the only one that has a grudge against Nielson—after the way he choked you—say, you never did give all the details regarding that. But I'll get 'em later."

"Chris, don't go. I'm asking that you call this off."

Chris chuckled suddenly. "My mind's made up now. I've had a heap of fun bucking Hawk Nielson. I'd like to put just one more stunt over on him."

Despite Whitlock's protestations, Chris slipped into his coat, buckled his cartridge belt about his waist, then donned his Stetson. Five minutes later he was in the saddle, riding towards Nielson City.

Whitlock returned to the house and, heaving a long troubled sigh, dropped into a chair. This should be his night of triumph, but the elation he had expected didn't come to him. How long he sat there thinking over certain deeds in his past life he didn't know. He only knew, now, that he was more worried than he had been in many years.

"Damn my soul," he muttered, "I haven't given that boy a square deal. I was so wrapped up in my own ideas——"

He broke off at a sudden spluttering of the wick in the oil lamp; the fuel was practically gone. Whitlock rose, got a kerosene can from one corner, and replenished the bowl. After a moment the lamp burned brighter. Whitlock sat down and consulted his watch.

"By the A'mighty!" he exclaimed. "We should be

leaving to meet Chris right soon. Wonder where the devil Dusty and Gabe are?"

A stumbling footstep at the doorway partly answered Whitlock's question. He glanced up to see old Gabe coming in.

"'Lo, Vard," Houston said in a quavering voice.

"Where in the name of the seven bald steers have you been?" Whitlock snapped testily.

Gabe didn't reply at once. He closed the door and stood looking at Whitlock, his eyes dull, almost opaque, as though trying to concentrate on the query that had been put to him. "Oh, I jest been ridin'," he finally answered vaguely.

"Riding, yes, but where? I figured you'd gone over to the hawgback. We didn't hear you leave. Dusty's out looking for you now. Just where'd you go?"

"Rode into town," Gabe said evasively. "You don't never let me go to town at night. I wanted to see was anythin' doin'——"

"In town! Did you see Chris on the road coming back?"

Gabe shook his head. "Didn't come back by the road. Sort of cut across country. I was goin' to the hawgback, then . . . I dunno . . ." Gabe rubbed his forehead in a puzzled way. "I reckon I must have changed my mind and come here. Y'say Chris went to town? Oh yeah, I 'member. . . . What was it? . . . Somethin' 'bout Hawk Nielson—sure, fifty thousand dollars——"

"My God," Whitlock said under his breath, "he's gone batty again."

"Y'know, Vard," Gabe continued childishly, "it ain't right for Nielson to have all that money, but Chris will take it away from him, won't he? It was Hawk that stole my 13-Bar, but we'll show him, won't we?"

"We sure will, Gabe," Whitlock replied calmly. Generally, when Gabe had one of his "queer" moments, Whitlock humoured him: steady conversation usually brought the old fellow back to normal after a time.

Gabe laughed suddenly, an eerie, shrill sort of laugh. " Crickey! Vard, we're goin' to get a real revenge on Hawk Nielson for all them things he done to us, ain't we?"

" I don't know about that, Gabe," Whitlock said slowly, voicing the dominant thought then occupying his mind. " The more I think about it, the more I feel maybe I haven't done right by Chris, deceiving him like I have all these years——"

" Don't see thet it makes no difference," Gabe croaked nastily. " Ain't Chris a Nielson, the son of thet ol' Hawk? Bad blood in him, I tell ye! Sometime it would have come out and he'd get to stealin' from you and me. He might even get my 13-Bar. I wouldn't trust him. Chris might even kill us like he killed Tod Ranson and Steve Taylor thet night——"

Whitlock swallowed hard. Gabe was worse that usual this time. He spoke slowly, enunciating each word clearly. " Chris didn't kill those two, Gabe. It was Hawk——"

" Prac'ally same thing," Gabe said pettishly. " Have you forgot how you and me planned to make Hawk Nielson suffer?"

" I never planned to make Chris suffer," Whitlock half groaned. " It's mighty serious to turn a son against his own father, make a thief of him. We've been selfish, Gabe, in not considering Chris's rights. When you come right down to it, we're as bad as Hawk Nielson. All he did was pile up money. You and me—well, we've maybe ruined Chris's life——"

" But look how Hawk treated you and me," Gabe flashed, his lined features working with fury. " Ain't nothing too bad to happen to him. He killed and he took my ranch and——"

" I've considered that," Whitlock said. Gabe came farther into the room and stood glaring malevolently at Whitlock. " After all," Whitlock went on, " I don't know as any of us were so pure those days, Gabe. It was up to every man to grab what he could. We weren't any too civilized. I don't say Nielson didn't have something coming to him for his actions, but I'm beginning to think it wasn't our place to bring it about——"

That was as far as Whitlock got. The words seemed to infuriate Gabe. He commenced swinging his arms wildly, and a crazy light gleamed in his eyes. " D'ye mean to tell me thet ye're going back on all the things we used to say—not going to punish Hawk as we planned ? "

" Sit down, Gabe, sit down," Whitlock said soothingly. " You wouldn't want to hurt Chris, would you ? "

Gabe refused to sit down, but his words dropped to a meandering cackle. " It's jest as I thought—jest as I thought ! Ye're not handlin' this business right. Ye got cold feet. What do me and you care about Chris ? Same bad blood as his father. We don't owe him nothin'. . . ." The words careened off in maniacal giggling. " He-he-he-he-he ! Thought ye could fool ol' Gabe, didn't ye ? I been suspicionin' ye was softenin' up—so I took care of things. Old Gabe fixed it, though, old Gabe fixed it ! We'll get our revenge and you'll be glad——"

For a moment Whitlock didn't realize the import of the words, then he jumped to his feet and faced the old man, who was gibbering like an idiot. " Gabe ! What do you mean ? Answer, quick ! "

A cunning light crept into Gabe's eyes as he backed away from Whitlock. " I fixed it, I fixed it," he repeated, laughing crazily. " Our time has come at last, Vard. We can laugh to-night. Old Gabe fixed it ! " The words were tumbling from his lips now as though he couldn't, even if he had desired to, put a stop to the admission. " Hawk Nielson will find his son to-night, Vard. Old Gabe ain't no man to double-cross and he ain't no man's fool—no, sirree ! I see'd you was weakenin', so I took things into my own hands——"

" Gabe ! What in God's name are you trying to say ? Out with it, quick ! What have you done ? "

Gabe giggled foolishly. " When I was in town I give a feller a note to give to Hawk Nielson. I didn't sign my name. I ain't crazy. I wouldn't give you and me away, Vard——"

" What kind of a note ? " Whitlock's face was ashen as he seized Gabe by the shoulder. " What did the note say ? "

" He-he-he ! In the note I told Hawk Nielson to watch his safe to-night. Thet's a good joke, eh, Vard ? Think how Chris will be surprised ! He-he-he-he ! " The cracked laughter of the old man was hideous. " We'll have our revenge, Vard. You can thank me——"

" Good God ! " Whitlock gasped. " Do you realize what you've done, Gabe ? There'll likely be a fight. Chris will kill his own father——"

" Oh no, he won't," Gabe said slyly. " I fixed thet, too. This mornin', when ye was all outside, a-sittin' in the sun, I drawed all the leads outten Chris's ca'tridges and plugged the shells with soap. Chris won't have nothin' but blank ca'tridges to shoot. But Hawk's gun will be loaded proper, and d'ye know what ? " Gabe's voice sank to a confidential whisper. " Hawk will kill Chris, sure as shootin' he will ! Hawk'll murder his own flesh an' blood. He-he-he ! Ain't thet a prime joke on Hawk Nielson, Vard ? "

The words ended in a startled gurgle as Whitlock grasped old Gabe by the throat. " You damned old fool ! " he almost sobbed. " Oh, you stark-crazy ravin' old fool ! Now you've done it ! "

At that moment Dusty opened the door and came in. " Hey, what's up ? " he demanded. " I been looking all over for Gabe, and here he is taking a whipping from you. Let him be, Vard. He's an old man. What's the idea!"

The words brought Whitlock to his senses. He released Gabe, who fell whimpering to the floor. "Gabe's had one of his crazy spells again, Dusty," Whitlock choked out. "He's spilled the whole business to Nielson—sent him a note, warning him to watch the safe to-night. What's more, he loaded Chris's guns with blanks——"

"Goddlemighty!" Dusty gasped, while Whitlock blurted out the rest of the story. Dusty seemed stunned at the news, incapable of movement as he sank, dazed, into a chair.

"Come on, pull yourself together, Dusty," Whitlock pleaded. He was gaining control of himself now. He whirled and leaped to his gun hanging on the wall. "There's only one thing left for us to do, Dusty, and we've got to act fast. Either we'll get there in time to warn Chris, or go down fighting with him. Hawk'll likely have a bunch of Forked Lightning hands waiting for Chris when he starts on that safe."

Old Gabe was just rising from the floor. The rough treatment at Whitlock's hands had partly shocked him back to normal. He stood swaying uncertainly before Dusty and Whitlock, a cloudy look in his bloodshot eyes. All memory of what he had done had fled from his mind. Even so, his reason was hanging by a slender thread that threatened to snap completely at any moment.

"Wha-what's the matter, Vard?" he asked querulously.

Whitlock's eyes blazed. "*You're* the matter," he snarled. "You've gone and had one of your crazy spells again, and spilled our plans to Hawk Nielson. Chris is in one hell of a mess. We're riding to help him—if we can."

Gabe brushed one gnarled hand across his eyes as though to dispel the cobwebs that clouded his muddled brain. "I—I—I don't remember doin' anythin' like thet," he whined,

" but if ye say I did, mebbe I did." Something like a sob welled from his thin breast. " I wouldn't hurt Chris for anythin'. I reckon I ain't fitten to associate with decent folks." Suddenly he braced himself. " All right, I'm ridin' with ye. If this is my fault, I aim to do what I can to help. I can still shake loads outten my six-shooter. I've jest got to help Chris."

" Come on, then," Dusty urged. " Grab your shooting iron. Every gun will help ! "

A few minutes later the three men were in saddles, riding hard. Gabe wasn't used to such a gait nowadays, but he managed to keep abreast of the other two despite the torture of the jolting to his ancient frame. He was resolved to do his utmost to undo the wrong he had brought about.

Whitlock was quirting his pony unmercifully. " With luck we might get there in time to warn Chris," he yelled to Dusty.

Dusty called back some sort of answer, but the words were lost in the pounding of horses' hoofs and the swift wind along the dark road to town.

22

MADMAN'S REVENGE

IT must have been about eleven-thirty when Chris reached town. Saturday being the traditional pay-day, there were more people on the streets than usual to-night. All the saloons were running full blast; various places of commercial enterprise were still open to accommodate such people as couldn't do their buying earlier. Lamps shone brightly from windows in many stores, throwing broad rectangles of light across the plank sidewalks. There weren't as yet any street lights in Nielson City; that was something that still awaited the piping in of natural gas. Horses and wagons were scattered at hitch-racks along the street; now and then a rider loped along the unpaved thoroughfare.

Chris pulled his pony to a halt when he reached the edge of town and yanked his Stetson low over his face. He scanned the faces of various people moving along the sidewalks, half wondering if Hawk Nielson might be seen. He felt certain Dorada wouldn't be on the streets at this hour. He crossed Texas Street, as his pony advanced at a slow pace, along Butterfield, past the Cascabel House with its usual loungers hanging around the hotel corner or bar entrance. At the corner of Butterfield and Mesa streets a medicine man with flaming gasoline torch, costumed Indian, a guitar, and wagon strove to peddle his "Panacea for All Ailments" to a large crowd of men and a few women.

On the next street corner to Chris's left he saw the Nielson Office Building, the windows of the lower floor dark and sombre. On the second floor there were three windows facing on the main street. Lights shone from two of the windows.

Chris gazed wistfully up towards the bright yellow oblongs of illumination. " Wonder how late Dorada stays up ? " he mused. " Hope she doesn't get interested in some book that'll keep her reading half the night. I remember she said once that Hawk generally turned in early and slept like a rock. I hope so. I sure want 'em both sound asleep before I enter that building."

His horse moved on past. Farther on a small photograph gallery was still open, and through the window next door he saw several cow-hands seated at the counter of an all-night lunch-room.

" Damn," Chris told himself, " I'm going to hate to leave here. Someday I'll come back and square myself with Dorada, when I know more about my birth. Another thing, this money I'm going to get to-night, I don't want any of that. Gabe and Vard and Dusty can have their shares. I'm going to return mine to Nielson, some way. Probably I could just put it in an envelope and mail it to him, without any writing to say where it came from."

He passed another restaurant, two saloons, a general store, still open for business. Beyond Santa Fe Street the way grew darker, though a light shone in the window of the sheriff's office. At Geronimo Street, Chris turned his pony and headed back. When next he passed the Nielson Office Building the lights in the upper windows had been extinguished.

" I'll give 'em a little longer to get sound asleep," Chris considered, " before I start in."

He next pulled rein at the edge of the crowd surrounding the medicine man and listened to that worthy's glib flow of promised cures. Ten minutes passed in this way, then Chris once more turned his pony in the direction of the

Nielson place. Two doors from the Nielson Building was the Denver Chop House, another of the town's all-night restaurants. It was here that Chris halted his pony at the hitch-rack, where three other horses were tethered. Chris climbed down from the saddle, flipped his reins carelessly over the tie-rail, and stepped to the sidewalk. Here he hesitated just a moment. There were pedestrians on the walks on either side of the street, but at that moment no one was in Chris's immediate vicinity. The medicine man on the next corner seemed to be holding nearly everyone's attention.

An instant later, key in hand, Chris had stopped before the locked door of the Nielson offices. The key slipped smoothly into the lock, turned without a sound. The door opened easily under Chris's hand, and then he was inside. Moving with extreme caution, he withdrew the key from the lock, slipped it into his pocket. Then, after clicking off the snap lock, he gently closed the door.

He paused, listening intently. Excepting sounds from the street, there wasn't a sound to be heard. Through the wide windows on either side of the door he could see people passing now and then. There wasn't enough light from the street for anybody to spy Chris through those same windows. He glanced back along the length of the big room with clerks' desks on either side, now silent and unoccupied in the deep shadows.

"It's lucky I've been in here before and know the lay of things," he congratulated himself.

He glanced towards the far left-hand corner where a flight of stairs led to the living quarters on the second floor. There was no sign of sound or light from that direction either. Chris waited but an instant longer to slip off his boots, then started noiselessly towards Hawk Nielson's office at the rear of the building, moving with all the stealth of an Apache Indian.

The door to Dorada's office was open, and he passed through that, feeling his way with cool certainty in the darkness. A moment more and his hand had touched the knob of Hawk Nielson's door. Here he had a brief moment of doubt: Nielson's door might be locked; but perhaps the key that had opened the front door also opened Nielson's office door. But Chris's doubt was dispelled at once: Nielson's door was unlocked. He stepped quickly within the office and again closed the door. Then he paused to take stock and a long breath.

A certain amount of moonlight penetrated the rear windows. Chris looked quickly around. The room was a large one, with Nielson's roll-top desk placed between two windows at the rear wall. In the left rear corner stood a big steel safe. Diagonally opposite, in the right corner, was a closet with closed door. Three chairs, in addition to the desk chair, stood about. A kerosene lamp was suspended above Nielson's desk.

Chris went to the windows—one in a side wall and two at the rear—and pulled the shades all the way down. Again he stopped and listened. There wasn't a sound to be heard, except dimly the noises from Butterfield Street. Cautiously he reached up and slowly, slowly lifted the chimney from the hanging oil lamp. That accomplished, he drew a match from his pocket and quickly scratched it on the seat of his trousers. The match flamed, he touched it to the wick, turned low, then as carefully as before replaced the chimney.

Once more he took a long breath and strained his ears. Nothing unusual was to be noted. He turned quietly to the big safe in the corner, then started towards it, testing each step before he put down his feet, that no board might creak from sudden pressure of weight.

"There it is," he whispered to himself. "Unless Vard is mistaken there's fifty thousand dollars there." He drew from one pocket a slip of paper on which was written a string of figures. "The sooner I get to work, the sooner I'll be out of here."

He stooped before the door of the safe, eyeing the shining round knob with its attendant circle of notched numbers, and below, the lever which would release the door lock when the proper numbers had been dialed on the knob. The shade from the hanging lamp allowed sufficient light for Chris to plainly read the numbers.

He stretched one hand to the knob, then glanced at his slip of paper. "Let's see, start at 93 . . . then right to 68 . . . now left to 87 . . . right again to 42 . . ." The mechanism of the combination lock worked noiselessly as the tumblers fell into place. ". . . now down to 73 . . . then right to 29 . . . only one more to go . . . left to 51. . . ."

Still moving cautiously, he grasped the steel lever and exerted pressure, then pulled. The heavy safe door swung back without a sound. . . .

Meanwhile Whitlock, Dusty Snow, and old Gabe, by pressing hard, had reached Nielson City. Whitlock cursed when they had to slacken speed so as to avoid attracting attention, but all three wisely pulled their ponies to a leisurely walk. They were just passing the crowd about the medicine-man show when Whitlock spoke tensely: "Did you hear shots then, Dusty?"

Dusty said no and after a swift glance along the street added, "I don't think anybody else did either. Probably your imagination. You're half expecting to hear guns——"

"All the more reason I might have heard 'em," Whitlock jerked out. He breathed a sigh of relief when farther on he caught sight of the darkened exterior of the Nielson Building. Then, abruptly, a light sprang into being on the second floor.

The three riders didn't wait to pick out any particular place to leave their horses. They'd already spotted Chris's pony standing before the Denver Chop House, and knew that Chris was by now inside Nielson's office. They dropped from saddles, crossed the sidewalk, tried the door to the Nielson entrance. It was opened, and they stepped quickly inside. Here they paused a moment, ears strained towards the upper floor.

"Somebody moving up there," Whitlock whispered.

He stopped only long enough to snap on the automatic lock, then his ears caught voices at the far end of the building, voices that reached him but faintly through the closed door.

"Come on," he whispered. "That must be the girl upstairs. It sounds to me like Chris had Hawk cornered in his office. Move as soft as possible. We don't want to bring in folks off the street if we can get away without . . ."

The three moved quickly and none too silently past the rows of desks. . . .

Within Nielson's private office Chris had, a short time before, succeeded in opening the door of the safe. Instantly his gaze found what he sought: in a large compartment at the bottom of the safe, below the smaller compartments and drawers above, was a small canvas satchel. Chris had just reached one hand to the handle when he heard a noise at his rear, then came Hawk Nielson's grim tones:

"Stop right where you are, mister, and reach high!"

Chris, half stooping before the open safe, swivelled on his heels in time to see Hawk Nielson just stepping from the doorway of the closet diagonally across the room in the opposite corner. Hawk's face bore a ferocious scowl, and his right hand gripped a six-shooter pointing straight towards Chris.

"You, eh?" Nielson growled. "I'm not surprised any.

So you were going to make a fool out of me, eh? By the time I was waiting for Vard Whitlock to bring Doc Gallatin here, you hombres would be far away with my money——"

"I don't know what you're talking about," Chris said quietly. He was still in his stooping position, head turned over one shoulder towards Nielson.

"You don't know how to bring off a job of safe-breaking, either," Nielson sneered. "A smart thief would have examined this closet before he got to work. I was expecting that when you first came in——"

And that was as far as Nielson got. Chris had flung himself to one side and came up, facing Nielson. Nielson's gun roared, a split second before flame left the muzzle of Chris's weapon. Chris hadn't tried to kill the man; he wanted merely to hit his gun arm, and a feeling of surprise flashed through him when he saw he'd apparently missed.

At the same instant Chris felt a shattering blow in his right forearm. He'd been moving too fast to make a good target. He was still on the move. As the gun dropped from his right hand he scooped it up in one swift movement with his left. Again Nielson's gun mushroomed a flame-and-smoke explosion, but not before Chris had thumbed a second swift shot. And for the second time he had apparently missed. This time Nielson had shot him in the left arm, and Chris's gun clattered to the floor.

"So!" Nielson exulted. "There is something I can beat you at, eh, Chris Whitlock?"

"Sort of looks that way," Chris forced out with a thin smile. He stood, helpless, against the wall, both wounded arms dangling uselessly at his sides. Powder-smoke swirled about the hanging lamp.

Nielson took another step towards him, gun ready for another shot. "By God!" he rasped. "This is a showdown I like. I always knew you weren't unbeatable, could I only find the right game. All right, where's your pals? You're all going to prison——"

"They pulled out a couple of hours ago," Chris said faintly. "They didn't have anything to do with this." He could feel the warm, sticky blood running down his arms, and felt himself growing weaker every minute. It required every bit of his will-power to stay erect.

"Don't lie to me. You'll tell the truth and tell it fast, or I'm blasting you, sure as hell!"

"I tell you I don't know where they are," Chris insisted. His eyes had commenced to close. He fought to keep them open.

"Speak up, damn you! Where's Vard Whitlock and the other two?" The gun raised menacingly in Nielson's hand. Then he tensed at the sounds of footsteps in the outer office.

The next instant Vard Whitlock, Dusty, and old Gabe flung wide the door and rushed into Nielson's office.

Hawk swung his gun-barrel in a short arc towards the three men. "Stick 'em up!" Hawk thundered.

For an instant Whitlock, in advance of the other two, looked as though he was inclined to make a fight of it, then he caught sight of Chris, slumped against the wall, eyes closed, blood dripping from his hands. Something of terror appeared in Whitlock's eyes, and he dropped his gun and flung his arms high.

"Don't shoot him again, Hawk," Whitlock yelled frantically. "My God, Hawk! That's your own son you plugged!"

Nielson jerked as though he himself had been shot. A strange look appeared in his eyes. "My son?" he exclaimed unbelievingly. "*My* son!"

Whitlock nodded violently. "Your own son, so help me God! I stole him from you the night he was born. Another baby was substituted by the Moquis, so you wouldn't know. I've got papers to prove things. I was wrong, Hawk, but——"

From upstairs came Dorada's voice: "Dad! Are you down there? What's happening? You said you were going out. Dad! Speak to me if——"

"It's me." Nielson raised his voice with an effort. "You stay up there. Nothing for you to worry about." Anything else the girl might have asked he didn't hear as he turned unbelieving eyes on Chris, propped unsteadily against the wall. "My son—Chris, my own son . . ." he muttered, his features working with emotion, as though he couldn't believe the evidence of his ears. "I might have known it," he continued dully. "He—he looks like his mother, and he's built big, like me. I should have realized, Vard, with you hating me like you did, you'd do something like that. . . ." His tones tapered to silence. The gun in his hand was slowly lowered, as Nielson appeared dazed by the turn events had taken.

Dusty and Whitlock still held their arms in the air. Old Gabe, half hidden behind them, hadn't even troubled to lift his hands. Something was happening to Gabe Houston. He felt the blood rush to his head, then something gave way—his brain snapped suddenly. At sight of his ancient enemy, Gabe Houston's unsettled mind deserted him altogether, and he turned violently insane.

"Yes, Hawk Nielson," Gabe screamed, "Chris is your own offspring. We've made you pay for robbin' us. We've taught him to steal from you!"

With an effort Nielson roused himself. "Taking what would have someday belonged to him, anyway, doesn't make him a crook," he protested. Nielson was still trying to grope his way out of the sudden bewilderment that had overtaken him.

"No, it wouldn't make no difference to you," Gabe raved,

" 'cause you're a thief your ownself. A dirty killin' thief! Jest like a plague of locusts, ye are, always devourin' up the range. What's happened is your own fault. You brought it on yourself! It's the dirty thievin' Nielson blood what's responsible. But, damn you, we're squaring the account——"

The words went uncompleted as Gabe savagely raised his six-shooter, momentarily catching Nielson off guard. The gun flamed three times in swift succession.

Dusty and Whitlock had lowered their hands and leaped for the old maniac to stop him, but they were too late. Nielson staggered back, tried to raise his gun, and failed. Quite suddenly he dropped forward on hands and knees, fighting doggedly to rise again. He still retained his gun, but seemed powerless to use it.

Gabe had leaped to one side, his gun swinging in a wide arc to cover Dusty and Whitlock. "Keep back, damn ye," he shrilled crazily, "or I'll give you both the same. This is old Gabe's hour. Hawk got his just due. Now I'm goin' to kill Chris! He's a Nielson—got the same thievin' blood in his veins. Old Gabe'll put an end to all this stealin'."

Dusty and Whitlock had backed away, alert for the first opportunity to leap in and wrest the gun from the old maniac, but he was watching them both with all the cunning of a madman. Chris had slumped half-way to the floor by this time, his broken arms making him powerless to stop old Gabe, and only half conscious of what was taking place. Nielson was still fighting on hands and knees to rise from the floor. He groaned and struggled; beads of perspiration stood out on his forehead, his features were contorted with anguish as he strove to gain his feet.

Gabe stood apart from everyone, gun still covering the room, gloating fiendishly over his fallen enemy. Nielson's efforts appeared futile; it seemed as though he'd drop unconscious any minute.

Gabe's malicious cackle grated through the room. He swung his gun towards Chris. "Goin' to kill you now, Chris! Ye been a good boy, but it's old Gabe's duty to kill you before you take to thievin' and ruinin' folks like Hawk. I'm goin' to kill you, Chris."

At these words Hawk Nielson made a last supreme effort. Bracing himself on one hand, he slowly raised his gun until it bore on the madman. Then his finger squeezed the trigger. A sudden spurt of orange fire darted from the gun muzzle.

A look of stunned surprise spread over Gabe Houston's face. He started to speak, but a violent gush of blood choked off the words. His knees buckled suddenly and he crashed to the floor. There was a spasmodic drumming of his booted toes, then he lay still.

Hawk Nielson had saved his son's life.

Dusty had darted to Chris's side. Whitlock crossed the room, caught Nielson's arm, and helped the big man into his desk chair. Nielson seemed to crumple before Whitlock's eyes. His face was ashen.

From the front of the building there came the sound of excited cries and a pounding on the door.

Hawk struggled to speak. The room was swimming with powder smoke. "Don't let folks come in here," Hawk gasped to Whitlock. "We'll tell 'em . . . it was . . . accident. Keep your mouth shut . . . you and me . . . we both did wrong . . . we'll talk . . . later. . . ."

Abruptly his eyes closed and his head fell to one side.

From the front of the building there came the sharp sound of splintering wood, then there was a rush of people into the room, Dorada, in a long blue wrapper, in the lead.

Whitlock never quite knew how it happened, but in no time at all the room was cleared. He swung back to the centre of the room, his eyes anxious. " I've sent men in all directions to round up doctors."

Chris was seated on the floor now, in a pool of blood, his back against the wall. He forced his eyes open. The room was revolving at a terrific rate. Holding his will sternly against the pain, he spoke to Dusty and Dorada, who were bending above him : " Nev' mind me. Go see what you can do for Hawk—for my father. I . . . I can't lose my father now . . . after I've just . . . found him. . . ."

Then he, too, passed into unconsciousness.

Dusty stood staring at Whitlock. " Good Lord ! what a mess this is. Hawk's done for, I reckon." He turned to the girl, saw that her eyes were wet. " Miss Dorada, do you think maybe——"

" This isn't the night for thinking," Dorada said. " No time for that. Run upstairs. You'll find bandages and other things. We'll do what we can now, until better help arrives."

23

CONCLUSION

BUT Hawk Nielson didn't die, after all. It was a long hard battle to save him, though, and only the big man's marvellous vitality pulled him through. Chris's broken arms had nearly healed even before Hawk was completely out of danger.

As soon as possible, Hawk was moved from the doctor's house out to the Forked Lightning Ranch. Dusty, Whitlock, and Chris accompanied him as a matter of course, despite the sheriff's insistence that they should be jailed. The sheriff didn't know quite what to make of the whole business, as no one would talk about what had happened, but the law officer felt certain in his own mind there'd been a plot to murder Hawk Nielson. He wanted to make arrests.

However, Dorada stopped that move on the part of the sheriff. Whitlock had told her the whole story, and after she recovered from the shock of learning she was no relation at all to Hawk, the girl efficiently took charge of all Nielson's affairs until such time as he'd either recover or the business should be handed over to Chris.

Practically the first thing Nielson said when he recovered consciousness was that no charges were to be made against anyone, that Dorada was to continue in her capacity as secretary, and that final decisions on anything that came up were to be left to Chris and Dorada, either singly or together. Following that, he set about making a new will.

Dorada, from papers given her by Whitlock, learned something of her own family, but not much ; all her parents' near relations had died even before they had. Chris, at first, felt as though he should hate Whitlock for what the man had done, but somehow he couldn't bring himself to do it. They had been like father and son so long, and Whitlock's regrets were so sincere, that Chris couldn't find it in himself to harbour any resentment.

Hawk, too, after the beginning of his recovery, did a great deal of thinking over his past life, and when Whitlock finally came to see him, Nielson held out a welcoming hand, saying, " Vard, you took him away from me, but you did a prime job of bringing him up, and you returned him to his father in due course. We'll call it an even score and try to forget the past. It's more than time I was forming some real friendships. There's a place on this ranch for you and Dusty. In a way I wish I could square things with old Gabe Houston, too, but he's better off where he is, under the circumstances."

Then there were long days of convalescence on the Forked Lightning gallery while Chris grew more and more acquainted with his father. Sometimes Whitlock took part in the conversations, and stories of old days in Ordway were called to mind. There was no longer any source of friction between Nielson and Whitlock now.

In time Hawk himself made the whole story known in Nielson City, and he didn't spare himself in the telling. It was the only way in which to set gossiping tongues at rest. There were many people who, getting the truth at last, thought Hawk Nielson had got off too easily. There were many more who concluded that Vard Whitlock should have been made to suffer. But who is to say ? True, Hawk had lived a hard life, but he had lived it in a day when a man had to live hard in order to exist. Hawk and Vard had both suffered for their misdeeds. Undoubtedly they deserved some years of happiness at the last.

At any rate, Hawk Nielson had achieved his greatest

ambition: he had a son. And then he was struck forcibly by another idea: why not also a grandson? The thought came to him one sunny Sunday morning as he sat on the ranch-house gallery, still swathed in bandages. Dorada and Chris had just crossed his line of vision as they started out on a ride among the hills. Both were laughing happily. Hawk hailed them from the gallery, and they came loping up to draw to a halt a few yards from Hawk's chair.

Chris said, " What's on your mind, Dad? "

" I've been doing some thinking about next summer's rodeo," Hawk said gravely. " I've an idea we're going to stage that show for a good many years to come."

Both Chris and the girl wondered what the elder man was leading up to.

Dorada nodded. " The rodeo seems to become more successful each year."

Hawk cocked a bushy eyebrow at Chris. " How long," he asked, " do you figure you can continue to take top money in the events? "

Chris laughed. " Until a better man beats my time. There's no telling—it might be *you* next year."

" Bosh! " Hawk growled. " From now on I'm reconciled to second money. But someday *you'll* have to give way to a younger man, Chris. It would be damn nice if his name was Nielson. What do you two think? "

They agreed it would be a fine idea, Dorada colouring slightly.

" That being the case," Hawk chuckled, " I figure it's about time we held a wedding here, just as soon as I get on my feet enough to take charge of the doings—provided you two haven't any objections."

And they didn't have—not one.

(Allan) William Colt MacDonald was born in Detroit, Michigan in 1891. His formal education concluded after his first three months of high school when he went to work as a lathe operator for Dodge Brothers' Motor Company. His first commercial writing consisted of advertising copy and articles for trade publications. While working in the advertising industry, MacDonald began contributing stories of varying lengths to pulp magazines and his first novel, a Western story, was published by Clayton House in *Ace-high Magazine* in 1925. MacDonald later commented that when this first novel appeared in book form as *Restless Guns* in 1929, 'I quit my job cold.' From the time of that decision on, MacDonald's career became a long string of successes in pulp magazines, hardcover books, films, and eventually original and reprint paperback editions. The Three Mesquiteers, MacDonald's most famous characters, were introduced in 1933 in *Law of the Forty-fives*. His other most famous character creation was Gregory Quist, a railroad detective. Some of MacDonald's finest work occurs outside his series, especially the well researched *Stir Up The Dust* which was published first in a British edition in 1950 and *The Mad Marshal* in 1958. MacDonald's only son, Wallace, recalled how much fun his father had writing Western fiction. It is an apt observation since countless readers have enjoyed his stories now for nearly three quarters of a century.